BEAST

BEAST

• A NOVEL •

CHAWNA SCHROEDER

an imprint of
GILEAD PUBLISHING

Beast by Chawna Schroeder
Published by Enclave Publishing, an imprint of Gilead Publishing,
Wheaton, IL 60187
www.enclavepublishing.com

ISBN: 978-1-68370-026-5

Cover designed by John Hamilton
Edited by Bethany Kaczmarek
Interior designed by PerfecType, Nashville, TN

Printed in the United States of America

DEDICATION

This book belongs first and foremost to the real
Majesty
To him belongs the honor and the glory.

And

To Esther & Tatianne,
who never gave up on this story.

ACKNOWLEDGMENTS

In many ways, *Beast* has been a book sixteen years in the making, and as might be imagined, the list of people I should thank is quite long. Indeed, the number of people who have contributed to my journey would be impossible to list here, if only because my memory will fail me at some point. So to all of you who have contributed to this journey, whether in critiques, encouragement, or advice—thanks. God placed each of you in my path at exactly the right time, and I am grateful for the part you have played. I stand on the shoulders of giants.

However, that said, there have been a select few whose influence has been unmistakable, and if it hadn't been for them, I wouldn't be writing this acknowledgments page in the first place. So my deepest thanks goes to:

My parents, Jim and Barb Schroeder: I'm indebted to you forever. You taught me how to dream big and then tirelessly, unquestioningly supported me year after year after year in order that I might have the freedom to pursue those dreams.

The rest of my family: You didn't merely tolerate my many crazy flights of fancy but often joined in right beside me.

Sharon Hinck: Next to my parents, you are probably the person to whom I owe the most. You took me under your wing when I was just starting out, and without your endless encouragement, I probably would have given up on this writing journey long ago.

My other writing friends and critique partners through the years: There are too many of you to name, but know that you each have pushed me to be the best writer possible and have kept me accountable. I might have wanted to throw my manuscript in the trash after you finished with me upon occasion, but in the end, you also kept me pushing my pen across the page.

My many writing teachers, whose instruction or classes significantly advanced my writing craftsmanship.

Esther: your unbounded enthusiasm for *Beast* kept me going in ways that few others could. You will always be my first fan. And yes, you were right about the title. You win.

My cheerleading squad, who have rooted me on as I pursued this crazy profession and listened patiently to writer rants you probably didn't fully understand: Kay & Dale Mundt, Chuck Gustafson, Betsy Rose, Jan Olson.

Steve Laube, because you believed in this story—both eight years ago, enough for it to give it a Genesis award, and now, by taking a chance in publishing it. I pray your expectations are not disappointed.

Everyone at Enclave & Gilead, for patiently working with this newbie, answering my zillion questions, pushing me to make this story even better, and then turning my whimsical imaginings into something tangible.

Finally, since this book began with a dedication to God, it is only appropriate to end with my grateful acknowledgement of him, for he is the Alpha and the Omega, the Beginning and the End.

My Lord, you were there in the beginning, supplying the ideas and the words to a story I didn't want to write. You were there in the middle, refusing to let me walk away during the long, dry waiting period. You were there at the death and resurrection of this chapter of life, surprising me with a climax beyond imagination, a climax worthy of a story. And you are here at the end, laughing at my joy—even as you prepare me for the next chapter. There are no words to express my gratitude. May I *never* forget what you have done, this book forever standing before me as a witness to your faithfulness.

CHAPTER 1

RAID

I am Beast. I serve Master.

When he calls, I come. When he commands, I obey. When he rages, I cower at his feet. By his word I live; by his word I die. So I stay to the shadows, sleeping in the pen with Master's dogs and fighting them for the scraps that fall from Master's table. Sometimes I win. Most times I don't. Then long nights follow. Cold nights, when wind pierces the wood.

Tonight, Master's dogs curl up together in the corner away from the wind. I try to join them, but the Others growl and snap. I go away to the pen's far side and wrap my fur around me. It is long, but it covers only my head, and the extra coat Master gave me is full of holes. The Others' fur covers all of them. This is one reason why I am Beast, not an Other.

Light comes after a long time, but it is cold light, angry light. My insides hurt. I curl into a tighter ball, but the hurt does not go away. Maybe some of Master's pack will come, and he will call me to do the things only I can do. Then Master will laugh, I will have food, and the hurt will go away for a little while.

The house door opens—it creaks—and Master's mate calls. "Warrior, Mongrel, Huntress, Arrow."

The Others immediately rise, yapping and jumping against the pen's boards.

Mate does not call me, but I uncurl anyway. Pressing my forepaws into the dirt, I swing the rest of me forward, my useless hind leg dragging behind. I am not as quick as the Others, but they have four good legs, and I have only three.

Without looking at me, Master's mate tosses bones to the Others. Her mouth is thin. I wait by the boards, face to the ground. I do not know why I wait. A thin mouth says she is displeased, and my insides always hurt more when Master's mate is displeased. Day will be cold and long.

"Beast, come."

I raise my head. She called me?

Her fingers grasp the gate, her mouth thinner. She did call. I bound forward.

Mate opens the gate enough for me and me only, then closes it on my useless leg. I yelp and roll forward. My leg, my leg! I curl into a ball, forepaws to my useless leg, water running down my face.

"Quit your whining." Mate hits my back with a stick. "Hurry up."

I slink toward Master's house but not fast enough. Mate's stick finds my back twice more before I reach the flat rock by the door. She raises the stick to strike again. I cower.

The door opens. "Enough, woman!" Master steps between his mate and me. "Get back to your work."

She scowls but turns away.

Master pats my head. "Don't worry about her, Beast." He goes into the house. "Come, girl."

I swing myself across the stone floor, and Master shuts the door behind me.

The inside is warm and thick with the smell of food, and I would thump a tail if I had one like the Others. My movement must be fast so that no one steps on me, for both strangers and the men of Master's pack fill the room. But perhaps more people will mean more food.

A stranger-man at the long table snorts and points at me. "What's that?"

"Beast." Master pulls out a chair, and it scrapes against the floor.

"But *what* is it? Human? Animal?"

"Neither. Both. It's a beast. Watch." Master breaks a loaf of bread and tosses part to me.

I catch it in my mouth. The bread is dry and hard, but it is food, and I feast.

Master breaks off another chunk. "Beast, catch." He throws it across the room.

I bound over the uneven floor and leap to catch the bread as it bounces off the wall.

Some of Master's pack chuckle, and a stranger says, "Impressive."

I think that means I did well. I chew on my reward.

The men hunch again over the table and stab fingers at something on it. I am forgotten, but I don't mind. The wind cannot bite here. I curl into a ball in the corner and watch the fire burning low in the hearth.

I think of a place where I am a favorite, where I lie by the fire and bones with meat are set before me every day. Could there be such a place for me? What would I have to do to earn such high favor with Master?

The men at the table become louder and louder. Master's pack is fighting the strangers. Fists pound. Voices yell. I huddle in my corner. Master is angry. I do not like it when Master is angry. Blood—usually mine—will flow.

One from Master's pack rises and stomps out the door. Outside. There I can hide until Master's rage goes away.

I slink toward the door. A stranger tips a chair over and a pot flies over my head, shattering against a wall. I dart behind pans by the hearth. My useless leg bumps a smaller pail. Gray powder spills across the floor.

"Beast!" Master's footsteps pound. "What are you still doing in here, you stupid animal?"

Whimpering, I flatten myself to the floor. *Please, Master. Don't be angry. Please, Master. I'm sorry.*

He grabs my fur and hauls me out from behind the big pots. "Out!" He kicks me outside and slams the door behind me.

Water from above splashes down on my head, and the wind bites hard. But Master's hand did not find his belt. That is better than I thought possible.

I drag myself off the stone by the door; neither Master nor his mate must find me here. The sky's water pelts harder as I crawl under some bushes near the edge of the woods. Master will not know I am here. The pack and strangers will leave. His anger will go away. Then I can return.

I sleep, but in my sleep I no longer lie by the fire or eat meat. Master is angry, so angry that he cracks his whip at me because I spilled the water bucket on myself. I am cold and wet, but Master does not see. He wants me to drink all the water I spilled, but the water rises faster than I can drink, and the more I drink, the more I thirst.

The water is to my neck. Master's whip cracks louder and nearer. I jump with a yelp, and the angry Master of my sleep goes away—I'm back outside under my bush, my whole underside wet from pooling water.

Crack!

My head jerks to the left. Fire! Not a little one like in the hearth, but a big one that eats the whole house with huge, crackling bites. The night is cold but not that cold. Why does Master surround his whole house with fire? And Master is not the only one who does this. Many houses of Master's pack have big fires.

Two shadows sprint around the house. The fire lights the faces—Master's mate is first, but the second is a stranger. The stranger grabs Mate. She screams. The stranger strikes her and drags her away beyond the fire.

He struck Mate! No one strikes Mate except Master himself.

Now other voices pierce the thickness of night. Loud voices. Scared voices. Strange voices. I cower under my bush. I don't know what's going on. The night is angry. The air smells wrong—thick and sharp. The wind blows hard and whips the leaves above my head. Where's Master? Why isn't he stomping around, yelling, beating back these strangers? Why is the night red instead of black?

Crack! Master's housetop drops into the fire.

I whimper and watch, unable to look away from this thing that should not be. Shadows jump against fires, shadows with no form, shadows with loud voices. One black form becomes two, then four, then more and more, until there are so many shadows that they blur back into one. Screams are fewer now, whimpers and yelps more—like the sounds that leave my own mouth. But they are Master's pack. I am Beast. Why do they act like me?

A whip cracks. A voice yells. The black blur of shadows moves, slinking beyond the red flames. A scream breaks out at the far end and then is suddenly silent. I shudder. I've heard that before, when I went hunting with Master. One of the Others caught an animal. It wiggled and screamed. The Other bit down on it. The scream stopped. So did the wiggling. Even when Master took the animal from the Other, it did not move. That night my insides hurt so much I could not eat.

My insides hurt the same way now.

The black blur of shadows disappears, and the crying weakens until only crackling fire is left. Then even that fades until there is only a little red left around the bottom. The sky lightens.

Black spikes stand where Master's house was. I wait for him to come stomping, yelling, with the belt in his hand.

He does not come.

I crawl out from under my bush, my useless leg dragging through the mud. It is quiet. Too quiet.

I creep to Master's house. Black and gray-white powder covers everything. The floor. The hearth. A few pots and pans. The black smears onto me as I swing across the floor. Still nothing moves or speaks. And I know.

Master is no more.

CHAPTER 2

CAPTURE

S trangers.

Like a sharp bark, the warning splits my sleep. My fur bristles; my body stiffens. I do not move, do not even open my eyes. Only breaths slip in and out, as if I still sleep. But I am awake, taking in everything around me. The light of a half-gone day warms my back. The smell of dirt and heat and sweat mixes with the taste of fire. The snap of twigs and light thud of steps come near me.

"What is it?"

I should run. I should hide. But there is no time. The strangers are almost at my side.

"Is it even alive?"

Bad Beast. Stupid Beast. I should have smelled them, felt them long ago, before I heard their voices so clearly. The least of the Others would have. But the night—it was so long. I only wanted to curl up by the hearth for a few breaths. Instead sleep took me to places where I was a favorite, a place that can no longer be. Master is gone.

A foot nudges my back. I lie still and do not whimper. Maybe the stranger will think I am nothing and go on by.

"I think it's dead. We should keep moving." The voice quivers, like a brown leaf barely holding to its tree in the wind.

I wait, coldness lapping at my middle. Only one voice has spoken, yet there is another. I feel him, smell him.

"She lives. Take her." The second stranger speaks, and his words command like Master's.

Now my body trembles. They will not pass me by. Only one thing is left to do.

"Are you sure? I mean . . . it looks dead to me. And even if it is alive, what would such a scrawny . . . thing do for us?"

"I said take her."

"If you say so." A hand brushes me. "But if anyone asks, it was—"

Attack!

I spring to my feet and snap at the stranger. My teeth miss the hand, but I am close enough to taste the dirt on it.

A short man of fire-hair yelps and bolts away from me. He fears me. He should. I have fought the Others and won. Crouching low, I flatten my paws against the blackened stone and deepen my growl.

Fire-Hair scrambles back, behind the second stranger, a tall man of the night's darkness. This Nightman shows no fear and even dares to laugh. "Take her, Alaric. What can 'such a scrawny thing' do to you?"

I want to set my teeth in Nightman, but I must wait. Too soon or too late and my attack will do no good.

Fire-Hair creeps forward, hand outstretched. "There, there. Be a good . . . thing and calm down." He still fears me, no matter what Nightman says. I can smell it.

I lower my head in preparation. Wait . . . wait . . . wait . . .

"That's right. We won't hurt—"

I ram into his chest.

He stumbles backward. His hands fly about like a bird in a net. I snap at them and claw his face, trying to get my teeth at his throat. Fire-Hair howls.

"Quit squawking. She didn't even draw much blood." Nightman grabs my middle and lifts me up before I can snap at him.

I snarl and claw air.

Nightman laughs. "You'll have to kick harder than that."

Fire-Hair rises, blood streaked across his face. "That thing has an evil spirit. Maybe the Devil himself. Let me destroy it." Something silver flashes—he points a knife at my exposed underside.

I fall still.

Fire-Hair approaches me. "You know what this is, devil-child? Good." He raises the knife.

"Put that away before you cost us a year's profit."

The knife stops and Fire-Hair's eyes narrow. "What do you mean?"

"I know a dozen men who collect oddities. A child with animal instincts like this would fetch a pouch of gold from them, even more on the auction block."

Fire-Hair watches me; I watch the knife. "How much?" he says.

"At least three times more than a healthy slave—and since you helped captured her, you'll receive an additional share."

"For this *thing*, this devil-child?" The knife point grazes my cheek.

Yelping, I jerk my head back.

Nightman growls. "More, if you quit damaging the goods."

Fire-Hair flattens his mouth, his eyes still narrow. I don't move, the knife too near. Finally he steps back and tucks the knife away, though closer to his hand than before. "I still think we should kill it. There'll be no restraining the Devil."

"Enough superstition, Alaric." Nightman drops me.

My useless leg reaches the ground first, and pain splits up it. The rest of me sprawls across the stone. But I am free and leaving now.

Before I can get my legs under me, Nightman pins me to the ground with his knee. No. He can't have me. I twist and swipe at his leg. Nightman catches both of my forepaws and yanks them behind my back, tying them together. Then he shoves me away and rises; I am not a threat to him anymore. "Bring her. We're finished here."

Squirming, I try to get my good hind leg under me. Yet what good will it do? My forelegs are bound, and without them I cannot run or even walk.

Fire-Hair stands over me. "Don't give me any problems, devil-child, or you'll regret it."

I snarl and receive a boot to my side for it.

"Enough, both of you." Nightman doesn't even look back at us.

Fire-Hair mutters words I don't know and slings me over his shoulder with a grunt.

"Quit cursing. Camp's not that far."

"You're not the one carrying the Devil." Fire-Hair stumbles away from the house.

His shoulder presses into my middle, and my head feels as if bugs crawl inside it as ground already walked passes by. I twist and lift my head.

The deep forest closes in on us; the leaves swallow the remains of Master's house and all I've ever known.

"Camp," as Nightman called it, is only an open place in the deep forest. No houses. No pens. No paths. Only many strangers together in small packs, and much noise. I do not like it. I want Master's man-pack. I want my pen. I want the Others.

Fire-Hair dumps me on the ground beside people bound with rope. Stragglers, Nightman called them. They all move back one step from me, with hisses of "devil-child."

In the center of the camp, a man-pack gathers around a big fire, as Master's pack would after a good hunt. One man there comes toward us. "Tracker." He nods at Nightman. "I see your hunt for strays has not been wholly unprofitable."

"No indeed. I even caught an oddity that should bring a handsome price on market day." Nightman nudges me with his foot.

I push myself forward with my good hind leg and bite at his ankle.

The stranger rubs his beard. "Spirited, isn't it?"

"That's what makes her so valuable." When I snap at him again, Nightman presses his foot down on my back, pinning me to the ground. "You can take the others and chain them up with the rest of the slaves. I'll handle this one personally."

"As you want." The stranger shoves one of the stragglers forward. "Let's go."

"Alaric." Nightman shifts his weight. "Grab me a sturdy rope from the supply wagon." He points to a wood box nearby.

With his eyes on Fire-Hair rather than me, Nightman lifts his foot up, no longer crushing me to the ground. I twist from under him and roll-tumble toward the trees any way I can.

"Not so fast." Nightman grabs my fur, snapping my head back. "I'm not done with you yet." He yanks upward.

I yelp and shove my good leg beneath me. That eases some of the pain.

"You learn quickly. Good. Now understand this: running only makes it harder for both of us." He hooks my foreleg and pulls me across the camp.

I hop along on one foot, but I am not as fast as he is. Often my leg falls behind and drags across the ground, stones scraping it.

Nightman tosses me at the roots of a tree and takes a coil of rope that Fire-Hair holds out to him. I growl and snap; Nightman only pushes my face to the ground and loops the rope around my neck. Does he fear nothing?

After he ties the other end of the rope to the tree trunk, he cuts the rope binding my forepaws. He is not wise. I spring to my feet and lunge at him, despite the stingers prickling my paws.

The rope snaps taut, cutting me short.

But I need only a little further! Nightman is not more than a step away. I yank and pull and stand on my hind legs to claw the air with my front ones. The rope bites into my throat.

Nightman shakes his head at me, his shoulders drooping. "You might as well save yourself. Pulling all night won't get you anywhere I say you can't go." Then he turns his back—he knows I cannot reach him or he would not do such a thing.

I slump to the ground and growl as he goes away. But Nightman is right. Here I am. Here I stay. Master may be no more, but I am under command. If not Nightman's, Fire-Hair's. If not Fire-Hair's, another's. There is always another.

The light fades until only darkness is left. Darkness and the smell of roasting meat. My insides snarl and claw. The bread from Master was so long ago.

Off to the side, whispers gather. Restlessness spreads through a second pack of mates and cubs grouped along the camp's edge. I've seen a few of the dark forms among Master's pack, but many are strangers. None look at me; they watch a man moving among them—Fire-Hair, handing out chunks of bread. He does not seem to hear the words of the mates and cubs or feel their grasping hands. He stops before me, just beyond my claws' reach.

I do not rise, but neither do I cower. Fire-Hair is not Master. He is the man who took me from Master's house. I bare my teeth with a snarl.

Fire-Hair snarls back. "You made me appear the fool today, devil-child. So now you'll eat what you sowed." He kicks dirt into my eyes.

I howl and spring away, pawing my face.

"Enjoy your feast."

I shake my head, growl at his retreating form, rub my face against my legs, and growl some more. But for what? Fire-Hair has left, taking the bread with him. We fought. I lost. Now a long night will follow.

Putting my back to the man-pack, I nose around. On the far side of the tree there's a small clump of grass. Not what I hunger for, but I tear the blades from the ground. It doesn't taste very good. Something bumps into me. I sniff it. Not an animal. Not a rock. Bread? I raise my head.

A she-cub sits less than two bounds away. "Go on. Eat it," she whispers.

I need no more commands. I drop the food between my paws and rip a piece off with my teeth.

With a sigh, the she-cub pulls her legs to her chest and rests her head on her knees. Her insides growl at me. I'm eating her food. I swallow the bread in my mouth; it hits my insides like a rock. She gave up her food. For me. But that makes it mine now, doesn't it? I take another bite. It doesn't taste as good. I tear off one more chunk, lay it aside, and nudge the rest toward her. I am Beast. What I need is little.

She looks at me, at the bread, and back to me.

I push the chunk as close to her as I can. She doesn't take it; she fears me. I crawl backward, out of attack distance.

She picks up the bread, and a burst of firelight shows her smile. "Thank you."

CHAPTER 3

TABBY

The bread from the she-cub fills the hole of my insides only a little. That is almost worse than none at all. I close my eyes, but sleep won't come and give me visions of bones and warm fires. Instead, every sound tugs me back to wakefulness. Leaves tremble in a wind smelling of wood smoke and wet ground. The man-pack's voices rise and dip against the snapping of fire. Soft moaning and snufflings drift from huddled mates and cubs. In the distance there's a howl, and something deep inside me echoes it. The howler and I are both alone, without our packs this night. But unlike the howler, I have no pack to join, nor will I find another. I shift my useless leg, its ache tightening all of me. No pack accepts weak ones who take more than they give—ones like me.

Unable to lie still any longer, I rise and sniff the ground. No stray berries or crumbs of bread hide in the dirt.

"My name's Tabby."

I swing toward the voice out of the darkness.

The she-cub who gave me the bread lies on her side, her arm curled under her head. "Sorry. I didn't mean to scare you. I only noticed you couldn't sleep either. It doesn't seem to bother them." She nods toward the rest of the mates and cubs. "But there's no end to the rocks."

My head cocks. Isn't the ground always covered with rocks?

Tabby rolls onto her belly and rests her head on folded arms. "The slavers are talking about moving us tomorrow. No more villages to raid, I suppose. It'll be nice to start moving, except that means we'll reach the border town in a few days, goods for the highest bidder." Her slender form shudders. "I've never been to a slave market. Have you? They're not allowed where I come from, but some of my . . . some people I know were once slaves."

I edge nearer. Why she is talking to me, I don't know. But since I'm now without a pack, her words may protect me from the packs that would turn on *me* as prey.

"I'm not afraid for me. Really I'm not." But Tabby's voice wavers as she pushes dirt around with a finger. "I was only visiting a friend, and Father will send for me. I know he will. But the others—whole families were taken. They have no one else."

Tabby's pack will fight to get her back? She must be strong and cunning for that risk.

"But you arrived alone." Her head jerks up and she looks at me with the intensity of a stare-down, one I cannot meet. "I know that rumors say you're some kind of mongrel, half animal and half human or maybe half devil—not that I believe it. But you still have to belong to someone, right? Someone who would come for you too?"

Someone come for me? My pack is gone or scattered. Master is no more. Not that they would risk anything for me, even if they still walked the ground. The pack comes first, and I am not worth the danger of a fight. I sigh, resting my head on my forepaws.

"I guess that means no. I'm sorry. I wish I could help you somehow—help all of you." Tabby rolls onto her back and says nothing more. Perhaps she has found the sleep she sought.

I should try to catch it too. I curl up with my back to the wind, which seems to whisper Tabby's many words in my ears again.

If only a pack such as hers could be mine.

Fingers of light slip through the leaves as I struggle to keep up with the mates and cubs. The shorter bushes snap back to slap me in the face. Mud slips and squishes beneath my paws. My useless leg drags heavier than usual, and I must run many times to stay with the pack.

The he-cub ahead of me stumbles forward, yanking my rope, which is tied to his waist. I plant my feet and the rope cuts into my neck, already rubbed raw. The he-cub regains his footing. I swing quickly after him to keep the rope limp between us.

A few minutes later, we shuffle into a small, open area. The slavers yell that we can stop, and the mates and cubs drop to the ground, seeking any shade they can find. I lie down, curling into my usual ball. The men pass food and water among themselves. They don't offer any to the mates and cubs, much less me.

A bee buzzes. A bird flits by. I shift my position, my nose twitching. Could it be? I push back up onto my feet and creep forward. My nose catches a heavy scent—berry bushes! And still loaded, from the smell. My stomach rumbles and my mouth waters, already tasting the sweet tartness that is not yet mine. Crawling on my belly, I push under some bushes and spot fat, black clumps—just beyond my reach.

I wiggle back. The he-cub I'm tied to is stretched out in the shade, his arm draped across his eyes. I bump my head into his shoulder. He swipes at me but misses, mumbling. "Lemmebe."

Can't he smell it? Hundreds of berries are only a jump away, enough for everyone. I grab the rope between my teeth and yank.

The he-cub rolls over and growls. "Quit it."

I yank again.

"I said stop that." He sits halfway up and swats at my head. I duck. Whispers and nudges pass through the line of mates and cubs.

Why don't they understand? I disappear through the bushes, pull on my rope, come back, and tug on the rope again.

"You stupid animal, you're going to get us all into trouble." He raises his hand to strike me.

"Wait." Tabby lunges out of the pack and grabs his wrist. "I think she's trying to show us something."

Finally! I dart to the bushes and push through them as far as my rope will go.

"Give me a little slack." Tabby follows and her eyes widen. "Berries." She whirls around and waves for the others to follow.

Whispers pass backward, and then everyone is up and moving toward the bushes. A slaver rushes forward to stop them. Nightman grabs his arm. "Leave them be. They're not going anywhere."

The slaver tries to stare down Nightman, but Nightman is stronger and does not let go until the slaver shrugs his shoulder. "Whatever." He stalks away. Nightman stays, leaning against a tree and chewing on some bread.

All around me mates and cubs grab at berries and stuff their mouths. I clean my branch and move to the next bush. It has already been picked clean. I join some cubs at a third bush, but they push me away. I try another spot and another, each with the same result.

A growl grows in my throat. I found the berries; I will eat my fill. If I must fight, I will. Baring my teeth, I move toward the nearest group. Would a nip on the leg be enough to clear the way?

Tabby breaks away from the group and plops on the ground in front of me. Berries fill her skirt. She pops a few into her mouth. "Take some, if you want. I have more than enough."

I stay back, eyeing the food. Does she mean it?

She takes some and holds them out to me. "Go on. You have to be as hungry as the rest of us. After all, you walked all morning too."

I lean forward, my nose quivering.

"Here." She picks up my front leg. Turning up its mud-smeared and scratched bottom, she dumps the berries into my paw.

I shove my face into them. They are gone before my hunger is.

Tabby laughs, a sound I have not heard from any of the mates or cubs since I joined them. "What a messy bunch we make. I can see berry juice all over your face, even your nose, and I can only imagine I look as bad. My old nurse would be scandalized and order a hot bath instantly, along with an equally hot lecture on propriety." Her smile fades. "But things never quite happen the way you expect, do they?" Her hand falls to her lap, her eyes no longer seeing the berry-picking chaos in front of her.

I push around some berries that fell to the ground. Tabby's smiles and laughter are nicer. Could I bring them back, like I sometimes did with Master? I pop a berry into my mouth, careful not to crush it, and spit it at the back of the he-cub in front of us. Juice splatters across the shirt.

I shoot another berry at a she-cub, and it catches her face as she turns.

"Hey!" She scoops up a nut from the ground and throws it at another she-cub across the way, who returns the shot with a handful of mud. Soon mud, nuts, leaves, and even a few berries fly from every which way.

Tabby, giggling, flattens herself on the ground next to me as the slavers rush into stop the fight. "Of course, the unexpected can be good." She faces me, smiling again. "Thanks."

The walk that fills the rest of the day is long, but the berries— and the memories of Tabby's smile—keep my legs moving on the mostly downhill trek. Then the light begins to dim, and we break out of the bushes into an open area with a wide dirt path in the middle of it; I could not reach both edges of the path at the same time, even if I lay down and stretched out my legs. Here the slavers make a new camp, and I am once more tied to a tree near Tabby. The whole back of my neck hurts, and every time the rope rubs across it, pain flares up. I slather some mud across the burning skin and try not to move.

A slaver passes out water and hard chunks of bread. That and the berries Tabby saved nearly fill the hole in my insides, and I curl up on the ground next to Tabby with a sigh. Tonight will not be quite as long.

As the men settle around the fire with loud talking, Tabby props her head on her knees. "It won't be long now. This"—she nods toward the dirt path—"should be the main road north to the border town between Rumbal and Ahavel. A two- or three-day walk, I'm guessing."

Her words mean little to me, but I listen anyway. It makes me feel like part of a pack, even if I'm not.

"We'll probably have to wait for the auction a couple of days after that. So five days. Five days and I'll be back in Father's arms. Back home. With hot baths, plenty of food, and shoes!" She wiggles her bare toes.

Five days. Then she'll return to her rightful position in her pack, and I . . . maybe someone will have a place for me among their dogs?

"Don't worry." Tabby rests her cheek on her knees, turning her face to me. "Whatever happens, I won't leave without you, one way or another."

Me? My head rears up. She is offering to take me into her pack?

"Father is sure to bring more than is needed for me. I know he will. So all I have to do is talk him into buying you too."

If only . . . but no. This won't be. I shake my head. Not that Tabby won't try to do what she says, but a powerful pack like hers will make her see they're better off without me.

"Don't you like the idea? Don't you want to go with me?" She stops. "I just realized I don't know your name."

My name? Does she not see what my name should be?

She reaches her hand toward me. I jerk back, curling into a tighter ball, a whimper escaping me. *Don't hurt me. I didn't mean to make you angry.*

"Shh. Don't be afraid." She pushes some fur out of my face and tucks it behind my ear. Her touch is light, soft, unlike anything I know. My body uncurls and I lean into her hand, now resting on me.

"We're very alike, the two of us. Both lonely, neither fitting in with the rest, taken from different ranks of people." She laughs softly. "Not that anyone could tell by looking at us. But somehow I feel you understand."

And somehow, perhaps for the first time during her words, I feel so too.

"That's it. I will call you Sarah."

Sarah?

"If you don't like it, you don't have to keep it. But until you *can* tell me what you want to be called, that's what I'll name you." She squeezes my paw and then, pulling away, she curls up on her side, still smiling. "Goodnight, Sarah."

Sarah.

A human name.

If only it could be mine.

CHAPTER 4

BORDER TOWN

For three days I have walked. For three days I have followed the he-cub in front of me. For three days I have eaten his dust, stared at his heels, matched his pace, never slowing, never slacking, never stopping.

Until now.

But standing on this hilltop, I balk. The land stretches out before me, so endless, so . . . empty. No trees. No bushes. No place to hide. Only patch after patch of tall grasses, yellow and green. With one look I see farther than should be possible.

A whip cracks over my head, and Fire-Hair yells, "Keep moving!"

I will not. I cannot. This is a hunter's land. The weak, the hunted, cannot live here.

The he-cub tugs on the rope, and farther down the line, Nightman strides uphill toward us.

"I said move!" Fire-Hair kicks at me. I cower but do not leave my spot at the forest's edge. He raises his whip.

"Stop!" Nightman plants his feet between Fire-Hair and me with such force, they kick up dust. I back up, pawing at my face. "I'll handle this. Animal minds like hers don't think the way the rest do."

Fire-Hair doesn't lower his hand. "They all understand the sting of a whip, animal or not."

"You'll have to damage her to get what you want."

"And damaged goods don't sell as well." The whip snaps into the dirt. "So you've said. Over and over. I don't know how Pete puts up with you, even if you're old friends or good at tracking strays."

Nightman stands, face and body unchanging.

"Fine. Five minutes to persuade it." Fire-Hair flops in the shade and pulls out his knife, rubbing the edge with a rock.

Whirling toward me, Nightman drops to one knee and grabs my throat, forcing me to balance on my hind legs. Then he brings his face so near to mine I could spit in his eye. Maybe I should.

As if knowing what I wanted to do, he tightens his grip, forcing my head up higher. "Don't try anything if you know what's good for you."

I growl but don't spit or claw at him.

"Now you're going to quit making this hard for both of us and march when I put you down. You understand?"

I refuse to lower my eyes in submission. Nightman is *not* Master.

"Or would you rather I hand you over to him"—he jerks his head toward Fire-Hair—"and have me apply two for every one of his on your friend down the row. Tabby, isn't it?"

My head jerks toward the mates and cubs, who have settled on the ground wherever they stood. Most of the heads bow in defeat and tiredness, but one face is lifted toward a bird circling in the sky. My insides wrap themselves around each other.

"Have I made myself clear?"

I meet Nightman's gaze once more and then lower my eyes from his face. He has won. For now.

"Good." He releases me, and standing, faces Fire-Hair. "We can go now. She'll move when you say so."

"If it doesn't—"

"She will." Nightman walks back down the hill.

Fire-Hair turns to the mates and cubs. "Everyone up. On your feet now!" The whip cracks.

Moaning spreads through the line. Mates and cubs stumble to their feet. My paws dig into the dirt, but when the order is given, I move with the rest. If I don't look at the emptiness, maybe it won't crush me.

But then again, maybe it will.

The light begins to fade, and I slink along the dirt path, trying to think I am back in the forest. There the shadows and light would dart in and out between the trees, chasing each other among the leaves, before the light sleeps and darkness works. But here cold, black fingers stretch out across the land. Grabbing. Devouring. Farther and farther they reach, as if the emptiness of this place does not fill its craving. My shoulders hunch forward and my paws hit the ground quicker so that I almost land on the heels of the he-cub in front of me.

A cluster of gray mounds rises up ahead of us, batting away what is left of the light. A shudder passes through my neck down to my toes. The mounds look like little more than heaps of stones held together by mud, yet I know. This is Tabby's "border town."

We cross a river on wood planks fastened with ropes and pass more dirt paths. Other man-packs join ours, many accompanied by strange creatures. A he-cub drives a group of dog-sized animals with fluffy white fur. Masters ride four-legged giants with long faces and stringy tails that they call "horses." A spotted monster with horns releases a low moaning sound as it pulls a rolling wood pen. I duck on the other side of the he-cub, away from that animal. What kind of place have I been brought to?

Then we pass a wall into the town, and my steps slow once more. This place is all wrong. It does not smell like wet leaves during a warm day but like a bone of meat left out too long. The place sounds hard, with clicks and clacks rather than swishing and rustling. It looks wrong too. Flat stone replaces dirt, and there are no trees or bushes or any grass—green, yellow, or brown. Instead, stone mound presses against stone mound, as if they want to keep the light out.

The pack is no better. A gray-faced mate clutching a wailing cub passes by without ever turning her dull eyes toward us. He-cubs throw stones the color of their clothing until a slaver scatters them. A gray dog, all bones and bristling fur, glares at us with the yellow eyes of a hunter.

We turn into an open place. Still no grass or leaves. More light does squeeze through here, but it is still tired and gray. Maybe living here turns everything gray. I lift up a paw. It is brown and muddy and scratched up as always.

The master slaver bangs on a door in a wall—both gray— and a wrinkled face peers out a small hole. "What do you want?"

"What does it look like, Marc? Flower selling?" growls the master slaver. "I want to board my slaves here."

"You know I don't accept new ones this late, Pete." Wrinkle-face begins to cover the hole.

"And I know you always have a price. What is it this time?"

Wrinkleface leaves the hole half open and squints his eyes. "Triple the rate."

"That's thievery and you know it. I'll give you an additional half."

"Two and a half."

"Double."

"Deal." The hole vanishes, and after some scuffling, the door swings in with a creaking moan, as if it hurts to open.

The master slaver nods to the other men. Mates and cubs are prodded to their feet and through the door one at a time. The line creeps forward, stopping often so a slaver can release the next mate or cub from the black rings binding them together. Then Wrinkleface scratches something on a flat board with a feather, and the mate or cub is put in a pen of gray bars. She-cubs go into one pen, he-cubs into another, and mates into a third. All are already full—no room to sit, much less lie down—and each new person shoved inside results in a gust of grumbling.

The he-cub before me is taken to the he-cub pen, and I want to run. But Nightman holds my rope tightly.

Wrinkleface squints down at me, nose wrinkling. "What is *that*?"

Nightman shrugs. "An oddity we stumbled across." He tugs on my rope and pulls me toward the she-cub pen.

I hang back. He can't put me in there. They'll step on me.

Wrinkleface blocks our way. "It can't stay here."

"Why not? Once I put her in a pen, she'll not bother you, as long as you leave her there." Nightman digs into a pouch and pulls out two flat but very shiny pebbles.

Wrinkleface reaches for them, but Nightman closes his hand around them. "She needs a pen of her own, however. The empty one next to the girls will be fine."

"Why should I waste good space like that?"

"Do you want to explain to your customers how their merchandise became scratched and bitten?"

Wrinkleface eyes me. I growl, baring my teeth. If looking fierce will keep me out of crowded pens, I will make myself look fierce.

"You have a deal."

Nightman gives him the shiny pebbles. "Come on." He leads me to the empty pen and swings open a door of bars.

I balk. Once in, there will be no getting out again. Not until they let me out.

Nightman lowers his voice for my ears only. "Don't make me put you in." Then he kicks my backside, though it is more like a shove than a kick.

Tabby pushes against the bars separating our pens. "Come on, Sarah. It's okay." She stretches an arm toward me as far as the bars will let her.

I swallow the dirt coating my mouth and swing inside. The door clangs shut.

I'm trapped.

CHAPTER 5

FOR SALE

ather will be here. He will. He's only been delayed. There are too many crowds. Or his horse went lame. But he will come."

Tabby sits curled up in the corner of her pen, whispering the words again and again. But they are not for me. She does not see me or feel my presence, even though her hand rests against my back.

"Father will come and buy us. We'll sit in a warm house and eat! As much as we want. And tonight a real bed. Sheets. Pillows. Blankets. All soft, all clean. Wait and see." Her hand trembles. Not from outside cold, for the air is warm and unmoving. From coldness on the inside. I know. I feel it too.

Tabby leans forward. "Father?"

Masters and mates wander between the pens. They talk and point and circle, pale people in bright clothing, as if that will make up for their colorlessness.

"I could have sworn . . . but no. Not yet." Tabby sags back against the wall. "So we wait. But it won't be long. He'll be here soon." Her voice lowers, but my ears catch her soft words anyway. "He must."

Another tremor. Her inside coldness is growing. So is mine, but not for the same reason, for I cannot think like Tabby. These people avoid me, do not want me. Why would her father? No, he will not take me into his pack. He will look once at my matted fur and useless leg and then turn away, just like the others.

Nightman saunters through the main door, now open to let the colorless ones come and go. His darkness makes him a solid branch protruding from swirling mists, yet only I seem to see him as he walks from pen to pen. Many times his face turns toward Tabby. Is he thinking to add Tabby to his pack? A growl forms inside me, and I press against the bars to be as close to Tabby as possible. Tabby should have better than him.

Something in his face changes. He nods once. To me? To himself? Then his normal blank hardness returns, and he leaves.

Tabby gasps, her fingers clutching my ragged coat. My head jerks toward her, but the smile on her face says that danger did not pull the gasp from her. She grabs a bar and pulls herself to her feet.

Who does she see? I cock my head. Not the man with a bear's bulk and hair that birds would nest in. Nor the man who is the color of the coldest days and dressed in river clothes—blue and flowing. Then I find a man of short height, little hair, and uneven walk. I look at Tabby twice, but there is no mistake. He is the one. This is her father, the great leader of her pack? For several moments, he tips his head, smiles, frowns, and makes other small gestures toward Tabby as he wanders around. She gives him the same. Then she points at me. He squints and frowns.

I press my head to my forepaws. *I do not look like much, but I will serve you. I will do all you say. You will not find a reason to be angry with me. Just take me.*

He shakes his head at Tabby and stops by the mates' pen, his back to us. He does not want me. But when he faces us again, Tabby frowns at him and folds her arms. He pauses at the she-cub pen. His eyes go from Tabby to me and back to Tabby. He bows his head, lowering his gaze in submission. I frown. This man takes orders from Tabby?

Tabby squeezes back into her corner. "That was Adeo, Father's steward."

I do not know what a steward is, but the man is not the pack leader. He serves the leader—and Tabby too, from what I saw.

"He says that as long as he thinks he has enough money for me, he'll buy you too."

He will take me? I raise my head. Adeo walks out the door and stops. He leans forward, talking to someone. Nightman steps forward. A vine of coldness creeps back inside me. They press their heads close together, then Adeo nods and backs up. They bow to each other and Adeo leaves.

Did Nightman tell Adeo about me? Will Adeo not take me now? Nightman wanders inside and slouches against the wall near my pen, pulling out a knife to sharpen, as one waiting. He does not look at me. He does not look at Tabby. He does not look at anyone, but my instincts tell me he sees and hears more than he appears to. Every movement and noise is noted, from the mates squabbling over a she-cub to the men gathering at my pen.

Until now, a master might glance at me as he walked by. But now several men, alone or in packs, stand before me. Not men like the ones looking at mates and cubs. These are stone-face men with whips and knives at their sides. Predators. My inside cold becomes worse than ever before. I turn my back to them. Then the noise dies. Not to a whisper. To utter silence.

My fur bristles as I shift where I lie. Tabby scoots backward, squeezing herself against the bars between us. Everyone, even Nightman, has turned toward a man standing in the open door. Unlike many around him, his clothing is dark and muted, the colors of deep forests. But his face tells of much time in the sun. Here is the leader among the predators. A master hunter. His gaze roams restlessly from Wrinkleface to the colorless ones to pens. Then it reaches me and stills.

I scrunch against the wall behind me, my paws digging into the stone under me. He strides over to my pen, everyone parting before him. He looks at me. I look at him. One eye is green. One is blue. Both glint with the want for prey. Our wills lock in battle, two dogs scrapping for the leader's position.

Nightman slides his knife into his boot and saunters over to Two-Eyes. "Disgusting, isn't it? I caught that creature, thinking she'd make me rich. But look at her now." He spits at the ground. "Completely ruined, not worth the smallest coin."

"Perhaps."

Nightman shrugs. "Your waste. Don't say I didn't warn you." He wanders away.

Two-Eyes keeps his gaze on me steady, daring me to look away first. But I will not, cannot. That would say I am weak, that he can do with me as he wants. And with one hand clutching a whip and the other clenched in a fist, this is a master I do not wish to serve.

"Marc!"

Wrinkleface scurries up, bowing toward Two-Eyes. "Yes, milord? You called?"

"I want to see the beast. Up close." He tosses his words over his shoulder like scraps, nothing to the feasting master but everything to the dog waiting under his table.

Wrinkleface waves his hands about, as if he cannot find the scraps he knows were tossed to him. "But milord, I was told that the creature is quite fierce and likely to attack if I release it."

"So you say." Two-Eyes turns slowly. "*I* say you fear that release would lower your profits."

"No, milord. Of course not. I just . . ."

Two-Eyes strokes his whip with one finger.

Wrinkleface spins around. "Bran!" He claps his hands twice. "A rope now!"

A twig of a he-cub lugs over a rope almost as thick as his arms.

"Catch the beast and show it to Lord Avery."

"M-me, sir?"

"Your name is Bran, isn't it?" He unlocks my door and shoves the he-cub inside.

The he-cub helper clutches the rope as if it will keep me from attacking. Wrinkleface holds the door closed with only one hand. Two-Eyes stands waiting, expecting me to come when he says, even though he could not stare me down. Beyond them all, the door is open to the town.

Tabby presses against the bars. "Please, Sarah. Let him take you. Don't make it hard for him and go quietly."

She does not see. Her master will never want me; Nightman will see to that. And I cannot bow to Two-Eyes. He will devour me.

Tabby continues to plead with me, saying this is the only way, but her words are a whisper in the wind. There *is* only one way, though not the one she thinks it is, and I must take it.

The he-cub steps closer and closer. He fumbles with the rope. I bolt.

"Sarah, no!"

I ignore Tabby. Her escape is sure. Mine is not. I bypass the he-cub in two bounds and a third slams my paws into the bars. Wrinkleface stumbles backward. The door bangs open. People scramble away. I charge forward with long, sweeping swings. The town with its hiding places is mine.

A whip snaps across my path. Two-Eyes.

I veer away, but his whip wraps around my leg with a sharp sting. I stumble, nearly hitting the ground nose first. Black boots with scratches across the toes plant Two-Eyes between the open door and me.

"No one has ever escaped from me." He grabs me by the throat and lifts me up to his eye level. "No one ever will. I *always* take my prey, alive—or dead." The glint in his eyes brightens.

Then I know. I saw Two-Eyes wrong. That glint is not hunger for prey. He gains that easily enough. No, Two-Eyes craves more: the challenge of the hunt. And I have given him exactly what he wants.

He tosses me aside and throws a handful of shiny pebbles near my head. "For your trouble." He strides out.

Wrinkleface scurries forward, snatches up the shiny pebbles, and jumps backward, as if remembering I'm there. "You there!" He points at Nightman. "Put it back."

Nightman doesn't argue. I thought he would, but he only grabs me by my coat's neck and shoves me back into the pen before he walks away, shaking his head. I slump in my corner. Two-Eyes has picked up my scent, and now no matter how far or fast I go, he will always be right behind me.

Tabby slides her arm through the bars and rests her hand on my paw. "Oh Sarah, why did you have to run?"

CHAPTER 6

THE HIGHEST BIDDER

Before a big storm, the wind stops. Twigs do not twitch. The water has no ripples. The slightest rustle of leaves raises the fur in alarm. That same feeling now thickens the air with the leaving of Two-Eyes. Those in the pens beside me huddle far from the bars between us. Mates cling to masters, who watch me with narrow eyes. All circle wide around my pen, and no one speaks above a whisper.

And they whisper of me. I feel it more than hear it. *Monster. Beast. She-devil.* I have been banished to the edge of the pack. Soon I will be chased out of it forever. Already a man-pack gathers beyond the door to send me away. Restless. Rumbling. Like an approaching storm.

Tabby feels it too. Her hand tightens on my forepaw. "It won't be long now."

The last of the colorless ones wandering inside join the restless men, and the door is shut. A man glides out from among the shadows of crates stacked in a corner, his footsteps silent even to my ears. His long fingers curl like bird claws, and a beak-nose hangs over his flat mouth.

Wrinkleface nods at him. "Jambres."

"Marc." Like his looks, Hawk's voice is sharp and pointed. "The list?"

"Here." Wrinkleface offers him a yellowed roll.

Hawk pulls it flat and stares at the black marks worm-wiggling across the surface. "Any place you want me to start?"

"The creature." Wrinkleface points his thumb at me over his shoulder. "It's been nothing but trouble. The sooner it's gone, the better."

"Understood." He clutches his roll in his claw-hand and glides silently out of the door, ready to swoop down on his next prey.

Outside, the restless man-pack becomes still. Inside, Wrinkleface approaches my pen and opens the door for a man who came in when Hawk left, a man whose hands could crush my neck. I cower in the corner. What will happen now? What do they plan to do with me? A whimper forms in my mouth, but I push it inside.

Tabby leans down so her mouth is nearly at my ear. "You'll be fine, Sarah. He's only going to take you out for the auction so Adeo can buy you. I'll follow in a few minutes, and together we'll go find Father."

That does not make my trembling less. She might think this is what will happen, but it will not. She did not see Nightman talking to Adeo. She did not see Two-Eyes when he thought of the hunt. He will not end his pursuit of me until I am his—or dead.

The man of life-crushing hands ties a rope around my neck and yanks on it. "Move."

I glance once more at Tabby. If Two-Eyes takes me instead of Adeo, I will never see her, never feel her gentle hands, never hear her soft words again. I will be on my own, never to be one of a pack.

"Soon, Sarah. Very soon." She squeezes my forepaw once more and lets it go.

I follow the man out of the pen, out the door into the open space between the houses. Except the space is no longer open. The man-pack—or is it several packs?—fills the area with more people than I have ever seen. The pack of Master was not few, but this group makes his seem very small. If this is where the slavers came from, no wonder Master's pack was destroyed.

"Come on." The man tugs on my rope, and I swing up a short hill of planks to the one spot still open—a square of boards raised above the ground.

Hawk paces in one corner. "Hurry up."

The man leading me grunts and forces me up onto a wood block in the center.

I cling to it, pressing my belly flat against the top. Everyone can see me; everyone *does* see me. Including Two-Eyes. He sits on a horse near the back, his arms folded and eyes half closed. A predator seeking to appear harmless to its intended prey.

Elbow poking, pointing, and laughing begin. "What is that? A half-breed—half devil, half dog?"

I want to growl and snap, but there are too many. If they attack, I'll be torn to pieces, like scraps thrown to the dogs. My head dips, and part of my fur falls across my face. Why didn't I run when I knew Master was no more?

Hawk paces in front of me. "Let the bidding begin. A beast-child, age unknown. Intelligent, with sharp instincts. Strong, quick, and in good health. Perfect for the Tournaments. Opening bid at one hundred. Do I have two? Two hundred. Do I have three? Three. Do I have four?"

The hands of stone-faced predators wave. Hawk spews more words faster and faster, pointing and nodding. Two-Eyes doesn't twitch. Adeo stands to one side, his hands at his sides. My head hangs lower. Tabby will be angry that her words were not obeyed, but in a few days she will think of me no more. Unlike me. I will think of her every day.

"Thirteen-fifty? Thirteen-fifty. Fourteen? Fourteen hundred? Fourteen hundred."

Hands continue to go up and down, but they are fewer now. Adeo raises his.

My head jerks up. Do I see what is not there? But Adeo's eyes are now on Hawk and there! He raises his hand again. Maybe I will be with Tabby once more.

"Two thousand. Do I have two thousand fifty, sir?"

Now only two are left—Adeo and another stone-faced man. The man nods slowly at Hawk.

"Twenty-one? Twenty-one hundred, sir?" Hawk peers down his beak-nose at Adeo.

Adeo starts to shake his head but then stops at a ripple in the crowd of people. Nightman edges out of the shadow of a building and nods to Adeo. Adeo's shoulders straighten and he stands taller. "Twenty-one hundred." Nightman wants Adeo to continue?

"Twenty-one fifty? Twenty-one fifty? No?" The beating of Hawk's words slow to a glide. "Bid for animal-child now closing at—"

"Five thousand." Two-Eyes breaks into Hawk's voice.

No. No! NO! I clutch the wood block I stand on as Two-Eyes nudges his horse forward. One hand grips a strap that goes into the animal's mouth, but the other rests on his whip. "Five thousand for the beast."

Hawk and I both look at Adeo. *Buy me. Don't let him take me.* He shakes his head. "Too rich for me."

My shoulders hunch. I knew it. Two-Eyes waited only for the other packs to tire from fighting each other so he could take his prey unopposed.

Hawk turns back to Two-Eyes. "Animal-child to Lord Avery at five thousand."

Two-Eyes rides forward, the pack parting before him. They know better than to step between a predator and his prey.

I am pulled to the edge of the raised square, and a growl grows inside me. I will not win against Two-Eyes, but I am Beast. I lived with the Others. I know how to fight and that you fight to the end.

But Two-Eyes knows how to fight too. He stays out of my striking distance. We will fight when he wants, how he wants.

"Want to run? Good, I hope you do." He strokes his whip. "But though you may run and run fast, my arrows always fly faster." He yanks on the strap, turning the horse around. "Lorcan, send it back to the Keeper. He'll know what to do."

A thin man steps forward, his smile offering sharp, yellow teeth to back up his master's bite. "With pleasure, milord." Even in his words, Fang's grin cannot be missed. He flips a knife up into the air and grabs it again before it falls to the ground, then stabs it into his belt.

Two-Eyes kicks his heels into the horse, which rears and then charges out of the open area. At his master's departure, Fang's smile widens. I retreat with a growl. Fang grabs my forepaws, flips me over, off the raised square. My back hits the ground, all air crushed from me. I should run. I can't move.

Fang grabs my hind legs and swings me into a wood cage sitting atop a wagon, closing the top before I can right myself. I swipe at him anyway. He jumps out of the way, his teeth reappearing. "Good try, animal." He saunters away, flipping his knife as he goes. "Deliver it directly to the Keeper."

"Yes, sir." A man I cannot see clicks his tongue, and with a jerk, we start rolling away.

My head sags against my forepaws. I could not touch him with teeth or claws, not even once. Now Two-Eyes can do with me as he wishes. I will never outrun or outfight him.

"One thousand." Hawk's voice calls over the rumbling. Tabby steps down from the wood block I stood on only a little while ago. Adeo stands at the edge of the raised square of wood and helps her to the ground. She is once more back in her pack's protection.

A loud clattering bounces against the gray houses, and a man in silver and blue rides in on a giant horse of white, right toward the raised wood. He jumps off before the animal stops and strides toward Tabby and Adeo. Tall and powerful. Yet this master does not have a face of stone or a whip at his side.

Tabby spins toward him. "Father!" She flings herself into his arms, and he swings her around, holding her close.

My insides clench. This isn't a master of any small pack. This is the master of *Tabby's* pack. What was almost my pack. I bury my face under my forepaws, unable to watch any longer.

CHAPTER 7

TRAINING

The wagon, as the men call the rolling pen, rattles any thought of sleep from my mind. The sleep I want—need so much. I can still see Tabby's father swinging her around, and only the blackness of sleep will remove that from before my eyes.

But the wagon bounces. And jolts. And jerks. Then when we pass the border town's walls, the men yell at the horse to go faster. I clutch my cage's bars with my forepaws, the wagon throwing me side to side.

The sun rises high. We change horses. The sun lowers back toward the earth, turning everything blood-red. I still cling to my cage. Finally the wagon slows its pace as the light falls prey to darkness.

My paws let go of the bars. They ache. So does the rest of me, even my teeth. But maybe the wagon will soon stop and the men will let me stretch my legs. Inside the cage I have enough room to roll over, but not much more.

"Who approaches the castle of Lord Avery? State your name and business—and be quick about it!" The voice sounds far away.

"I am Soran, the servant of my Lord Avery, and I bring back goods from market for him."

"Approach."

Clanking and groaning, as of a giant monster, fill the night, and the wagon rolls forward under iron teeth. I huddle in my cage, not moving to even take in air. Those teeth could crush me—crush anyone—with one bite.

Footsteps echo against the all-stone ground, and a man waving a firestick comes near. "So, Soran, what did the old fox find this time? Fresh flesh for the Tournament?"

The driver shrugs. "You might say that, though it's unlike anything I've ever seen."

The firestick man peers down at me. "That? I hope he paid a pittance."

"Five thousand."

"Five?" The man whistles. "But it won't last a fortnight."

"I bet three days, especially if he uses an accelerated regimen—and he probably will; I was ordered straight to the Keeper."

"Makes sense. The Royal Tournament *will* be here in three weeks. Which means . . ." The fire flickers, its light twisting in the man's eyes. His voice lowers. "It would be better for this one if it doesn't last the fortnight."

A shudder makes my shoulders jump. What does Two-Eyes plan, that even his own pack speaks of it in vague words and low voices?

"Don't let his lordship hear that, or you'll be the one on the wrong side of his whip," says the driver.

"Isn't that the truth?" The firestick man waves us on, and the wagon rumbles forward.

Tall stone walls rise up around even taller stone buildings toward a black sky. Sharp footsteps echo against the stone ground. A distant firestick flickers. Stone grinds against stone within me. When the wagon stops again, I am lifted to the ground before a low, crouching building. There is a light in one window, a glowing eye glaring at the intruders of its sleep.

A couple of sharp knocks brings a man as old as the trees to the door. He tilts to one side, as if some of his roots have come loose from the ground, but the ragged ridges on his face tell of the many battles he has survived. "Ah, the lord has sent another specimen, has he?" The Keeper peers at me with one eye, the other long lost to another predator.

I shrink back, fur bristling.

"And what a fine specimen it is indeed," he croons. "Back strong, frame sturdy, eyes clear and bright, spirit unbroken. Yes, this one might be . . ." He whirls back to the men, waving his arms. "Be your heads stuffed with feathers? Bring it down to the pens." He hobbles inside.

The men lift my cage and by the time we are inside, the Keeper is already partway down some dark stone steps, his firestick's light barely touching the walls. We follow him down, down, down. The darkness darts around the weak light, taunting it, and creeps up my back. I tuck myself into a ball as best as I can. Are the walls closer together down here than up above?

The stairs flatten. Barred holes and small doors dot the walls. A screech sends me against the bars of my cage—there are other animals here. Green and red birds. Shivering rabbits. A pacing dog with a shaggy coat. And those are only the ones I can see.

"Hurry up now. The empty cell is back here. Vacated only two days ago. Was sorry to lose that one. It showed such promise." He rattles keys and unlocks a thick wood door.

I scrunch backward, the fur along my legs and neck rising. Not another pen of stone. I need trees. Sky. Sun. Grass. Dirt.

The men dump me into the narrow room. My shoulder hits the back wall. I crumple to the floor. The Keeper shuts the door, cutting off all but a single splinter of light squeezing through the gap. No, no, no. I struggle to my feet. They can't leave me here. I slam my paws against the door again and again and howl with all I have.

There's a rap on the door. "Sleep. Training begins soon." Then footsteps go away, taking with them the last of the light.

No! I career around the small space, blacker than the

blackest night. There must be a way out; there must be. I pound
at the walls, claw at the floor. But the floor is stone, the walls are
stone. Even the low ceiling is stone. Only the door is not.

Panting, I kick, claw, ram against the wood. The door doesn't
even shudder when I throw all of me against it. Paws raw, body
sore, I slump to the ground, darkness creeping along my skin.

❦

Do I sleep? Maybe. Maybe not. It is always dark, whether my eyes
are shut or open, whether I sleep or wake. And quiet too. Once
I think I hear another animal. Or do my ears hear what is not?
This place is so full of . . . nothing. I curl into a tight ball, wishing
it would all go away, wishing for Tabby's soft touch.

What is she doing now? Sleeping in a bed like she spoke of?
Eating with her father, talking, laughing? What I would do to be
under their table, waiting for the scraps to fall, or sleeping among
their dogs! But I thought I knew more than Tabby. She told me
to stay, but I ran. Now I will always run, always looking back for
predators. For Two-Eyes. Maybe I should lie down and let him
take me.

Footsteps thump against stone. Or so say my ears. There is
nothing out there but darkness. Endless darkness.

My door opens and light burns into my face. Too bright! I
bury my face in my paws.

"Come, Beast. Much to do, you know. Tournament coming
soon and all that."

I peek out. The Keeper holds only a firestick high above my
head. But how can that be? That light looked so weak coming
down.

"Broken already? Tsk, tsk. I would have thought better of you."
He pulls out a roll. "Not even interested in breaking your fast?"

My nose twitches despite myself. Fresh bread. Not a rock-
lump like the slavers gave. Soft, still-warm bread. Water fills my
mouth.

He backs away, holding the food out. "That's right. Come along."

I shouldn't, but the lump is so big. Two meals' worth. I dart forward. He jerks his hand up and throws the bread. I leap after it, snatching it in my teeth before it bounces on the floor.

"Not bad! Not bad at all." The Keeper hobbles toward me.

Snarling, I hunch over the roll and chew on it. If he tries to take it now, his hand will have more ridges and fewer fingers.

But he no longer seems to want it. "Reflexes good and quick. Excellent height. I'll have to make use of that. But speed. That's the key. We need more, or we'll never outrun the lord."

Outrun Two-Eyes? I overfill my mouth with the rest of the bread and sit back on my hind legs. That isn't possible—is it?

The Keeper pats my head, slipping a chain around my neck before I know what he does. "Come on. We have work to do." He tugs on the chain, leading me back upstairs and outside.

All the things I've missed rush forward to greet me. Light. Wind. The smell of dirt and water. Leaning back, I lift my face to the sky. The shadows slip from my back and cower beneath me. This is where I belong. Not in that black hole of endless night.

The Keeper tugs on the chain, his hand tight around a long rod with which he replaced the firestick. I do not move. I need to drink in the light. I need to taste the wind.

He whacks the rod against the stones in front of my paws. I jerk back.

"Keep up. Next time I strike." He marches me around the low building.

Behind it, traps await their prey. A deep dirt pit. Twisted poles and logs, a tangled thicket waiting to ensnare. Wobbly planks leaning against a wall ready to crumble. And I smell enough water to drown the biggest animal—probably held by the long bucket on the far side.

The Keeper goes straight to the pit and climbs inside, pulling me after him. The dirt is very soft. With each step my paws sink in. I lean back, but it shifts under me and I slide toward the center.

"There." The Keeper taps the stake in the middle where he attached my chain and walks along the top edge of the pit. "Now run."

I sit there and blink at him. Run? On this?

"I said run!" He hits my side with the stick.

I spring away and face him, snarling.

"Snarl, growl, grumble. You stay." His stick smacks my back again.

I swipe at it, and he thrusts the end into my face. Hard. My head snaps back and cracks against the stake. I slump to the ground.

"Get up." Approaching from behind me, he strikes me again. "Now."

I stumble to my feet.

"Run." He prods with his stick, though not as hard this time.

My paws swing forward and I bound around the circle with an uneven gait, my useless leg bouncing around.

"Faster."

Faster? But my chest already heaves. I cut across the pit.

"No, no, no." The stick beats my right side, making me stumble. "You must stay to the edges. Now faster."

I don't want another prod from his stick, so I stretch out my good legs to their full length, tucking the useless one up against my body as best as I can. The Keeper stays near, his rod ready when I slow or drift toward the middle.

The light warms my back; no breeze finds its way into the pit. My fur clings, thick and hot. The Keeper drives me on, around and around the pit. Finally he calls, "Stop!"

I drop where I stand, panting.

He sets water before me and pats my head once before he walks to the stake for the chain. I turn my back to him and lap up the water, my nose in it as well as my mouth.

When I lift my head, the Keeper tugs on the chain. "Come. We have more to do."

More?

───※───

"Stop."

When the word leaves the Keeper's mouth, I slump to the ground. Swimming. Climbing. More running. Jumping. The Keeper has made me do it all. But no more. I cannot even raise my head to drink the water he sets before me.

He watches me for a moment, then nods. "Enough." He tugs on my chain. "Come."

I push up, my legs all trembling. A little farther. One more step. The buildings are fuzzy along the edges, and my belly nearly drags on the ground. But if I keep my head down, I can shuffle forward.

A whip's crack splits the air, followed by the scream of an animal—yet not quite of an animal. My paws dig into the cracks between the stones, every hair bristling. The Keeper stops too, cocks his head, and hobbles to the right, away from the low building. Toward the screams. Toward the whip.

A chill like I felt in the dark room of stone creeps along my body. I don't want to go that way. Can't. The Keeper pulls me forward anyway.

Crack! "Arrr . . ." The scream drops into a moan as we round the corner.

Two-Eyes, a half smile on his face, raises the whip. A man leans against a wall, his face puffy and gashed, his bared back a bloody mass of welts. A swordsman holds back a crying mate. Fang, holding three other whips, grins at his master's work. I immediately curl into a ball. My insides try to push out of my mouth not once, but again and again.

A hiss-crack rips through the air, and a shudder rips through me. My claws dig into my paws, my forelegs covering my ears.

But it doesn't keep the sounds out. The mate's cries. The whip's hiss-crack. The man's screams.

"Another escapee? Where'd this one make it to?" The Keeper's voice barely creaks above the whip and screams.

Fang chuckles. "Delt, if you can believe it."

The Keeper whistles. "That's almost to the eastern border." Hiss-crack, moan.

"Such is the lure of Ahavel." Hiss-crack, moan. "You'd think the fools would learn. It always ends the same way." Fang jerks his head toward the whip.

"Give me my animals. Train much better." The Keeper tugs on my chain. "Come."

He need not ask again. I bound forward, ahead of him. Anything to leave this place. Still the sound of the whip pursues me—the sound of the whip and the silence that has replaced the screams.

CHAPTER 8

The Tournament

Day chases day until they blur together so I can barely tell where one ends and another starts, like a pack of dogs running together. The Keeper comes for me, gives me some bread, and then takes me outside, around the low building to the pit and other traps. Then I run around the pit or along the top of the crumbling wall. Or climb up slick plank hills. Or jump over logs or swim in the big bucket.

The first day the water made my fur bristle. By the third, I jump in whenever the Keeper lets me. Not only does the water cool me down, but I can do it best. My useless leg does not slow me in water like on land. Faster speed, fewer blows.

But if the Keeper does not beat me as much when I swim, he strikes more—and harder—when I run or climb. My left side is often tender. My right side always is. But I am not in the black hole at these times. The sun, the wind—I cannot get enough of them.

Then one day the Keeper does not come.

I pace my stone pen, sleep, and pace more. My insides rumble. Still no Keeper, not with food, not to let me out. Have I awakened long before he is to come? I cannot tell in this darkness. No light appears to say day is here. I try to sleep again. My insides rumble louder.

Thump. Thump.

My head lifts. Footsteps—and a splinter of light. Finally! I leap to my feet.

The light fades. So do the footsteps. I am still trapped in my pen.

I stand in the darkness, blinking. Is he going to leave me here? But I did all he told me to do. He even patted my head. Said I am ready. Why does he not let me out? I scratch at the door and whine. Nothing. Not even a "Quiet!"

I pound harder and howl. But no one comes.

I slump against the door, alone.

"All as ordered, milord."

My head pops up. The Keeper! He is back. I push toward the light squeezing through the crack in the door. The thumping of many feet against stone reaches my ears.

"Yes, yes. All ready. This one or that—you can have any choice."

"All?" A single word, said as a question, yet commanding. Two-Eyes.

I back up a step, fur rising on my neck. If he is here too, it is not good.

"Isolation. Fasting. Everything as you ordered. Even for the beast."

The footsteps stop nearby. I crouch in a corner, a growl building. Two-Eyes brought this. No light. No food. No run outside in the sun and wind.

" 'Even for the beast'?"

"Not ready. Not ready at all, milord. It's cunning. It's fast. But not ready yet. More time needed before it peaks."

"No matter. I promised this would be the greatest Tournament. Nothing will be spared. I want it, along with your six best."

"As you wish, milord."

Footsteps in the confident beat of Two-Eyes go away, and the Keeper calls out. "You two—do you sleep with your eyes open?

Take the stag. And you! Haul the pheasants up." Thump! "And careful! Your neck if there's damage."

"What about the beast thing?"

"I'll take it. It'd probably slip from your fingers before halfway to the field. Yes, yes. Much too cunning for men with feathers for brains." The Keeper rattles his keys, but only after the other footsteps fade does the door open.

He looks me up and down, head bobbing. "Yes, yes. This is the day." He nods to himself once more, and a smile—a real smile!—slinks onto his face. "My work is complete. If any creature can outrun the lord, this is the one."

People everywhere! Curled in a ball, I watch them between the wood poles of my new pen. Many man-packs seem to have gathered in this open place of grass, like the first day I met Two-Eyes. People going, people coming in bright clothing, in brown clothing, among red-and-gold cloth buildings, among the open places.

In the pens beside me, other animals pace. I wish Tabby were beside me, yet it is good she is not. At least I am surrounded by real grass and dirt instead of the stone or wood of the walled buildings behind me. And on the far side beyond the people are trees—a whole forest of them, clothed in orange and gold and green! If I can reach them before Two-Eyes reaches me, maybe I can outrun him.

A loud blast rings across the field; a short man blows into a long shiny thing. The people quiet, sitting on chairs and wood benches and blankets spread on the ground. Several men with bows line up at the front. Two-Eyes stands near the center of them, at ease, a master in control.

A man dressed in red and gold faces the line of men and spews words that make no sense to me. All are quiet except a few at the line's far end; they shift and mutter, unsettled by a latecomer. I rub my eyes against the back of my paw, but that does not change the latecomer's form. Nightman. What is he doing here?

The speaker finishes and moves to the side while men carry the cages of pheasants among tall grasses at the far end of the field. The line of men slide arrows against their bows' long wood arches, points to the ground.

"Archers, ready!" calls the speaker, raising an arm. Bows lift. The speaker's arm drops to his side.

One bird after another bursts from the grasses. Twang, twang, twangtwangtwang. Arrows shoot through the air, a swarm of bees—stingers first. The pheasants fall one after the other. My insides lurch with each thud.

The fallen animals are brought forward. Two have black-feathered arrows and are given to Two-Eyes. One has a blue-feathered arrow; Nightman gets that one.

More animals from pens next to mine are let out. First birds, to be shot by the line of bowmen. Then come the land runners—deer, wild boars, bears. Most bound for the woods, pursued by men on foot. One rabbit doesn't want to leave its pen and must be prodded to go. Moments after it limps into the forest, Two-Eyes comes back, carrying high its unmoving body. I hide my face after that.

Soon the sun is straight up and the last animal, the stag, is released. I press my body against the back of the cage. The stag is fast. The stag is strong. Surely if an animal can escape, it can. A bird circles above, screeches, and flies toward the forest. Leaves rustle. A blast rings out, calling the other hunters back. Even the stag could not escape.

Trembling, I rise. My legs do not want to hold me up, much less move, and I must run next. But if even the stag is not fast enough, how can I be?

When all hunters have returned, the speaker calls, "Time for the midday meal."

The man-pack rises. Words flow together in a storm rumble. Hunters check weapons. Smoke and hot meat and bread scent the air. I pace in my cage, but no one comes to let me out. I lie down again.

Several of the hunters wander by. Desire brightens their eyes, even the ones who look tired when they first stand over my pen. They are ready to hunt me. Nightman, with another man, also stops.

"So this is our grand challenge that's supposed to take a half-day?" The second man pokes a finger at me between the bars. "What do you think?"

Nightman stares at me as if he was not the one who caught me, who drove me and saw to it that I would be on that wood block in the border town. "I don't know. I half expect her to run for the smell of water and become trapped on the bluffs like the others."

"And if it doesn't?"

"The briars will take her, especially with matted hair like that." He shrugs. "The animals just don't understand the only way out is the one they instinctively avoid—the narrow path in the middle. They fear the open areas with no brush." He walks away. "It almost seems a pity."

"Is that so?"

"Hmm . . ."

Any more words are eaten by the man-packs' noise. I rise and press myself against the front bars of the cage. The trees' branches wave and the leaves rustle, calling me, saying I'll be safe among them. The trees do not know Two-Eyes walks among them like a man in his house. He is a master predator. Nothing can outrun his arrows. After the earlier hunts, I know that more than ever.

But it is hard to shoot what you cannot find.

CHAPTER 9

FLIGHT

A blast calls the man-pack together. People race for places to sit, crowding along the edges to see. The hunters line up, Two-Eyes once again in the center. His shoulders are rigid as he checks his tools, from the knife strapped to his side to each arrow he carries. He changes bows with a man behind him. The first hunts were games. Now the predator appears. He will not let go his prey.

My insides roll over each other until they form a rock in my middle. Because of Nightman, I know more than I did—but will it be enough?

The speaker steps in front of the hunters and the man-packs. "The final hunt of the day is a beast-child. Human in form, this creature combines animal instincts with almost-human reasoning, providing a most challenging hunt. Therefore, the winner will be awarded five hundred gold pieces along with the body."

A murmur rumbles through the crowd.

"And if the beast-child can be captured and brought back alive, that amount shall be doubled."

The noise grows so loud that any other words go unheard. The speaker turns away, and a man rests a hand on my pen's latch. They will let me go soon. I edge forward, ready to bolt when the hole is big enough.

"Hunters, ready!"

The men shift their positions, bows in hand.

The speaker nods to the man by my pen. He pulls a pin. The door opens. I bolt.

With long swinging bounds, my leg chews up and spits out the land as I head toward the woods and the scent of water. *Faster, faster!* The Keeper's words push me harder, and I stretch out my legs even longer. The open area drops behind me. Trees wave their branches in welcome. Bushes embrace me. Dirt and grass give way to a floor of leaves. I turn away from the scent of the water and toward the briars.

A blast rings out, and shouts arise. The hunters are on their way. My legs stretch to their full length. I run as if the Keeper is behind me swinging his stick, with Two-Eyes and his whip just behind that.

A narrow strip of dirt cuts in front of me. The open area. I swing onto the path and follow it, though my body does not want to. But I cannot win over the briars. They would catch my fur and hold me, making me easy prey for the first hunter to find me.

I follow the path, bounding between the trees along its edge. Leaves long fallen crunch beneath my paws. A vine wanders across my path. It won't be long. Soon Two-Eyes, Nightman, and the others will know I am not among the cliffs by the water. They will look for me elsewhere. I need more space. I need more speed. I need more time.

None of them are mine.

My pace slows, my chest heaving as pain stabs my side. I can no longer go like this. A hiding place, one where the hunters won't look for me and can't track me, is my best choice. Maybe my only choice. But where? There are only trees, trees, and more trees. No bushes or tall grasses. Not even any low places in the ground.

A bird flies up to a tree and hops from branch to branch before disappearing among the leaves. What if . . . I bound forward. There! An old tree leans against the tall one next to it. I pull myself onto the trunk, its rough bark biting into my paws. When

I jump on the tree, it shivers only a little; it should hold me. I walk up to the top, an easy climb after the Keeper's slick planks.

Staying on the branch is harder. I slide my forepaws forward, then pull up my good hind leg, my useless one dangling beside. The branch sways and begins to bend. I need to reach the next tree. I cannot go back to the ground. I must jump.

My paws push off, my eyes always on where I want to go. My forepaws grab. My good hind leg hits—and slips. My paws grapple to hold on. But it is too much. I tip backward . . .

. . . and jerk to a stop, my forepaws still clinging to the branch. My insides pound to get out, but my body slowly grasps that I am not about to hit the ground and lose all my air. Still, my forepaws do not like holding all of me. Maybe I should drop to the ground, climb up again, and—Crunch-crunch. Crunch-crunch. My ears pick up the soft sound. Someone is coming, is almost here. I don't have time to climb the old tree again. I must go up from where I am.

My hind legs swing my body. Back and forth. Back and forth. Almost there. I tip back until I'm almost upside down, swing my good leg over the branch, and pull myself up. I made it! But that is not enough. Any hunter can find me here. I crawl toward the big trunk, climb up onto a higher branch where more leaves will hide me; and press myself to the tree on the side farthest from the path.

Crunch. Crunch. The soft footsteps stop below me. The wind tugs at the leaves, giving me a glimpse of the man below, a bow in his hand. Two-Eyes. Slowly he pulls out an arrow, places it on the bow's string, and then stands unmoving—looking, listening, maybe even smelling for my nearness.

My paws tighten their grip on the tree. I do not let air go in or out of my mouth. I don't dare. Two-Eyes may keep his eyes on the ground now, but a single sway of a branch or rustle of leaves would turn them upward.

Two-Eyes waits on, ever the patient hunter. Around us, the forest stills. No wind teases the leaves. No bird calls to another. The thick taste of brown leaves and wet dirt fills my mouth.

The rough coat of the tree bites into me. My hind leg, holding almost all my weight, aches. I shift my paw some. The leaves of my branch shiver.

His head jerks up, but his back is to me, so Two-Eyes doesn't see me. Yet. Then he starts to turn.

A squirrel bounds forward, chattering at him loudly.

Two-Eyes grinds out words I don't know and don't want to know, from their growling sound. Letting the arrow drop, he scoops up a rock and throws it at the squirrel. It darts out of the way, pulling more growling words from Two-Eyes. He stuffs the arrow in the pack on his back and marches away.

I lean against the trunk, my air rushing out of me. I am safe . . . for now.

I keep walking among the tree limbs. It is not as fast as on the ground, but I am beyond where most would look for me. Twice more I wait as hunters pass by below. None come as close to finding me as Two-Eyes.

The light lasts longer up among the branches, but it still goes away, and in the half-shadows, I nearly crash to the ground when I miss a jump. So I climb down. I wish I could curl up and sleep, but the longer I can go without stopping, the less likely Two-Eyes will find me.

Darkness slows my steps, but a cool breeze ripples by, the familiar scents of earth and leaves pulling on me. No black pits, no cage, no Two-Eyes tonight! I am back where I know the paths and hiding places.

Silver light creeps between a blackness darker than overturned dirt. The unseen animals of night chirp and click and hoot with each other. The path widens as the trees grow farther apart. I near the end of this part of the forest. I cross over the path to head back among the thicker trees.

Crunch. Quiet. Crunch.

I stop and cock my head, the sound so soft I almost miss it. But the footsteps are there. Someone creeps toward me. I bound back across the path and crawl under some prickly bushes.

Nightman emerges from the shadows, bow slung over his shoulder. Crouching, he presses a hand flat to the ground, as if he expects to feel through it what moves around. What is he doing still out? Most men do not hunt at night. He turns his head toward the bushes I lie flat under. Does he know I am here? He nods once to himself, and rising, slips back into the shadows from which he came.

I stay where I lie. Nightman must be nowhere near when I come out. Another animal scurries past in the dark. The silver light shines on unbroken. The bush taps on my back. I finally rise. But though I do not see or hear or smell Nightman, he hunts me even now in the place where I wanted to go. Now I must walk ground I have already walked today.

Snap.

I dive among the roots of a tree and huddle in its shadow. Nightman steps back into a spot of silver light, his darkness made deeper by it. He creeps toward me. The night swallows him again.

Tracker. The slavers called him Tracker. Because he can find and follow animals—like me. I must get out of his way. Now. I circle far to the left and then to the right. Tracker cuts off my path of escape each time. It's almost as if he knows where I will go next.

But I will not let him take me. He will drag me back to that gray place, and if he does that, Two-Eyes could claim me again. I shudder, the echo of the whip and screams gone silent still in my ears. I will leave the shelter of the forest before I go back to that.

Turning around, I follow the path to the forest's edge.

CHAPTER 10

—◆◆◆—

REUNION

The forest ends as light warms the edge of the sky.
I rest in the shelter of the final row of trees, staring
at the patches of grasses. Such horrible openness, yet I
must go into it. Tracker is at my heels, looking behind
every tree and under every bush. And if *he* looks for me yet, will
not Two-Eyes be looking too? No, these grasslands will be the best
hiding place—after a sleep. I cannot run more than a few steps
now, and run is what I must do if I tread the open spaces. So I
burrow between an old log and some bushes—may it be enough
to hide me from Tracker!—and try to sleep.

But sleep comes in short bursts. Every twig-snap, every leaf-
rustle is Tracker almost on me. Or so my ears say. My eyes say it's
only a few birds and other animals passing by.

Darkness returns and I swing down the path, my steps
soon falling into a steady beat. Plant forepaws, swing forward.
Plant forepaws, swing forward. Past patches of yellow grasses.
Past black rumpled dirt with nothing growing in it. Past a
house. I never see any animals or people. No masters, no mates,
no cubs. That is good, except it makes me feel like the only
one alive.

The sky goes from black to gray to blue. I may be alone now,
but men made this dirt path and they will use it. I swing off the

road and find a stream. I drink my fill and settle among the trees clustered next to the water. Day passes. I sleep little.

The next three nights go much the same. More grass and dirt patches. A few houses. A town to circle around. Once I spot Tracker and must change which way I go.

By the fifth night, hunger pinches my insides and my legs drag from lack of sleep. I want the forest. My useless leg keeps me from being a good hunter, but with time I can catch or find *something* to eat, and fewer people would mean more sleep. Why did I let Tracker drive me from among the trees?

But it is too late to go back. I push on. Light comes again. Only a pile of big rocks among the tall grasses offers me a place to hide. It is not much, but it is better than the path. I curl into a tight ball by the rocks and shiver. The cool air of night is not warmed much by day's light. But I am so tired that I sleep, cold or not.

The slowing of a horse's steps awakens me. The light is weakening, and the shadows are now larger than me, though the air is warmer than when I fell asleep.

The horse stops. "Which way now?" A master rides a horse, and he is not alone.

I roll onto my underside and dig my paws into the ground. If they see me, I must run.

"Left, to Cordal."

My fur prickles. I know the second voice, the voice that grins: Fang. Does that mean Two-Eyes is also near?

"Not to Delt?"

The second man's words stop me from looking for Two-Eyes. I've heard the name Delt before.

"Delt has a border guard to catch any runners headed for Ahavel. If the beast goes that way, they'll snare it. But if it crosses lines between fiefs and another lord catches it"—Fang's voice flattens, losing all grin and gaining all teeth—"twenty men lost their heads the last time that happened."

The second man gulps. "Cordal it is then." There's a slap, and the two horses turn down the left path.

Delt—that's where the man made it to, the one Two-Eyes was whipping. And beyond Delt is . . . something. From the way everyone talks, if someone could get beyond Delt, he would be safe, at least from Two-Eyes. I turn my face to the path on the right.

My path goes through the middle of a man-pack. In the shadow-light before darkness, the houses hunch over like a pack of sleeping dogs, and for a long time, I only look from one to another. Is this Delt? I do not know, but I must walk as if these sleeping-dog houses might awake and attack me. I do not want to make the mistakes of the man Two-Eyes caught.

I scramble from building shadow to building shadow, creeping ever closer to the blackness beyond the buildings—a forest. Even if this is not Delt, I will be safe if I can reach the trees.

"Halt!"

I dive into the shadow of the last building. That word cannot be for me. I cannot be taken now, when I am so close. I will fight the whole man-pack if I must.

"I said halt!" A swordsman marches across the path, away from me. I crouch closer to the ground. Should I run now or wait?

"Keep your voice down. You'll scare her away." A low growl rumbles from the other side. Tracker is back. Will I never escape all these hunters?

"Who are you? What's your business in Delt?"

"Name's Mason, and you're still talking too loud."

The swordsman stalks toward the voice. "I'll talk as loud as I want until I get some answers."

"I'm tracking a beast-child." Tracker shifts, barely more than a black hump in the shadows. "Now be quiet. She's nearby, and I don't want to lose her again." He slides forward, and silver light glints off a ready bow.

The other man lowers his sword and steps alongside Tracker. "A beast-child?" His words are softer now, so that I must strain my ears to hear them. "Like the one that escaped from the Tournament?"

"The very same." Tracker moves away from me. The swordsman follows. Both their backs are to me.

This might be my only chance to reach the trees before Tracker finds me. I crawl around the building, set my face to the woods, and run.

"There she goes!"

An arrow whizzes above my head.

Not good. Not good. Not good. I plunge into the forest, zigzagging between the trees. Faster, faster. I dart between two trunks and skid to a stop. No more trees shelter me; I stand at the top of a bare hill overlooking another small town. Why aren't there more trees?

Branches crack and leaves crunch behind me. No time to figure it out now. I bound down the hill, pebbles sliding under my paws. Shouts ring out behind me. Hide, hide, hide! An old tree stands behind the first house I reach. Most of its leaves still cling to its branches. Leaping straight up, I grab the lowest branch and climb up and up and up until I dare not go higher.

Men gather at the top of the hill, as if a wall keeps them from coming closer. Tracker alone approaches. He circles around the nearby house twice and stops under my tree, listening, waiting, his darkness blending into the shadows below my feet. My paws tighten around the branch. If I jump from here, could I land so I can still run?

Then Tracker moves on, circling the next house, prowling shadows between buildings, and stalking anything that moves. He reaches a larger building which spills much light and noisy laughter into the night. He goes inside. Why did he do that? He must know I would not be in there. Maybe he needed something, because soon he steps out again and continues his prowling until I can no longer tell him from the shadows.

I swing down and drop lightly to the ground in a crouch. Where to go? What to do? The forest offers protection, but men still pace its edge. Tracker stalks among the buildings. I'm tired and hungry. What ever made me think I could outrun Tracker, Two-Eyes, all who hunt me? Maybe I should put myself before

Tracker. End this running, the days of hunger and nights of no sleep. Maybe I should . . .

No. Master often gave me no food, and the cold kept me awake many nights. I lived through all of it. I can live through it now. I can find a good sleeping place. I can hunt down food. Food is always around where a man-pack is.

From building to building I go, sniffing for any lump of bread or hunk of meat. The first house is empty and has been a long time. At the second house I rouse some dogs and must keep going—Tracker might hear them and come back. The third house is closed up tight.

The next building is the noisy one Tracker went into. I start to swing around it, staying out of reach of the light's fingers. But a big pack usually means more food, and my nose tells me that is true here: bread, drink, roasting meat. My insides rumble as I sneak around to the back. A door is open, light stretching across my path.

I press my side to the wall and edge forward. I must be fast. I must be quiet, as if I stalk an animal that can run from me. No one can know I am here. Otherwise they might tell Tracker or give me to Two-Eyes. I peek in the doorway.

The room is empty of people—and full of food. A pot bubbling over a fire. Barrels of potatoes. Bread and cheese and a leg of hot meat on a table in the middle. I pad inside and lean my forepaws against the table. All that food, laid out for the taking.

A mate walks in from another room. She looks at me. I look at her. She grabs a black rod from by the fire and swings it at me. "Get away from there!"

I chomp down on the closest food—the leg of meat—and run for the door. A he-cub steps into my way.

"William! Shut the door. Quick!"

The door slams. I spin around. Now I'll have to go through the people in the other room. Maybe my charge will surprise them and they'll let me through. I have to leave before someone tells Tracker I'm here.

The mate steps between the other room and me and waves the rod side to side so I cannot slip by her. "No one steals from my kitchen."

I crouch low, growling, wanting to attack. But the meat is tearing from my teeth and I need this food. I cannot go much farther without it.

The he-cub nears me from the side, and the mate steps forward. I back up, pushing a pot toward the he-cub. He dodges it, letting pot bang pot. The mate creeps closer and pokes the rod at me. It has a sharp point and hook on the end. "Drop the meat." She jabs at me. "Drop it, I say!"

I jump to the side, digging my teeth into the meat. My shoulder bumps the wall. I'm cornered, with nowhere to go. A door cuts off one way out. Men gather in the other doorway. Now Tracker will come and take me away, back to Two-Eyes.

Someone cries out, and a she-cub wearing the color of early leaves pushes through the group. "Child, wait . . ." A man grabs for her, but she slips out of his grasp.

Dropping to her knees, the she-cub flings her arms around me. "Sarah!"

At the human name, I drop the meat at last. This is not any she-cub. It's Tabby.

She presses her head against mine. "I can't believe it's really you. We tried to get you. We talked to that awful lord that bought you. Tried to buy you back. He said you died. I knew he was lying. But no one would listen."

I twist out of her arms. No. This can't be. My head shakes back and forth. Why did I have to find her here? She'll want me to stay. I will want to stay. But I cannot. I am Beast and I must run and run and run.

"Tabby?" A deep voice too big for the room surrounds us.

"Father." Tabby jumps up. "Look—it's Sarah. Lord Avery *was* lying. She is alive." She grabs the hand of a tall man.

Everyone steps back before him; this is a man in control. He may not carry a whip, but he will not fear me and I could never outrun him, even if my legs could move. But they cannot, not from this man more powerful than Two-Eyes. I shrink back, face to the floor.

I feel his giant presence kneel before me, and his hand rests upon my head. "So this is Sarah, who has caused so much trouble." His finger slides down to my chin and nudges my head upward.

I don't want to look up, but the power of his hand makes me. Not that his touch is hard or painful, like when Two-Eyes grabbed my face. This power lies below, rippling, compelling without force.

His eyes, like the sky after rain, take me all in, from my useless leg to the ridges on the left side of my face, left by a fight with the Others. His thumb rubs across them. I want to pull back—yet I don't.

Then he drops his hand. "You took what was not yours, Sarah. You should be punished." He rises.

I look at the meat I dropped and lower my head. He is right. Take another pack's kill and pain will be yours. I pick up the meat, shuffle forward, and drop it at the mate's feet. My insides twist as I lie down for my punishment.

"Mistress Klein, what would be fair recompense for the meat as well as for the disturbance of your kitchen?"

"Oh, Your Majesty . . ." The mate twists the rod in her hand.

"How about this?" He offers her two flat, shiny pebbles of yellow color.

"More than fair, Your Majesty." She bobs before him.

Majesty smiles and offers the bone to *me*.

But I took another's kill. He should whip or beat me. Not give me food.

"Go ahead, Sarah. I'm giving it to you."

I bite into the meat and back away.

"Eat, and if you need more, you need only ask. Tonight we celebrate your safe return to us."

CHAPTER 11

AN OFFER

Tracker!

My eyes pop open, all of me coiled to run. But his dark form does not lurk in the corners of the kitchen, now filled with light from the outside. I slept all night.

Bad Beast! Stupid animal! I use all the names others have called me as I push to my feet. The bone, the warm fire, and Tabby's chatter must have driven Tracker from my mind. But while I slept, Tracker would have kept hunting for me. Even now he probably knows I am still in the town. It will be hard to hide from him in the full light of day. I must get to the cover of the forest. Soon. I paw at the door leading outside. How to open this thing?

"Oh, you're awake."

I turn around, dropping to a crouch.

The rod-swinging mate of last night steps in from the other room, carrying dishes. She puts them on the table and wipes her hands on a cloth. "You're wanting to go out? Here, let me get the door for you." She steps to the door, staying a full pace from me, and flips a latch.

I lean forward, ready to spring out when there's room for me to go.

But instead of opening the door, she moves the latch up and down, up and down. "I hope you don't hold any hard feelings.

About last night, that is. I'm a hard-working woman. I can't afford to lose much, or me and my boy would be out on the streets. So when I saw you sneaking around my kitchen taking food, I thought you were—well, I didn't know you were a friend of King Elroy's."

I curl my paws against the floor and stare at the door, a growl forming at the clicking of the latch going up and down, up and down. Enough words! Let me out!

"No hard feelings?" She reaches out, taps the top of my head, and jerks it back. "Good. Glad we got that cleared up." She opens the door.

Finally! I bolt outside. The cool air makes my skin tingle, but the sun's light is warm, and birds twitter, calling me back up to the trees. All around, people are beginning work. Windows and doors open. Smoke grows from fires being stirred up. A mate hangs clothes on a line, and a she-cub scatters seed. I dig my paws in and circle around the back of the houses. I should have left long ago. At least no one seems to see me as I swing by.

The houses end and I turn to the main path again. The forest darkens the hilltop, now only paces away—and not a sign of Tracker anywhere. Maybe he went on after all.

"Good morning, Sarah. A beautiful day for a walk, isn't it?"

I whirl around, dropping into a crouch. A man sits on a large rock in the shadow of a single tree, a long rod of wood resting across his knees. Majesty.

Everything tells me to run. Majesty provided me food and protection. He will expect something in return. But what could a beast like me have that he would want? I am weak, useless, not good at anything. Now he has caught me running away. My body lurches back one step and drops into a cowering position. What will he do to me now?

He rises and walks toward me, his large fingers coiling around the rod. A beating from such a rod can leave me limping many days. In the hands of a master like Majesty—will I ever walk again?

"You're trembling." He kneels before me and stretches out a hand.

Here it comes. I drop my face to the ground, a shudder shaking all of me, and a whimper escapes my mouth. *Please don't beat me. I didn't mean to make you angry. I'm sorry. Please don't hit me. I'll do whatever you want.*

"Shhhh . . ." His hand strokes my head. "Don't fear. You're safe with me."

I peek over my forepaws. The rod now rests at his side, and he leans down so far he is almost at my level. A master at a beast's level. He dips his head toward me. "Why would I want to hurt you?"

Over Majesty's shoulder the line of trees wave their branches at me, so near and yet beyond my reach.

"You were running away."

Not a question. A statement. He understands now. I jerk back into a ball, my shoulders hunching. Soon the blows will fall.

"Oh Sarah." His hand pulls my head up. Like last night, his grip is not hard or painful, but I recoil anyway. "You aren't my prisoner or my possession. You are free to go. I won't stop you." He drops his hand and leans back so I have a clear path to the forest.

I can't move.

"But Tabby and I would love you to join us, if not now, then later. You are always welcome under my roof and at my table."

After all I did, after seeing all I am, he is offering to take me into his pack, to protect me from other predators like Two-Eyes and Tracker?

No. His words cannot be for me. I am Beast. He's . . . Majesty. A master. Like Two-Eyes. I bolt for the forest. Faster, faster! If he takes me now, he will give me a beating or a whipping or both. Noise fills my ears, but it is the noise of my gasps. Not the angry shout or pounding step of pursuit. I glance back. Majesty trudges downhill toward the houses.

He is letting me walk away.

I slow, head swiveling between forest and Majesty. He let me go, doing his words. Two-Eyes would not have done that—or even Master. My insides lunge after Majesty. Could he, would he take me back? Everything says that can't be. But everything I know said he would not let me go either, yet he did. I turn around and swing down the hill. As I near Majesty, my steps drag. What will he do when he knows I've come back?

"Definitely a beautiful day for a walk." Majesty does not slow or speed up but strides forward steadily, striking the dirt with the rod every two steps "But I believe we've tarried too long this morning. Tabby is going to wonder what happened to us."

I cock my head. Is he talking to me?

He smiles back at me. "Well, hurry up. We can't keep her waiting, now can we?"

He is! I bound forward and take my place at his side.

They took the extra coat Master gave me. They dowsed me in hot water. They scrubbed until my skin tingled. And I let them, because Tabby asked me to. But my fur will not be cut.

Crouched under the bed, I snarl at the three in front of me—a mate with a knife, her she-cub helper, and Tabby, kneeling between them and me. My fur is my only protection against the cold, and the white days will be here before my fur can grow long again.

"Come on, Sarah. This won't hurt. Not one bit. I promise." She holds out her hand in pleading.

I gnash my teeth at it. I should have never let Tabby lure me to this upstairs room when I returned with Majesty.

She leans back on her heels, batting away a loose hair from her face. "I don't understand. Why is this so hard?"

How can she understand? She sleeps inside, near fire when it is cold. I live and sleep out in the cold. I back up farther under the bed.

"We'll cut off only the ends where it's very matted," persists Tabby. "Then we can pull it back like mine." She flaps the end of the braid trailing over her shoulder.

I don't budge, the cool air prickling my wet fur. Plip-plop. Water pools around me. I should have fought to keep the coat from Master too. It might tear easily. It might have many holes. But it is better than nothing.

Tabby sighs. "At least come out so you can dry off and get dressed. See"—she pulls a bundle off the bed—"Father sent up some pants and a shirt." She flops out clothing like a he-cub wears. "I wanted to give you one of my dresses, but Father said it would be impractical because of how you walk."

I nose one corner of the cloth. Thick, warm, no holes. I could ask for nothing better to replace my old coat. But what if this is a trap so they can cut my fur?

Tabby glances over her shoulder. "Candice, you may put the knife away."

The mate dips her head. "Yes, Princess." She tucks the knife into a bag on the table.

I crawl out, ready to retreat under the bed again the first time someone reaches for the knife. But the knife stays in the bag. Instead, Tabby and the mate help the she-cub dress me. I stroke the soft cloth. A beast in he-cub clothing. I should not let them give me these. I should ask for my old coat. But the shirt and pants are so warm.

Tabby picks up the last item in the bundle and shakes it out. With a snap, the cloth stretches out blue wings, its span bigger than me. "A cloak. To keep you warm outside." Tabby drapes it across my shoulders, and warmth wraps around me.

I lower my head, my face flaming with a heat that has nothing to do with the cloak. This would keep me warm no matter how cold the day—or short my fur. Slipping out from under the cloth, I swing across the room. The black handle of the knife juts out from the bag, and I stare at it for a moment. Once I let Tabby do this, I won't be able to put the fur back on.

A floor board creaks behind me. "Princess, shouldn't we—"

"Wait." Tabby's single word stills any motion.

She won't make me do this. The first move is mine. I grab the knife between my teeth, return to her, and drop it at her feet.

Tabby kneels before me and slowly picks up the knife. "Are you sure, Sarah?"

I flatten myself against the floor, face down. If this is what she wants, I will not run from her.

"We'll be quick. I promise." She gathers my fur in a fist.

I squeeze my eyes shut. Tug. Tug. Slice. My fur falls back around my face. Shorter. Lighter. I shiver. If I cannot keep the cloak, the coming days will be very cold.

"All is well." Tabby pulls me up. "Now doesn't that feel better?"

No, but I will not tell her that.

"Come on. Let's show Father how well you cleaned up." She bounces out of the room and down the narrow path between doors—a hall, she had called it. But at the top of the stairs leading to the open room down below, her feet stop.

Voices—Majesty's and another man's—push up through the floorboards. "No . . ."

". . . I don't care . . ."

"Who is he to . . ."

Tabby lowers herself to her hands and knees beside me, and together we edge forward.

"Lord Avery says the beast-child belongs to him and demands its immediate return."

My paws root themselves at the grinning voice. Two-Eyes has sent Fang for me.

"Belongs?" Majesty's voice edges upward. "Setting aside the question of whether any human *belongs* to another, it seems to me that he has failed to uphold the rules of your own Tournament— that he himself must catch or kill his prey—and therefore he has no claim on Sarah."

"My lord bought that beast at fair market price. He insists—"

"Enough!" A chair crashes to the floor.

I whimper. So much anger. And when there's anger, blood flows.

"Shush, Sarah. It'll be fine." Tabby rubs my back.

"I have heard all I need to hear." The floor beneath me shudders at Majesty's commanding voice. "Tell Lord Avery that he has no jurisdiction over anyone in my lands and that I am under no obligation to return anything to him."

"My lord expected as much. Therefore, this is the answer he sends: 'To Elroy Aven, supposed king of Ahavel, hear this: Weakness destroys those too weak to destroy. So do not deceive yourself into thinking you protect this cowering creature from me. I will not be denied my rightful prey. If you will not relinquish the beast now, you *will* relinquish it later—at a price far greater to you and it. These are the words of Lord Avery of Morshe, Rumbal.'"

My forepaws curl around the edge of the top step. Two-Eyes is a mighty predator. He will hurt anyone standing between him and his prey. Maybe I should give myself up.

"My answer remains the same." Majesty's words stand like a rock; no amount of howling wind will be able to move him. "Sarah is under my personal protection. Whatever Lord Avery does to her will come back on his own head in the end. Tell him he would do well to remember this."

"As you wish." Feet stomp across the floor and a door bangs, as if Fang were angry. But a grin hid among his words. Majesty spoke how Two-Eyes wanted. I shiver.

Majesty sighs and a chair scrapes across the floor. "You two can come out now. He's gone."

Tabby jumps to her feet and flies down the stairs. I follow more slowly, and by the time I reach the bottom, she is wrapped in the arms of Majesty. "Oh, Father, you won't let that horrible lord hurt Sarah, will you?"

"Do not worry, Tabby. Lord Avery was taught that strength comes from domination and does not realize how little he truly controls. So whatever he might think, Sarah belongs here with us, and a volley of words will not change that." But he raises his face, forehead creased, and our eyes meet.

We both know that Two-Eyes will not stop with words.

CHAPTER 12

A New Home

"We're almost there, Sarah. We're almost home." Tabby half hangs out of the bouncing carriage, her cheeks glowing pink and her shoulders thrust forward like a bird about to take flight.

I crouch on the floor. Home. Tabby has used that word for both of us since we left the town where I found her five days ago. Do beasts have homes? I do not know, though I have turned the question over and over like a stone until it has lost all its sharp edges.

The carriage lurches, and Tabby tumbles forward. Majesty grabs her waist. "Hold on there, young lady." He hauls her back inside. "I know you're excited to see Melek again, but why don't you have a seat until we come to a stop? I don't relish the thought of picking you up off the road behind us."

"Yes, Father." She plops on the seat. "I just can't wait to be home."

"Is that so? I couldn't tell."

Tabby scowls at him, but that only makes Majesty laugh and soon she is smiling again.

"And what about you, Sarah?" Majesty bends down to me. "Would you like to see your new home?"

I scoot back, my gaze jumping from Majesty to the window

and back to Majesty. I would like to see, but I would need Majesty's help, and how can I ask that of him?

"I think that's a yes." He holds out his hand. "Come here."

I creep forward and he lifts me up. "There it is." He points over the houses lining a rolling river to the tall buildings beyond. To the buildings made of gray stone, with a stone wall around it. Like where Two-Eyes lived.

My mouth turns all dusty, and I can't move. Majesty and Tabby live there?

Tabby grins at me. "Isn't it beautiful? And now that you're here, it won't seem so big and empty. Not like before." She shakes her head, light fading from her face. "I was so worried about you, and then when word reached us that you were dead—that was when Father decided it was time to visit all his lords." Her smile returns. "Wasn't it fortunate that we were in Keseph when you crossed the border?"

Fortunate? I should have run when Majesty let me, before he could bring me here, to all that stone, those trapping walls, the endless darkness. When Majesty puts me on the floor again, I squeeze into the corner as far as I can get from the door, my eyes scrunched shut. But I still see and feel everything from the black hole of Two-Eyes. The teeth of the iron gate. The Keeper's stick. I can't go back. I can't. Not even for Tabby and Majesty. The carriage rattles over wood, clatters against stone, and rolls to a stop. Cold vines twist up my legs toward my middle.

The door latch clicks. "Welcome home, Your Majesties."

"Thank you, Adeo." The carriage rocks as Majesty gets out. "Sarah?"

Shudders rattle my body so hard I have to grind my teeth together so I don't bite myself. *Please, don't make me do this. I can't do this.*

Majesty settles next to me and pulls me into his arms, pressing my head to his chest. I'm so close I can hear the steady beating inside him—thump-thump, thump-thump. Unlike the bird thrashing inside of me, trying to escape.

"Sarah, don't fear." Thump-thump. "I'm here." Thump-thump. "I'll protect you. For always and always."

I lean into his tree-trunk solidness. Thump-thump, thump-thump. My own beating slows down.

He brushes the fur from my face. "May I show you one thing?"

How can I refuse? He's the master of my new pack. I must do what he asks. My head drops to my chest, even as my eyes squeeze shut again.

Majesty lifts me up and carries me out of the carriage. His breath warms my face. "Look, Sarah."

I grit my teeth and force an eye open. I gasp and lift my head higher. Yes, there is the wall and the gray buildings and the stone path the carriage crossed, but those are the only ways this place is like where Two-Eyes lived. Green grass fills the open place. Flowers bob heads of gold and orange. A few brown birds hop and twitter among some bushes. My forepaws uncurl; I did not know I had clenched them.

Majesty shifts his hold on me. "I'm sorry there aren't any trees, but there's a whole forest of them behind the castle, and you can visit it every day if you wish. Now are you ready to see the inside?" He turns toward the tall building.

"Father, may I show her?" Tabby squeezes up against her father's side and slides a hand around his arm. "Please say that I may." She leans against him.

"Very well." Majesty gently sets me on the ground and stoops to look Tabby in the eye, placing one hand on her shoulder. "But you must promise to be a good hostess and show Sarah every room, every hall, every nook and cranny."

Tabby cocks her head. "*Every*thing?"

"Everything, from the highest turret to the bottom-most passages. Do you understand?"

"Yes, Father."

"Good. And that leaves me free to examine the records immediately." Majesty straightens up and faces a man standing nearby—Adeo the steward.

He bows slightly. "As you wish, Your Majesty." He leads Majesty away, and as soon as they round the corner, Tabby sprints up the steps.

"Come on, Sarah. We have some exploring to do."

———✦———

Majesty's home: never could I have imagined anything so big, so full of light and color, so overflowing with good things! Warm fires and thick rugs; flowers and pictures—a little of everything is crammed inside, and at every turn, something new awaits me.

With my head turning back and forth, I follow Tabby up the narrow, winding staircase of the north tower. She races me through a wide hall. I peer over the low railing of a "balcony," as Tabby calls the stone ledge leaning over the giant room with Majesty's throne. Many clusters of trees could fit in there. Then again, all of Majesty's house is so big I could lose myself in it more easily than in the forest.

As we wander down another hall, my nose twitches at a warm smell. Is that what I think it is?

Tabby shoves open a wood door, and the scent of much food pours out. "Welcome to one of the best rooms in the castle—the kitchen."

I lick my lips, my insides growling at the sight of more food than I've ever seen in one place. It's stacked everywhere. On tables, in pots, in barrels, hanging from the ceiling, cooking over the fire. On the table nearest me, white wisps curl up from bread. Would anyone notice if I took one, the smallest one on the end?

A mate stirring food in a big, bubbling pot straightens up and nods to Tabby. "Good afternoon, Princess, and welcome home. Is there anything special I may help you with?"

"Nothing in particular. I'm just showing Sarah around."

Uh-oh. I step back into the doorway. Most mates don't trust me in a room with this much food, and they are right not to. So much for the bread.

71

The mate nods to me like she did to Tabby. "You look like you could use a snack, Lady Sarah. Would you like some bread and butter? The bread's fresh."

My head ducks. She saw.

"You're welcome to it if you want it."

As if I could refuse food offered. I nod jerkily toward the mate.

"Bread and butter coming up." She slices through the bread and accepts a yellow slab from a she-cub that is almost a mate.

Tabby leans over a pot above the fire. "How are the lessons with the healer going, Gwen?"

"Well, thank you, Princess." The almost-mate she-cub dips her head, face reddening. She slides the food onto the floor before me, the plate scraping against the wood. "It has been a privilege to study with Healer Yakov."

I hang back until Gwen returns to cutting food at the table. Then I snatch the thick slab of bread and take a big bite. My eyes slide close. It is even better than it smelled.

"Father thinks it is worth any problems to have a healer back in the castle."

"I hope my skills won't disappoint His Majesty."

"From what I've heard, that won't be a problem."

I swallow the last bite, and after licking the plate clean, I nudge it forward toward the feet of the mate. Backing up one step, I place my face to the floor. The bread was the best I've ever tasted.

"Lady Sarah, I . . . ." The mate loses her words.

I slink under the table. What did I do wrong now?

Tabby lights a stick in the fire. "Let me show you the cellar while we're here." She lifts up part of the floor. "Then we'll go outside and inspect the grounds." Stooping, she walks down the steps that were under the floor.

I edge to the hole and poke my head in it. Shadows twist and writhe as if the light from Tabby's firestick hurts them. The musty wet-stone smell leaves a bad taste in my mouth. A damp chill creeps along my back on spider legs.

"Come on, Sarah. It's perfectly safe." Tabby waves for me to join her.

Maybe safe for her. Not for me. Not for a beast.

Tabby puts a hand on her hip and waits. She is not coming back up until I come down. I slide down to the top step. Tabby does not budge. I slide down to the second step. Tabby waits. I keep climbing down. When I reach the floor, Tabby rewards me with a smile. "See, it's not that scary down here. Just dark and a little funny smelling."

She waves her firestick around, making the shadows leap and pounce. She points to some barrels and tells me what is in them, but the words miss me so I do not know what she says. I huddle against the bottom step. The ceiling is too low. The light too little. Is the Keeper hiding behind those boxes? I take in air through my nose; the bird beating against my insides has flown into my throat and will fly away if I open my mouth.

Tabby goes deeper into the room, taking the light with her. I turn to bound up the stairs to the kitchen but only reach the first one before stopping. What about Tabby? What if a predator stalks her in the shadows?

Something thumps from the way Tabby went, and she cries out.

I leap off the step and bound the way Tabby went. She kneels on the ground, picking up round things and putting them back in a box, the firestick stuck into the dirt floor beside her. She lifts her head. "There you are." She rises and slides the box back onto a nearby stack.

I drop to the ground. Tabby is unhurt. No predators lurk nearby.

"Before we go back upstairs, I've one more thing to show you." She turns to the stone wall behind her. Bags hang from pegs sticking out of it. "When Father insisted I show you everything, he wasn't telling me to be a good hostess. He wanted me to show you this." She grabs two empty pegs at the bottom, turns them toward each other, and pushes against the lower stones.

The wall rolls back into blackest darkness, and a whimper rolls around my mouth. She doesn't plan to make me go in there, does she?

"Most only see a wall covered with old wineskins and water

bags. But for us, it's much more." Tabby picks up the firestick and ducks inside the hole.

I put my head in after her but cannot go beyond that. My insides slosh around like water in a swinging bucket. Maybe eating that bread wasn't such a good thing after all.

Tabby doesn't seem to mind as she waves the firestick around. The flickering light lands on smooth rock walls with ropes stretched along them, latches, and a groove in the floor where the wall slid in.

"Hard to believe such dark and creepy place is safe, isn't it? But Father says we could live down here for a long time, even if an enemy lived in the castle itself. We could take food from the cellar without anyone ever knowing. And down there"—she points into the darkness—"an underground lake is fed by the moat. At least that's what Father says. I've never gone that far."

She steps back out, grabs the peg in the center of the stone block, and pulls the wall back into place. "Personally, I hope we never use it. But I guess it's nice to know we have a safe place to go if trouble does come."

Safe? Maybe for her. Endless terror for me. If I ever have to go there . . . I huddle on the floor, shivering.

"But enough." Tabby twists the two pegs out, and when she pushes all of herself against the stones, they refuse to move like most walls. "Let's get out of this black hole and find some sunshine."

The best words she has said all day. I bound forward, leading her all the way to the stairs.

CHAPTER 13

ᴛRACKED

"A re you sure you don't want to feed Abigail?"

Dust, heat, smells I don't know and don't want to know—all of it thickens the air until it almost refuses to go down the throat. But Tabby seems not to notice. She calmly holds up an orange stick to a horse, an animal many times her size and able to trample her if it chose to. And she wants *me* to put myself within striking distance of those hard feet?

The horse snorts and Tabby rubs its nose. "All gone today." With a last tap, she walks back to me. "Abigail isn't as wild as she appears. She just likes to show off. I can't wait until you learn to ride and we can go out together."

Me? Sit on top of one of those? I shudder and bound after her into good air. I drink it in. My useless leg may slow me some, but not that much. My feet stay on dirt and stone.

"Gwen must have a lesson with the healer today." Tabby leads me past the open gate where Gwen is just walking out, her red cloak bright against the gray stone.

"Father does so many things for reasons that most could never guess at." She shakes her head and climbs the stairs to the top of the wall. "Like Gwen. Father didn't pick her to be the new castle healer because she was the best one for the position. Rather, Father knew her work as a kitchen helper would not provide

75

enough for both her and her younger brother. But it happens that she is very good—she has a special gift of mercy, Father calls it."

We reach the top of the wall, and the wind gusts around us. Tabby sighs. "What a beautiful day."

The day is not what I see. I see how far down the ground is. My insides rustle, like leaves in the gusting wind. But my feet are on stone. That is more solid than the branches I walked among, and I don't have to jump from stone to stone like I did with trees. I move closer to the edge. The land stretches out and out, all dressed in gold and brown and red, with a strip of blue water.

Light warms my back, and I lift my face up, my eyes closing. The sounds around me sharpen. The soft padding step of the bowman passing by. The low splashing of the river as it rejoins the other half from its split around the castle. The banging and calling of the people in the town below. My rustling insides settle. This wall isn't here to hold me in. It's here to hold others out. Masters that want to hurt me, like Tracker or Two-Eyes.

The wind shifts. A cry rings out, then cuts off like that of an animal cornered by the Others.

I grab my middle, insides lurching. Run. Hide.

"Sarah?" Tabby's voice seems far away, on the other side of the castle.

But Two-Eyes is not here. Tracker is not here. Majesty is here. So is Tabby. My heaving chest slows. That cry isn't—

The cry was real. My eyes pop open. Someone is cornered.

"What's wrong?" Tabby kneels beside me.

Didn't she hear it? But though Tabby frowns, the frown is for me. I pull away from her and peer over the wall. Road, house, people, road.

"Maybe we should go inside. The wind is a bit chilly out here." Tabby's voice is light on top. But murkiness darkens the depths. She walks toward the stairs.

But I heard something. I know I did. My paws clutch the stone, as if that would make me see better. A man pulls a cart through Melek. Cubs play. Mates with baskets stop and chat with each other. Gwen, easy to find in her red cloak, turns toward the edge of town with a tall man.

"Sarah," calls Tabby. "Come on."

Gwen—she was alone when she left, but now a man walks with her down an empty path, his hand resting on the back of her neck. Gwen's body is post-straight. He looks both ways and pushes her into a house. This isn't right. I drop to all fours, bound past Tabby, and half-run, half-fall down the steps. Part of Majesty's pack—*my* pack—is in trouble. I skid around a corner, kicking up dust. The gate is still open. I charge.

Tabby chases me but drops farther and farther behind me. "Wait!"

I can't wait. My legs stretch to their full length. Past people. Under wagons. Around a well. My shoulder bumps something. Someone yells at me. I cannot stop to find out why. I turn down a narrow way between houses, away from the people.

A muffled cry squeezes into the open air. Gwen! I drop into a crouch and slink toward a house.

"I don't know what you are—"

Whack! Flesh smacks against flesh.

A growl rumbles in my throat. In. Now. But the door is latched tight. I circle. A small hole gapes between the wall and dirt. I claw at the ground. It's soft and pulls out easily, like a hole filled in not many days ago. My paws dig faster. The hole deepens. Part of the wall falls away.

The inside is dark, with a patch of light pushing through the roof here and there. A small body covered in red cloth huddles in the corner. The tall man stands over it. "Tell me."

"How can I tell you what I don't know?" Gwen's voice rises out of the depths of the huddled body. "I've never seen what you've described."

"You lie. I know that King Elroy has taken a beast-child. I know he has brought it here."

Beast-child. My paws still. This man is looking for me. Run. Hide. But what about Gwen?

"Last chance. Where is it? What does he plan to do with it?" The man steps toward Gwen. Light glints off silver metal. A sword.

I thrust myself through the hole. It is not big enough. It must be. I twist and tumble through with a grunt.

The man whirls around and sneers. "Now look here. The beast-child itself. Luck has smiled on me today."

Snarling, I slink back into the shadows. Wait. Let him move first. Watch. Learn where he will strike.

The man steps forward.

Left. He'll come from the left—that is the hand holding the sword.

"My lord will be pleased." The feet of Left-Hand scuff against the dirt. "He sent me for information and I shall return with a body." He lunges—from the left, as I expected.

I duck and ram into his left leg. He staggers back and stabs downward. I roll out of his way. Circle through shadows. Duck. Attack. Twist away. Lunge. Retreat. I crouch, panting, waiting for the next move.

Left-Hand swings the sword, much too long for the small space. Gwen scrambles for the door. She gets it unlatched, and it swings open, light bursting into the dim room. I blink. Left-Hand blinks. Gwen blinks. None of us move, as if the light holds us where we stand.

Outside someone shouts.

Gwen jerks and scuttles out. The man lunges after her. I throw myself in his way.

His foot strikes my side. His heel lands on my forepaw with a grinding crunch. The sword flies from his hand.

"You stupid animal!" He spins around toward me. "I'll strangle you with my bare hands if I must."

I limp back, my forepaw pounding in pain. My back legs bump into the wall behind me. I'm trapped, with nowhere to hide and unable to fight.

With a roar, Left-Hand charges. Suddenly he staggers and drops to the floor at my feet. A stone rolls away from him.

I look at Left-Hand, then at the door. A dark shadow disappears around the corner. Tracker? Can't be, and yet . . . I leap over the man and run into the light. The shadow is gone. But I did see someone, didn't I?

"Sarah!" Majesty runs up the road, several men with bows and swords behind him. Gwen is at his side, pointing at the house behind me. Two men brush past me and drag out Left-Hand, now waking from his rock-made sleep. I slink out of their way, into the shadow of the house.

"That's the man." Gwen nods to Majesty. "The one who took me. He said he wanted information about a . . ." Her head jerks toward me.

I limp back farther, my loose fur falling across my face. Smeared with dirt and blood, I am now seen for what I am. A beast.

Gwen jerks her chin up. "He wanted to know about a beast-child. I told him—and I'll say it again—His Majesty King Elroy harbors no such creature."

"You have answered well." Majesty turns to a man standing rigidly in front of the others. "Captain, take him away."

"As you wish." Captain faces the two holding Left-Hand. "Bring him."

"Blind! You're all blind." Left-Hand snarls as he is dragged by. "You can't even see what stands in your own midst. You all deserve to die." He spits at Majesty's feet.

Captain spins around and strikes him. "Silence. Or next time I shall personally separate your tongue from your mouth."

Left-Hand glares, but he says nothing more as the four men leave. Gwen kneels at my side. I cower.

"Shush. All will be well, Lady Sarah." She ties a plain square cloth around my upper foreleg where the sword grazed me and then tries to pull out the painful paw.

I yelp and jerk away.

"How is she?" Majesty stands over us.

"Nothing life threatening. Some shallow cuts, bruises, maybe

some broken bones. I'll need Healer Yakov's help with that one—
if you please, Your Majesty." She dips her head.

"I'll send someone for him immediately. Meanwhile, let's get
you two back to the castle." He leans down and scoops me up
in his arms before I can react. Then he glances up over my head
and nods.

A shadow shifts and slides away into the darkness between
houses.

CHAPTER 14

WINTER

The leaves fly away in gold swirls. Light grows weak, and a blanket of gray covers the sky many days. Finally, white feathers fall to the ground. And I watch it all from a warm spot by a fire.

This is more than I could have asked of Majesty. But he did not stop with that. Hills of blankets. Warm clothing. A room just for me. More food than I can eat. I should not have all this. Among Majesty's dogs is where I should sleep. But each time I try, day finds me back in a bed. So I stay in my room and sleep on the rug by the fire.

Even that makes Majesty shake his head and say, "Oh Sarah, what will we do with you?"

I always slink back at those words, but then he gathers me in his arms. I like it when he does that. No one can hurt me, it seems. But I know Two-Eyes and Tracker haven't given up, even though I never see either. They are hunters. They know how to wait out of sight until they are ready to attack.

Will Majesty's pack protect me when they do?

Curled up on a rug in a study room, I soak in the warmth of a fire. Nearby, Majesty and Tabby sit at a table and play with a peg board. Tabby's legs swing back and forth, back and forth, as she thinks. Finally she leans forward, pulls out one of the many pegs, and starts to put it into another hole.

"Are you sure you want to do that?" Majesty, settled deep in his chair, lets a smile lift one corner of his mouth.

Tabby stops, her peg hovering over the board. "I don't want to?"

"Maybe. Maybe not. It's your decision."

Scowling, she rams the peg back into the board. "I hate it when you make me second-guess myself."

I stretch and carefully swing over to the table. My hurt leg is good most days now, but sometimes pain will still shoot through it. Rising up, I rest my forepaws on the table's edge. Tabby tried many nights to explain the forest of colored pegs and how they are to be moved. But they are still only colored pegs in a board to me.

"Would you like me to get you a chair, Sarah?" Majesty starts to rise.

I shake my head. The floor is still the best place for me.

He settles again in his chair. "If you change your mind, let me know."

Tabby continues to glare at the board. The fire snaps and crackles. The wind races around in the dark outside with a clatter and a howl. I shudder. It sounds like a hunting pack ready to trap me, and—That's it! The pegs are two dog packs and their masters. Each hunts the master of the other.

Tabby moves a peg, opening her master to attack. My paw darts over the hole.

"What's wrong, Sarah?" Tabby cocks her head.

I don't move my paw.

Majesty rests his chin on folded hands and smiles. "She's trying to tell you that's a wrong move."

I nod twice.

"Fine." Tabby huffs as she replaces the peg. "*You* tell me where I should move."

I lick my lips and stare at the board. I see it. Majesty used words to make Tabby doubt. I nudge a peg and point to the hole she had first wanted to put it in.

"But Father said . . ." Her head jerks up. "You knew. You knew it was the right move all along."

Majesty chuckles. "Of course. That's why I said something. I'm your opponent—why would I want you to make the right move? It only makes my job harder." He puts a peg into the hole on its left. "Let that be a lesson for you. Never trust the enemy's words—no matter how good or right they sound."

I keep helping Tabby play, but in the end, Majesty still corners our master peg first.

"Excellent game of Catteran. With a little practice, you two will be hard to defeat." Majesty rises and pours himself a drink.

Tabby dumps the pegs into a hole in the board. "You'll still win."

"Maybe."

"Of course you will. You haven't lost in five years, and the last time you lost on purpose." She slides the board onto a shelf and faces me. "And Father does love to play Catteran. He has invited every visitor who knows the game for a round, whether lord, lady, or servant. I can still see the shock of the stable hand—Bartholomew—the first time you asked him to play, Father."

"He had nothing to apologize for. He was an excellent opponent, sharp and creative. Better than many of my lords."

I curl up on the rug again, my head resting on a foreleg. This is not the first time I've heard Majesty speak well of a person outside their presence. What would Majesty say of me? I want his words to sound like these. But there are so many things he has tried to teach me that I cannot do. His words probably would be *stupid, weak, useless*.

Tabby and Majesty give each other looks I do not know.

"May we tell her now, Father?"

"You think we should?"

Tabby nods so hard, her whole body bounces with it.

"Sarah, please come here." Majesty stretches out his hand.

I rise and walk toward him, my legs shaking like they are made of grass. What is going on? Have I angered him or Tabby somehow?

"Closer."

I reach his feet and lie down, head on paws.

"Always so fearful." Majesty lifts me up into his lap. "And you have nothing to fear from me." He wraps his arms tightly around me. "Sarah, I want to make you my daughter—just like Tabby."

My body stiffens, like meat left outside in the cold too long. Majesty did not say these words. Anyone can see I cannot be like Tabby, that I am only a beast.

"Actually, the adoption is simply a legality. A bunch of words and a couple of signatures to declare to everyone else that you're my daughter. Tabby and I both already consider you a permanent part of our family."

"Isn't it wonderful?" Tabby grabs my paw. "We're going to be sisters for always and always."

No. I twist out of Majesty's arms and back away. They make laughter. I am Beast. I will always be Beast. My insides shudder and begin to split apart.

"Sarah?"

Stop, stop, stop. I am not Sarah. I am Beast. Beast! Why can't they see that? They must see that. How can I make them see that? I shake my head, claw at my fur. Stupid Beast. Why did I ever think I could do this, be what they wanted me to be? Calling me Sarah does not make me Sarah. My claws dig into my head.

"Sarah!" Majesty grabs my forepaws.

I try to fight him. But I am weak. Weak and stupid. He is strong. A master. My master. Water spills down my face. I flatten myself to the floor, even as Majesty holds my forepaws tight.

When I stop fighting, he lets me go and starts to draw me to him.

I jerk away, curling into a ball with my back to him. I want him to hold me. I can't let him hold me. Beasts serve the master, not the other way around.

Majesty sighs. "What more can I do? There is so much I long to give you, but I will not force it on you."

Give to me? No. To Tabby, yes. To a Sarah, maybe. But not to Beast. He will see that and be glad I did not let him make me like Tabby.

When I do not turn back to him, he rises. "I will wait. Someday you will see. Someday you will be sure of me—and I will be waiting." A door opens. "Good night, Tabby. Good night, Sarah. I'll see you both in the morning." His footsteps retreat.

A fist pounds against wood, and I tremble harder. "Sarah, how could you?" A drawer slams shut. "You sleep here, eat with us, take Father's gifts—but you won't let him adopt you? How stupid can you be?"

Her words lash at me, hurting more than Master's belt ever did. *Stupid beast.* I tuck my head, water now flowing faster than ever down my face. She doesn't know, doesn't see I want to say yes, can't understand why I must say no.

"I'm going to bed." She stomps out of the room, leaving me alone.

CHAPTER 15

A WAGER

S pring thaw. A good time to get out, to escape the confining walls of the castle for a while. A visit to the lords will do us all good. At least that's what Majesty says. To me, it still feels cold—outside and in.

I hunker by the inn's fire. Its heat burns my face, but I am still cold. The outside air seeps through the cracks in the walls and sweeps across my back, making me shiver.

Tabby feels it too. First she stands with her face toward the fire. Then she turns so she faces away, only to turn again after a moment. But however she stands, her back is always to me with no word or look tossed my way. Many days have passed since Majesty said he wanted to make me part of his inner pack, but Tabby's anger still burns hot.

My head droops and I swing away from the fire. Maybe I should leave when warm days come again. Tabby no longer wants me here, and while Majesty treats me as he always has, a sadness is in his eyes when he looks at me—I cannot give him what he wants. Pulling the cloak tight around me, I curl up on the floor, away from Tabby and Majesty and the three swordsmen traveling with us.

Majesty finishes talking with the master of the inn and walks over to where I lie. Settling on the nearest bench, he stretches out his legs and leans back against a table, his eyes on Tabby. "Give her time, Sarah. She's hurting, confused, and scared—and she doesn't know what to do with any of it."

I stare at Majesty. Does he want me to leave too?

"She's vulnerable. Very vulnerable. And so many dark days are ahead." He finally tips his head toward me. "Keep her safe, Sarah. Don't do anything rash that might add to that hurt."

His words fall heavy on me. Majesty wants me to protect Tabby? But how am I to do that when she will not even turn her face toward me?

Tabby turns so that the fire warms her other side, her fingers jangling the pouch at her waist. No, that isn't right. That jangle does not come from the pouch. It is not loud enough, nor does it match Tabby's movements. My head tilts to one side. But the jangle is gone. Or maybe it was never there.

Scuffling feet and low voices skulk outside.

My fur rises on my neck. But it is nothing. Other travelers stopping for a midday meal. That is all. Nothing but—

Two-Eyes.

How do I know? I cannot say. But I know it's him. He's here. For me. I back up under the table, back into the shadows. If only he won't see me. If only he won't know I am here.

"Sarah?" Majesty leans forward to peer under the table at me. Then he raises his head to look at the door again. His hand closes around his sword, so tight that white spots show on his fingers. "So it begins." He stands.

The door bangs open. Several men with drawn swords burst in on a gust of cold air. I shrink back. Two-Eyes is not among them, but he is here. I feel it.

Majesty strides forward, drawing his own sword, and his three swordsmen follow his lead. Metal clashes against metal. Boots pound against the floor. I cannot see who is winning.

"Father!"

Tabby. A man I do not know drags her away. She thrashes against his arm, but her movements are all wrong. She does not know how to fight this man.

"Hold on, Tabby." Majesty fights against two men.

He will not get there soon enough. I swallow the stone in my throat and bound forward. The man sees only Majesty and his men.

"Look! The beast!"

"What—"

I throw all of me against Tabby's captor and bite his leg. The man howls. Tabby twists free. She grabs the closest thing—a metal pot by the fire—and smashes it against his head. Gray ash flies. The man slumps to the floor.

Tabby smiles—at me! "Thanks."

"Good job, you two." Majesty locks blades with another man. "Now get out of here."

"Come on, Sarah." Tabby ducks into the kitchen.

I swing after her and hesitate. This is not right. The room is empty of mate and master. Where are the kitchen people? The master of the inn?

Tabby yanks the door open. "What are you waiting—look out!"

A shadow falls across me. Fang looms in the other doorway, and I dart under the table. But though Tabby's warning is for me, Fang marches toward her. "Isn't this a treat? I've found myself a lovely young princess."

Though I can see only his legs from under the table, his words curl upward with a grin.

"Sorry." Tabby snatches something from a barrel by the door. "I'm not edible." She throws a potato at him. It falls harmlessly at Fang's feet.

"Resistance only makes victory sweeter." He moves steadily forward. Almost there . . . three more steps . . . two . . . I rear up and push over the table. Food flies and pots crash into him; the table slams onto his feet. He howls. I shove Tabby out the door into the cold air.

"We'd better split up. You go that way." She gathers up her skirts and sprints away.

I bound the way she pointed. Steps squish in the soft mud.

I spin around. A hand catches my throat and slams me against the inn's wall. Darkness slides across my sight. I blink, trying to see again.

One blue eye and one green eye stare into my face. Two-Eyes.

He throws me into the mud, face down, and rams a knee into my back between my shoulders. "I hope you had a good run, Beast. It was your last."

He yanks my forepaws behind my back and ties a rope around them. No! He cannot take me. Not now. I kick and twist and thrash and arch my back. Mud splatters everywhere and lands in my mouth. I cough and choke. Two-Eyes only chuckles. My head slumps forward. I cannot throw him. I need help. I need Majesty.

Creak-moan. A bowstring pulls taut behind us. Two-Eyes drops flat against me. An arrow thuds into the ground a few paces beyond us. He flips over, his powerful arm crushing me to his chest.

Majesty! He tosses a bow aside and strides forward, drawing his sword. I twist and kick, trying to free myself, to get to him.

Two-Eyes pushes up to his feet, holding me tight. My feet strain to find ground, but Two-Eyes dangles me high above it. I cannot reach it.

"Good move, Elroy, but I wouldn't try anything more." Two-Eyes flicks his free hand to his side. "Further surprises might cause my knife to slip in a most unfortunate way." A cold, sharp edge is thrust against my throat, under my chin.

A chill stiffens me.

Majesty lowers his sword until the tip touches the ground, his eyes never leaving Two-Eyes, his stance never easing. "What do you want, Avery?"

"I have what I want." Two-Eyes slides along the wall, his clothing scuffing against the stones.

Majesty steps toward Two-Eyes. "She's worthless to you."

Worthless? A stone crushes my insides. Majesty thinks I'm good for nothing—even for making laughter? I blink hard to keep water from slipping down my face.

Two-Eyes snorts. "You underestimate the value of conquering every challenge. Even the smallest crack can crumble the entire castle if left unattended."

Before Majesty can reply, Tabby skids around the corner. "Sarah!" She starts toward me.

Two-Eyes jabs his knife upward. I gasp.

"Go inside, Tabitha." Majesty's gaze does not stray from Two-Eyes. "Now."

Tabby looks from me to Majesty and then disappears from my sight. But no door slams. She hovers nearby. Still the knife slackens against my throat.

"I'll buy her." Majesty's voice remains rock solid. If he fears Two-Eyes any, it doesn't show. "Double what you paid."

Double? The ground and sky wobbles. Didn't Majesty just say I was worthless? Why is he offering so much to buy me?

"And lose my best source of entertainment in years? No, I have too many plans for this one." Two-Eyes starts creeping along the wall again.

The tip of Majesty's sword lifts off the ground. "Plans?" His voice is low and tight. "Like starving her until she can no longer run from you? Whipping her until she's half dead? Torturing her until she goes unconscious? Just so you can listen to her screams, fill your lust for blood? Over my dead body."

Two-Eyes digs his knife into my throat, forcing my head up. Wet warmness creeps along my skin. A whimper forms in my throat, but it can't squeeze beyond the knife blade. I'm caught between two powerful masters with no way out.

"A generous offer, Elroy. One I'd love to take. But unfortunately, I'm forced to decline at this time."

We are almost to the corner of the building. Where Two-Eyes plans to go from there, I do not know. But he has something planned, something that will include the hiss-crack of a whip—and its sting on my back. I lift my eyes to Majesty. *Please. I'll do anything. Find a way to be useful. Just don't let him take me!*

"A wager."

Two-Eyes halts. "What?"

"You're a betting man, aren't you, Avery? So if you won't let me buy her, wager her in a game with me. Sarah for my kingdom."

Silence. Even the wind has dropped, as if holding its breath.

Two-Eyes leans toward Majesty; the predator has picked up the scent of prey. "Tell me more."

"One game of Catteran. If I win, you relinquish Sarah and any claim on her. If you win fairly, I hand over my crown, my throne, my kingdom."

My eyes widen. He cannot mean those words.

"The ultimate game of strategy. Interesting pick." Two-Eyes tightens his grip on me. "If your word is good."

No, no, no! Don't do it! Don't risk your whole pack for me.

"You know it is, Avery. Of course, if you wish I attest to all this in writing . . ."

"I wish—with the additional provision that if I should lose by some obscure chance, I will return to my lands upright and under my own power."

"I do not find the same pleasure as you in turning the ground red."

"My gain. But the wager—shall we retire inside?"

"After you."

Tap, tap, tap, tap. The sound of the wood peg against the table fills the entire room. Tap, tap, tap. Two-Eyes clenches his fist around the peg and scowls at the board. He smashes the peg into a hole—only his control as a hunter keeps him from doing more.

And he hasn't even lost yet.

I pull my hind legs up to my chest and shudder. I sit across the room from him, waiting with everyone else for the game's end, but if he chose to heave the board at me, it would find me.

Tabby, sitting on the floor beside me, adjusts her cloak around my shoulders as it starts to slide off; Two-Eyes insisted my forepaws stay bound behind my back. She squeezes my shoulder and bends over to whisper in my ear. "Everything will work out, Sarah. You'll see."

I manage a nod, for her sake. At least her anger no longer burns against me.

Two-Eyes scowls. "Just move."

Majesty picks up a peg and plops it into a hole without hesitation. Another peg joins Majesty's pile beside the board.

Two-Eyes mutters harsh, growling words under his breath. Men belonging to both Majesty and Two-Eyes edge nearer the table. No one pulls out swords, but all rest hands on the handles, ready to do so.

My forepaws clench underneath the cloak. A clash of swords and fists would have been easier to watch. It would have been over sooner too. My insides growl, reminding me that the time for the evening meal is long past.

Two-Eyes, hunched over the board, suddenly smiles and moves a peg toward me. He didn't do that, did he? He just stepped into Majesty's trap, opening his master peg to attack.

He leans back. "Ah, the dust of defeat—what a bitter taste."

"Especially to the arrogant." Majesty drops a peg into place, sealing the trap. He cannot lose now. Not unless he intentionally moves his master peg one hole to the right.

Tabby bounces up and down at my side. "Father's won. He has won the wager!" Her words barely keep to a whisper.

I want to be glad too. But something is not right. Two-Eyes does not scowl or clench his fist in anger. Rather his face is blank, calm. Does he not see he has lost? Majesty is not blind. He will not move his master peg to the right.

Two-Eyes pushes a peg into a hole. His eyes glint, like a predator who has trapped his prey but the prey does not yet know it. "But there are worse things than defeat, aren't there, Elroy?" He shifts to the side, and my ears pick up a soft creak-moan—like a bowstring being pulled? But how, where?

A shadow shifts in the kitchen doorway. A bowman aims an arrow toward Tabby. One word, one flick of a finger from Two-Eyes and she'll be . . . Majesty can't let that happen. Not to

Tabby. But if he protects her, he'll lose his whole pack to Two-Eyes. No, Majesty must win. But if he wins, the arrow will fly straight into Tabby.

Unless it can't reach her.

I scoot forward and around Tabby, forcing her behind me. She grabs my shoulder. "Sarah, what are you doing?"

She does not see the bowman. But it does not matter. I do. My chin lifts and I glare at Two-Eyes. I am Beast. My life is not worth much. But better to fall forever still at the point of an arrow than at the end of his whip.

Majesty shakes his head, his shoulders drooping as if a great weight has been placed on them. "Avery, you would kill your own family to avoid defeat."

"I could." He leans back and stretches; he has won his prey. "But killing someone else's is far more effective."

"Yet you still don't understand, do you? In the end, you will never win."

"Never?" Two-Eyes clicks his tongue. "Such a strong word, Elroy, especially since I already have."

"Have you?" Majesty picks up his master peg and rolls it between his fingers. Two-Eyes narrows his eyes. The whole room leans forward. I try to brace myself. The arrow will fly in the next breath or two.

Majesty twists around and locks eyes with me. My chest tightens. He can't be thinking that. I shake my head. *No. Don't. You said it yourself. I'm only Beast. I'm not worth the whole pack.*

A single drop of water rolls down his cheek. "Oh Sarah, if only this would be enough to convince you of the truth."

He drops his master peg in the hole on the right.

CHAPTER 16

IN ENEMY HANDS

*A*s my first act as King Avery of Ahavel, I hereby sentence the traitor, Elroy Aven, to death."

In the sound-muffled darkness of the kitchen cellar, I live the moments after Majesty's loss again and again.

"And claim his daughter as my slave."

I shiver. From the coldness of the dirt floor I lie on? Or from the sights and sounds I cannot shake?

The leers on the faces of Two-Eyes and his men. Majesty's men leaping to his defense. The clash of swords. The thud of a falling man. Tabby's scream as she's grabbed.

A table overturns. Game pegs scatter. Blood smears the floor. I try to follow, but Tabby is gone before I make a few paces.

Doors bang. Majesty retreats, Two-Eyes chases. Then Two-Eyes comes back, throwing dagger words. I huddle under a table, hoping he will not see me. But he does. I'm thrown down here, tied to a post, and left to wait. Wait and wonder what happened to Tabby and Majesty, what pain they face—because of me.

Darkness gnaws at me, on the outside, on the inside, until a thin shell is all that's left of me. Majesty's gone or maybe already dead. His pack belongs to Two-Eyes. I am trapped, unable to do the one thing Majesty asked of me, protect Tabby. I do not even know where she might be or where I would look for her if I could get loose. Maybe she is dead too.

Why did Majesty lose the wager? Could he not see what would happen? And now it is too late.

Footsteps march across the floor above me. A door creaks, and gray light tumbles down the stairs before rolling to a stop at my feet. There's too much darkness around me—in me—for the light to come any closer.

"Get down there."

Hurried feet patter against wood, trying to keep their master from falling. The last step is missed. Tabby! She falls to hands and knees with a soft grunt.

I twist and yank against the rope tying my forepaws to the post.

At my whimpers, she looks up—a dark red bruise covers her cheek. "Sarah!" She lunges for me, arms wrapping around my neck.

I lean into her. She is alive. Breathing. Here! Maybe I will be able to do what Majesty asked.

Hard, steady steps pound against the stairs. Two-Eyes. "Friends in direst circumstances, once again united. Touching scene, isn't it?"

Men yank Tabby from me, and Two-Eyes plants himself between her and me. I jerk forward, trying to get to her. Did the rope slip a little? My forepaws work back and forth. *Come on! A little more!*

"Too bad your father couldn't be here for this little reunion, right, *Princess*?"

"I told you. I don't know anything. If Father had some secret hiding place, I haven't a clue where it is. Not that I'd tell you even if I did."

Majesty escaped? And Two-Eyes the master hunter can't find him? A spark of light pierces the darkness inside me.

"I'm beginning to get bored with hearing the same answer again and again." Two-Eyes steps toward Tabby, fist clenching. Her body quivers, a mouse in the shadow of a predator bird, but she doesn't back away.

I twist my paws and pull. Almost there.

"I hate it when I get bored." He strikes her.

She cries out. I jump forward. My paws pull free.

With one spring, I am on him. My forepaws claw his face. My teeth sink into his shoulder. My good hind leg kicks him in the middle. Two-Eyes roars and flings me away. My head whacks the post; I crumple to the floor.

"Sarah!"

His boots find my unprotected underside. I curl into a ball, clutching at my belly.

"You want to play rough, Beast? Then let's play rough." Two-Eyes spins away, coiling his whip around his hand. "Hang it up."

Men grab me. Chills prick my body; pain slices through my middle. I twist and kick and snarl.

Tabby lunges against Fang, who holds her back. "Let her be, you monster!"

"I might—if you'll provide that one little location."

"How can I tell you what I don't know!"

A barrel is pushed under me, forcing my back up for the whip, and my forepaws are tied to a nearby post. The ground is just out of reach of my hind legs.

Two-Eyes lowers his face close to mine. "Comfy, Beast?"

I growl and snap my teeth at him.

"Good. You won't be much longer." He disappears from my sight.

"No, don't—"

Hiss-thwack! The whip burrows into my skin with a burning sting. Two-Eye yanks it out. I clench my teeth and squeeze my eyes shut. I won't cry out. I won't. Thwack. Thwack. Pain spiderwebs my back.

"Please, please don't, please . . ." Tabby's words are swallowed by sobs.

Two-Eyes only growls and strikes harder. Hiss-thwack. Hiss-thwack. My head rears back. No. Crying. But a strangled gasp squeezes out, water trickling down my face.

"It doesn't have to be this way, Princess. Only a few words. No? Well, let's see if we can soften that hard heart of yours a bit more." The whip strikes harder and faster. The whip digs into my back, then Two-Eyes tears it away.

I pant for air.

Thwack! A scream wrenches itself from my mouth. Then another and another . . . the gate has been opened, and I cannot stop now. The walls echo with my cries. Thwack, thwack, thwack! Stickiness spreads across my back. *Stop. Stop. Stop.* Hiss-thwack, hiss-thwack! My body loosens, my paws unclench, my screams die to a moan. Pain burns too deep. Hiss-thwack. I have nothing left to give. *Tabby, Majesty, I am sorry. I tried, I tried . . .*

"Enjoy, Beast?"

I manage to open my eyes. Two-Eyes stands over me—when did he stop whipping me?

"I'm so glad you did. I'll try not to keep you waiting long for more." He vanishes from my sight. "We're finished here for now. Let's go. Bring the girl—no, wait. Leave her here, with a torch. Let her ponder the consequences of her actions."

Steps fade. The door thumps closed.

"Oh Sarah, I'm sorry. I'm so sorry." The ropes holding me up lose their grip.

I crumple to the dirt. New pain claws my shredded back. I want to scream. I can only moan. My paw digs into the dirt. Must. Protect. Tabby. Up. Forward.

The darkness takes me.

My forepaw curls and uncurls, seeking a way out of the darkness. The darkness is safe. My pain is far away. But I must get out. Must protect Tabby. Two-Eyes—he could come back. Whip her.

I roll to my side. Claws rake my back. I whimper. *Make it stop. Make it go away.* A single drop of water rolls across my face, and darkness tugs me down.

"Shhh . . . All will be well." A gentle hand strokes my fur. "You'll see. Everything will work out." The voice breaks, and a drop of water splashes against my face. Tabby.

I force my eyes open. My head rests on Tabby's lap. We are still in the cellar, but a couple of paces away, a small fire fueled by jagged boards burns low. Smoke thickens the air but pushes through the cracks between the floorboards above so it doesn't overwhelm us.

Neither Two-Eyes nor his men are in sight. Yet.

I struggle to my feet. A scream begs to get out. My teeth clamp together, trapping it inside. Who knows how long darkness has held me when Tabby should be the one sleeping? I shake my head, fur tumbling about my face. Think.

"Please, Sarah. Don't move around so much. You might start bleeding again."

She is right. I need to save my strength. Two-Eyes will come again. I settle next to the fire. It is warm, but not warm enough. I am cold, so very cold.

Tabby scoots next to me. "It's so quiet up there. I haven't heard any steps upstairs for a long time." She waves at the shadowy lumps of boxes and barrels. "Though I guess we don't have to worry about running out of food." She laughs, but it is short and sharp and dies quickly.

The fire snaps and pops.

"When you were lying there so still and I didn't know whether you would . . ." Tabby clenches her hands together on her lap. "Father would say I let myself get stuck in a mud hole these last few months. All mired down in petty things, stuff that doesn't really matter. I knew I was wrong, what I did, how I treated you. But I didn't know how to stop, how to get out of my mud hole, and truthfully, I'm not sure I wanted to."

She pulls a small box from her pouch, and wetness on her face sparkles in the firelight. "But I want to now. Sarah, can you ever forgive me for hurting you the way I did? You've done so much for me and I've been terrible to you. But I love having you around, I really do. Nothing would be the same without you. You're the feathers to my bird."

She opens the box. A gold bird and a set of gold feathers, both on gold strings, sparkle in the firelight. "I was saving this for when you came to your senses and agreed to become part of our family. But I think now is better." She lays the feathers by my paws and fastens the bird around her neck. "May I put on your necklace? I'll be careful."

I dip my head, and she takes that as a yes, because she puts it around my neck. "Official or not, we're sisters, for always and always. And I'll wear this forever"—she touches the bird— "to remind myself of that."

Water slips down my face. But it is not from outside pain. Inside pain. I want to take Tabby's words, but I cannot.

"Sarah?"

I shake my head. Not Sarah. Never Sarah.

"No? No what—no Sarah?"

I lift my face to her. Does she finally know what I mean?

"But what then will I call you? The only other thing anyone has called you is 'Beast' or—"

My head bobs hard.

"Beast? But you're not a . . . Oh Sarah. Is that why you didn't want Father to adopt you? You thought you were a . . ." Tabby chokes on her words.

I lower my head, fur falling over part of my face. She understands at last.

"How can you believe all those . . . those *lies*? You're not a beast or a monster or an animal or . . . or some half-devil. Don't you see? You're a person, just like me."

I shrink back. What is she saying?

She grabs my forepaw, pressing her hand to it. "One thumb. Four fingers. Palm. Knuckles. Fingernails." She points to each part, ending with my ragged claws.

I jerk my forepaw away. No. This can't be. I served the Master. Fought his dogs for food. Made his man-pack laugh.

"And our feet—see, they're the same too. And our arms and our legs and mouths and eyes and teeth. You don't have a tail or long snout or fur covering all of you. You don't even have pointed ears."

I start to touch my ears, then jerk away my paw—or is it a hand? No. It can't be.

"So what if you walk funny because your leg is maimed? And if you have some extra skin between your fingers so you can't spread them out like me? That doesn't make you any less human."

No! I turn my face away, a whimper growing inside me. This can't be true. Can't she see that?

Because if I am human, why did Master, Two-Eyes, the others call me Beast?

CHAPTER 17

Failure

url, uncurl. Curl, uncurl. In the red light of an almost gone fire, I stare at the scarred and dirt-stained skin. Paw? Or hand? Master called me Beast. Two-Eyes calls me Beast. But Tabby and Majesty call me Sarah. Who is right? Am I Beast? Or Sarah?

Tabby sighs and rolls over in her sleep. A clump of hair slides across the smooth skin of her cheek. I rub the ridges covering the left side of my own face.

No, Tabby is wrong. I am not a Sarah. Maybe I could have been once, a long time ago. But not now. I have been Beast too long. I limp away from the fire, away from Tabby, and curl up in a ball by a barrel. My eyes close, my insides hurting from all the emptiness.

Ka-thud. Something hits the floor above my head.

My head pops up. Tabby pushes up on an elbow. She heard the sound too. "What was that?"

I force myself to my feet and hobble over to the stairs. My ears hear nothing unusual. Someone must have dropped a pot or—Wait. I tip my head. A scuffle, like a man trying to move so no one hears him.

Tabby crouches beside me. I feel her presence more than see her; the light of the dying fire cannot reach this far. Together we wait.

Thud. The door opens above us. I press back into the shadows. Who is coming? Not Two-Eyes. He would not care how much noise he made. This person does.

"Princess Tabitha?" A board creaks under a foot. "Your father, His Majesty King Elroy, has sent me to bring you back to him."

I peer into the darkness. I cannot see more than a black form creeping about, but the voice—I know it.

Steps scuff dirt. "He told me to tell you, a bird needs its feathers and feathers need the bird. Only together can they take flight."

Tabby's grip tightens on my shoulder, making me wince. "The necklaces. Only Father knew about them. That means he must be . . ." She gasps. "The Protector. The one Father promised would be nearby if I ever needed one." She pushes away before I can stop her. "I'm here."

The dark form turns and bows. "Princess Tabitha. We need to move quickly."

"I know, but—Sarah."

"She's here too?"

"Yes, but . . ." Tabby's words choke her. "She's been hurt. Badly."

"Can she make it up the stairs?"

"I-I'm not sure."

I growl. No matter what this man says, I don't trust him. He will not carry me. I limp forward and climb the steps, ignoring my aching body.

The kitchen is dark, except for a few red coals in the hearth. Is this a trap? But no one—not Two-Eyes, not his men—jumps out to stop me. I crawl onto the floor. Tabby bounds out after me without hesitation, and the man follows, darkness clinging to him.

Tracker.

This man can mean no good. I crouch in front of Tabby and growl at him. He will not take her back to that gray town and sell her to another master. She belongs to Majesty.

"Sarah, what has gotten into you? This is the Protector; he's here to help."

Help? More like capture for his own use. I press my paws against the floor, ready to attack. I will not be able to fight long, but long enough for her to run.

"I believe your Sarah doesn't trust me, Princess. Unfortunately, we are out of time." He steps forward and reaches for me.

Thunk! Someone bumps around in the other room.

Tracker whirls, whipping off the bow slung across his shoulders. "Run! And don't look back!" Even as a whisper, his words press for action.

Tabby unlatches the door and glances back. "But how will you find—"

"I will. Now go!" Tracker places an arrow against the bowstring.

Tabby sprints outside into the night. I follow.

Shouting bursts out and footsteps pound against cold dirt behind us. "Halt!" An arrow whizzes over my head and sinks deep into a tree trunk.

I dart back and forth among the bushes, trying to keep Tabby in sight. Faster. Go faster! My chest heaves. Blackness sparks across my eyes. I stumble over a root. Pain rips through me so I cannot move. Must. Keep. Going. I crawl to my feet. Tabby. Where's Tabby? My gaze darts all around me. Silver snow. Gray trees. Black dirt. But no Tabby. I limp forward. Coldness wraps around me, and air from my mouth comes out in white puffs. Find Tabby. Find Tabby. My forepaws hit the ground that they can barely feel, and I swing my hind leg forward.

Nothing moves. Not even a branch twitches. My steps slow, then stop. Still no Tabby. Tracker must have found her. Now what? If I want to find Tabby, I will have to find Tracker—or let Tracker find me. Shivering, I curl up against a tree.

I do not wait long. A shuffling step and then Tracker slips around a fallen log. For Tabby, I will not growl, attack, or run.

He steps backward. "If I didn't know better, I would say you were waiting for me."

I tilt my head. Where *is* Tabby?

"If you look for Princess Tabitha—may the kingdom be

restored to her and her father soon—she isn't here." He limps forward; a dark splotch stains his pants. "Some of Lord Avery's men found her before I did."

Two-Eyes took her again? I spin around and run the way I came.

"Wait!"

Why obey his words now? He does not have Tabby, and she is all that matters now. My feet stumble, but I don't let them stop. Tabby ran from Two-Eyes. Two-Eyes whips those who run from him.

The trees end. I slow to a walk. The door to the inn's kitchen still stands open. I peek inside. Fang stands over the table, stuffing food into a bag. For once his grin is gone. A second man pounds up the cellar steps carrying a box. "This is the last of the worthwhile stuff."

"Grab a bag, fill it, and let's go." Even Fang's voice is flat. "His lordship isn't going to be in a good mood, and if we're late . . ."

"Don't say more." He fills the sack and ties it shut. "Ready when you are." They grab the bags and clomp into the other room.

I carefully swing inside. Broken boxes and wood dust are scattered across the floor. Something gnaws at my insides—and it isn't the want for food. I pass the open door of the cellar; they would not have left it open if Tabby had been there. The large room beyond is dark and empty. Where are Two-Eyes and his men? Where's Tabby?

A chilling breeze sweeps across the floor from the far open door and smacks me in the face. I shiver and know. Two-Eyes is gone. His men are gone. Tabby is gone. I'm the only one left.

Outside there is a slap of reins. I leap across the room. They can't leave me here. I have to go with them, be where Tabby is. Two horses pound down the road, the way Majesty, Tabby, and I came so long ago. I run after them, stretching my legs as far as I can. My back burns as if a fire lies on it. But horses are faster than beasts, and soon they cannot be seen or heard.

Still I go on. I must find Tabby. I must do this one thing right. When I can no longer run, I walk, and when I cannot walk, I stumble forward. My chest heaves. The air burns inside and out. Hot stickiness bleeds across my back. Pain pierces my side like an arrow. Rocks scrape my paws; redness spots the dirt. My feet trip, my body sprawls forward. But I cannot stop, not yet. I haven't reached Tabby. I claw dirt, trying to drag myself forward. My body won't go. It has taken me as far as it can.

My head slumps to the cold ground, and dirt swallows the single drop of water that falls from my face. One thing. That is all Majesty asked of me. And I failed.

Hooves pound the road. Run. Hide! But I cannot even crawl off the road. Let the rider come. It doesn't matter.

"Whoa!" The rider pulls the horse up sharply a moment before its hard feet would have crushed me. Tracker. No surprise there. He has found me again.

He slides to the ground and limps forward. "Don't run. I can't handle much more tonight."

I turn my face from him. What is left to run for? Take me. Sell me—if you can. I'm only Beast, a burden to the pack.

Tracker lightly touches my shoulder, as if waiting for me to pounce. One shudder shifts through me, and my body falls still. Even shivering is too much work.

He growls. "All I need." He scoops me into his arms and holds me close. Not crushing like Two-Eyes. Protectively, like how Majesty holds—*held* me.

Somehow Tracker, with me in his arms, climbs onto his horse, an animal as dark as he. "Come on, Storm. We have what we came for." He nudges it forward, back the way he came. Away from Tabby.

Away from anything worth living for.

———— ❧ ————

Trees. So many trees, their bare limbs grasping for what cannot be found, their twisted trunks curled over in defeat. Is there anything left but trees? It does not matter when I open my eyes. It is only trees and Tracker and his horse and me. No towns. No people. No animals. Only trees twisting in their own silent pain.

I let the cold darkness sweep over me. I cannot fight it, do not want to fight it. Only in the darkness do I not think of Tabby, and sometimes even there I cannot escape.

Tracker shakes me, pulls me back to the light. He hovers over me, he and the trees. He presses food to my mouth, tries to pour water over my thick tongue. Chewing is too hard. So is swallowing. I turn my face away, wait for the slap of Tracker's hand. But his fingers brush lightly across my cheek, soft words murmuring over me. Like Majesty might have done if he were here.

Majesty. My insides twist and knot like the roots of an old tree. He will be so angry when he hears what happened, angry that I could not protect Tabby. No, it is good that Majesty is not here. It is good that Tracker takes me far away, back to that town of endless gray. I curl into a shivering ball.

Light blurs into darkness. Maybe this time I will stay there.

But Tracker will not let me. He keeps dragging me back to the light, always ready with food, drink, and a light touch. Why won't he leave me alone? Doesn't he see it would be better for everyone if I stayed in the darkness? But just as I could not lose him when he hunted me, neither can I stop him from bringing me up to the chilling light now.

"Hold on. Don't give in to the fever yet. We're almost there." He bends over me, pours some water into my mouth.

Something has changed. I squint at him, past him. The trees. The green has come back. It is no thicker than a clinging mist, but it is there. I sigh, sinking back into the arms of darkness. At least the trees found what they wanted.

When I open my eyes again, Tracker carries me. He walks now, moving with long strides toward a house. Master's house? No. Fire ate Master's house. This one is bigger, taller. Why did Tracker bring me here? A door opens and a mate of night's color steps out. "Mason! You're home. And successfully, I see."

"The egg has not hatched yet, my love." His boots pound against a stone floor. "Princess Tabitha is still trapped, and this one emptied her quiver to protect the princess. Only a bowstring ties her to life." The door thuds shut behind us. "Has His Majesty arrived safely?"

"I have."

My head jerks toward the voice. Majesty's voice. No. I cannot face him. Not after I failed him. A wail rises inside me, but only a moan comes out. Why did Tracker bring me here?

Majesty leans over me and brushes fur from my face. "Sarah. My precious Sarah."

"I'm sorry, Your Majesty. I couldn't get to the princess. I tried, but . . ." Tracker shakes his head.

"You've done well, especially considering these trying days."

"My loyalties don't shift with the balance of power, Your Majesty. Lord Avery did not win that wager fairly, so you are still king, no matter what others may say."

"Will you two stop?" Tracker's mate pushes between him and Majesty. "We have to get this child in bed or the whole trip will be dust. Mason, lay her down in there, then fetch my herbs from upstairs."

Tracker carries me past a curtain and gently places me on a bed in the corner of the small room. I roll toward the wall; heaviness pulls my eyes closed. I hear Majesty approach.

Please let me go. I'm not worth the work.

CHAPTER 18

STOWAWAY

I want to be left alone, should be left alone. It would be better that way. Why can't Majesty and Tracker and his mate see that? But they do not go away or leave me behind. Not Tracker. Not his mate. Not Majesty. One of them is always at my side as I drift from shadows to light and back into deep darkness. Often they have food or water in hand. I would rather have another blanket. Coldness seeps under the one I have and prickles my skin until even my insides shiver.

"Come on, Sarah. Fight. Fight the fever." Majesty's voice pleads with me over and over.

I do not want to hear his words. I do not want to fight or do anything else he says. But he is Majesty. How can I say no?

Tracker's mate comes in. "Any change?"

"No." Majesty's word comes out hard, flat.

She places a hand on my forehead. "The fever should have broken by now. I don't know what to make of it. It's like she doesn't want to live."

"That makes my decision final." Ever the hunter, Tracker comes in without a sound, unseen until he wishes to be seen. "I'm going after Princess Tabitha."

His mate bumps the bed with her abrupt turn. "But Mason—"

"It's our only hope. I've watched these two since I picked her up. They created a special bond, and now Princess Sarah blames herself for what happened to Princess Tabitha."

Princess? My thoughts stutter. When was *that* added to my name?

But Majesty does not correct Tracker. "He's right. Go. With my blessing."

"Thank you, Your Majesty. I will leave within the fortnight, within the week if the weather is good. Maybe, if I hurry, I can save them both."

———— ❧ ————

"I'm going after Princess Tabitha."

Tracker's words finally pierce my darkness like an arrow lit with fire: He knows how to find Tabby. If I follow him, maybe I can help bring her back to Majesty, and I will be able to meet his eyes again. I roll over with a sigh and look around.

Shadows cling to the corners of the small room like spider webs, held at bay by a lamp hanging near the door. The chair next to the bed sits empty except for a lump of cloth and tangle of thread. Someone bangs around in the other room.

I push out from under the thick pile of blankets and slide over the edge of the bed to the cool stone floor. My back itches, but pain no longer claws it. I swing forward a couple of steps. My other leg drags behind as always, but at least I can still walk.

Pushing around the curtain, I nose into the main room. Again I think of Master's house. This room is bigger, but it has the same stone floor, the same wood chairs and table, the same warm hearth and scent of smoke and cooking food. Only the ladder going into the ceiling is not the same.

Tracker's mate pulls a pot off the fire with her apron and turns around. "What are you doing out of bed? Get back. Quick. Before death catches you."

I slink back a step and duck my head. She is definitely Tracker's mate.

She dumps the pot on the table and marches toward me. "Didn't you hear me? Climb back under those blankets. Now."

I sidestep her before she can back me into a corner. I've spent too much time in the bed. I need to move, run. But where to go? I need to stay near so I can watch Tracker and know when to follow him. And angering his mate would not be good either. I cannot take another beating so soon, and Tracker's mate, like Master's, looks more than strong enough to give a hard one.

She rolls her lips into her mouth and her shoulders shake. Finally laughter spills out. "My Mason was right. You are a willful one. I can see that now. No wonder he fumed and fussed so."

I cock my head. Laughter is not how I thought she would act. What should I do now?

She lifts up the blankets and waves for me to crawl under them. "If you would please, Princess Sarah?"

My toes curl. The stone floor *is* cold.

"Then I'll get you something hot to eat."

My insides rumble. She wins. I swing over and crawl back into the bed.

Boots stomp into the other room and a door thumps closed. "Evie, we're back," calls Tracker.

His mate, tucking the blankets around me, shakes her head. "As if I couldn't tell. Never have convinced him to use that same wood stealth in the house."

Majesty pushes aside the curtain. He's changed. Gone is the lightness and laughter. Now his shoulders stoop forward and shadows linger in his eyes. And why is he dressed in plain brown clothing like Tracker? He steps to the side of Tracker's mate. A smile spreads across his face, a face that has more lines than I thought it did. "Sarah, you're awake."

I dip my head away from him. How can he smile at me after the way I failed him?

Tracker's mate slips away, and Majesty settles on the edge of the bed. "For a while there, Mason and Evie thought you had given up completely." He brushes some of the fur from my face.

"But you've proven once more your strength goes deeper than what the eye can see."

Strength? His words swirl like leaves in the wind so I cannot grasp them. I cannot run or fight for more than a few minutes, and even if I could, my useless leg always slows me down. Strong are the Others, Tracker, Two-Eyes. I am not strong.

"I am honored that you gave so much of that strength for Tabby and me. But even if you hadn't, I'd still be glad you're here." Majesty rises and bends over me, pressing his mouth to my head. And though I do not want to, I lean into his touch, into his words.

Then he is gone, leaving the hunger for more gnawing at my insides.

How long must we wait? How many more nights must I twist in my sleep, my legs aching for a run? How many more days must I stare at the cobweb darkness in the corners of the room? Tabby is somewhere out there, caged by Two-Eyes, while I lie here protected, warm, well-fed. She should be the one here. I am the one Two-Eyes wanted. I am why he came, why the wager was made, why Majesty lost the game.

I thrash under the blankets, but I cannot go. Tracker must leave first so I can follow him—and he cannot go because storms rage.

Light fades into darkness. Darkness gives way to light. Still the wind howls, the water from the sky pelts the house, and Tracker paces the other room. I would be at his side, but his mate will not let me out of the bed for more than a little at a time.

So I wait. And listen. Tracker and Majesty often bend over the table in the other room, talking, when they think I sleep. Many of their words I do not understand, but I hold onto them anyway. What is meant may be made known to me later.

The storm finally stops. Tracker no longer paces. He goes in and out of the house all day, doors banging. Majesty opens a window by my bed so I can watch. My nose twitches at the thick scent of warm air, wet dirt, and damp leaves. I want to run, but I must wait a little longer. Tracker loads a wagon with blankets and pots and bags. He will leave soon.

"Everything ready?" Majesty's whisper yanks me from a light sleep.

"As ready as I can be, Your Majesty." Tracker scuffs and bumps around.

"What about Sarah?"

"If all goes well, I'll be back with Princess Tabitha in less time than a hunting trip would take."

"And if you two keep going on so, she won't be asleep much longer." Tracker's mate pulls the curtain across my doorway.

Good. I push the blankets off and dress in my he-cub clothes as fast as my clumsy paws will let me. The gold feather necklace from Tabby glints at the bottom of the pile. I lightly touch it, then jerk away. That belongs to Sarah. I am not Sarah. I push open the wood boards covering the window.

The outside is gray, caught in the time between dark and light. This is good. I can see without being seen. I plop down onto the squishy ground. A cool breeze wraps around me in greeting. I shiver, but my face lifts at its touch, my nose twitching. The days of heat and berries are not long off.

A door creaks. The voices of Majesty and Tracker come nearer. I bound across the ground—how good that feels!—and climb into the wagon. Some blankets are piled in the corner. I slip under them.

Footsteps squish past the wagon. "Don't worry, Your Majesty. I won't come back until your daughter is safe in my arms." Metal jangles from the front.

"I do not doubt it. But I wish I could go with you."

"No!" At Tracker's loud protest, the horse knickers and the whole wagon rocks, causing me to clutch the blanket under me. "Lord Avery stays his hand only in hope of pulling you out."

"Shh, girl, all's well." Majesty quiets the horse. "I know, Mason. I only express the longing of my father's heart."

"Forgive me. I spoke rashly."

"Pardon given. Go and return quickly, with all speed and strength."

"I will, Your Majesty." The wagon creaks as Tracker climbs up onto the front. "I swore at Princess Tabitha's birth to protect her, and I fully intend to keep that oath."

I cock my head. Tracker is a part of Majesty's pack? Then why was he with the slavers? Tabby—he was there to protect Tabby. Then reins snap, and the wagon jerks into motion, casting from my head Tracker's words and days now gone. For I am on my way. Soon Tracker will find Tabby, and I will bring her back to Majesty.

The horse's feet clop on wood, and a river rumbles below us. It sounds strong and fast, the kind of water I would not want to get caught in. Then we're over and the chirping and chattering of first light surrounds us.

The wagon stops. "Come on out. We're beyond sight of the house."

My body lumps like the rocks of the ground. Is Tracker talking to me?

"Sitting up front will be more comfortable than hiding under a pile of blankets, Princess."

I peek out. Tracker faces forward. Does he plan to take me back?

"The ride to town will be long. You might as well join me and help me plan how to rescue Princess Tabitha."

I crawl over the seat.

Shaking his head, he finally looks down at me. "Evie would kill me if she knew we'd let you come along."

He and Majesty knew I was here and said nothing? I flatten myself on the narrow board his feet rest on.

He lifts his head and stares straight ahead, solid and immovable as a cliff of dark rock. "I don't work with cowering animals."

I lick my lips and tip my head back to look up at the seat. I don't belong up there. But if Tracker becomes angry, he might send me back to Majesty. I awkwardly crawl up beside him. My useless leg hangs thin and twisted against his straight strong one. And I think I can help him get Tabby from Two-Eyes?

A cap plops on my head. "Tuck your hair under that. We don't want any unnecessary attention." Tracker slaps the reins against the dark horse's back and the wagon lurches forward.

I do as he says, keeping my gaze down, shoulders hunched forward. I still don't belong here.

The light grows warm on my back, and my forepaws ache from clutching the board I sit on. Tracker stares ahead, saying nothing. Is he angry with me for coming?

Hooves of fast-moving horses approach. My head jerks up. Where are they coming from?

Tracker glances over at me. "You hear something?"

I nod.

"Horses?"

Another nod.

"Probably Lord Avery's men. I expected that. We're close to Ahavel's border here." He peers ahead. "Can you act like you can't hear?"

What?

"If you can, keep your head down and do it."

My paws tighten on the seat. Keeping my head down is no problem. But acting like I cannot hear?

Four men turn a bend in the road, coming toward us. "Halt!" They surround us, forcing the wagon to stop. The lead rider in red and black pulls aside Tracker. "Name and business."

"Thomas of Riggings. I bring goods for market."

I cannot see the lead rider's face, but thick fingers—too thick for their gloves—grasp reins. Sausage Fingers flicks a hand toward another rider, who slips to the back, pokes through pots, and flips through blankets. What would have happened if I had been hiding back there still?

"Who's the boy?" Sausage Fingers circles around to me.

I keep my head bowed. Act dead, and predators will soon seek prey elsewhere.

Tracker rests his hand on my shoulder. "My helper. I call him John."

"Call?"

Tracker shrugs. "He's a stray I picked up about a year ago. Can't hear or speak, but he's smart and a hard worker."

"Very likely." Sausage Fingers grabs my face, forcing me to look up at him. "Who are you, boy? What are you doing here?"

A whimper and a growl tangle in my throat so neither can get out. This man is not my master. He belongs to another pack. I do not need to listen to him or do as he says.

Tracker shifts and tightens his grip on my shoulder. Something is about to happen.

A pot shatters behind me.

"Not even a flinch." Sausage Fingers shoves me against Tracker. "Find anything back there?"

"A few blankets, clay pots, a couple of sacks of old potatoes, and this." A small bag jingles as it is held up.

"That'll do."

"But that money belongs to me." Tracker leans forward. "I need it to conduct business."

"Consider it your proper fee for crossing the border." The riders clear out of our way, and Sausage Fingers waves us on. "Move along before I decide otherwise."

Tracker mumbles something and slaps the reins. We rumble away.

When the men can no longer see or hear us, Tracker nods at me with a half smile. "Not bad. Together we just might return Princess Tabitha to His Majesty alive and well."

CHAPTER 19

ᴵNFILTRATION

he heaviness is newly come.

The town looks like the others that were under Majesty's care. Open space. Clean houses. New green spikes pushing out of the ground around them. Early flowers adding patches of yellow and purple. A town full of light and color.

But a heaviness hangs in the air, and I think of the gray border town. I scoot nearer to Tracker. I may not trust him like I do Majesty, but he is strong and able to protect me—if he chooses to do so.

"I know, Princess. I feel it too." He clutches the reins tightly.

The heaviness is strongest in the big people. In the way masters' shoulders slump. In how mates keep cubs at their sides. In the frowns that crease faces and in the narrowing of eyes. And my ears, though they are to hear nothing, hear everything: hushed words, barely restrained growls, the lack of chatter and laughter.

Tracker turns into an open square, filled with other horses and wagons. Men unload sacks and barrels and poles and cloth. Animals penned in one corner bleat and moan. The noises ease some of the heaviness.

Tracker helps me down to the ground. "Do you know what to do?"

I nod. He told me his plans when we traveled. First we need more information. So I am to listen. Find any word on Tabby.

"Then go ahead. But be careful. If any of Lord Avery's men see you walking around, they'll know who you are."

The beast-child. A shiver slides down my back at the words Tracker does not say and does not need to say. I will walk as if stalking prey.

I work my way through shadows and around buildings. In and out. Back and forth. Every road and path and good hiding place around the square must be mine. I must be ready to run from Two-Eyes—or hide from Tracker, if he should turn on me. Around me, words are thrown about. Words about the cold and the storms. Words about the "fineness" of cloth. Words about whether crops will be good or if a baby will be born soon.

As I circle around the square, my cap keeps sliding off my head. I stop and tuck it away so I don't lose it. When I look around again, a nearby seller is backing into the shadows with a second man. No one else seems to see that, and from how they look over their shoulders, that is what they want. I creep into the shadows behind them.

"Careful, Joshua. That's treason these days." The seller's voice is very low, and I must listen hard to know the words.

The second man with a scruffy beard growls. "This tyranny is treason. Taxes have tripled in the past month, and what taxes leave, they take in extra fees or just outright steal. And worse"—he leans forward—"rumor has it that this new king holds the princess and will force her to marry him."

"But the princess is barely more than a child!"

"It doesn't matter to him." Scruff-Beard spits on the ground. "He only thinks of silencing us, the dog."

"May the kingdom be returned to His Majesty King Elroy soon!"

A swordsman wearing red and black saunters by. The seller moves some of his pots around. Scruff-Beard picks one up and looks at it closely. I wait unmoving; I need to know all these two do.

The swordsman continues on, but the seller keeps his eyes down. "The rumor is probably just that, trying to lure us out."

"Not according to my man." Scruff-Beard lifts another jar to the light. "He says a servant saw her in the castle's north tower." He pulls open a pouch.

The seller takes the shiny pebbles. "If it is true, she is to be the most pitied of all."

"Indeed she is." Scruff-Beard wanders away.

I press my back against the wall. Tabby is alive—and I know where she is! For a moment I consider just going, without telling Tracker. Think how pleased Majesty would be with me then. But no. I need Tracker, and if he wanted to hurt me, wouldn't he have done it by now? So I bound down a road and around a corner.

Shouting bursts out behind me. "Did you see that?"

"Yeah, I did. Halt!"

My head jerks around. Two-Eyes's pack! I sprint ahead and dart between the houses. Stupid Beast. How could I have forgotten to make sure my path was clear?

I turn into another crowded square and scuttle through clusters of people. A short stone wall sits in the square's center—a well. I leap onto the edge, twist around, and drop myself into the hole, only the tip of my paws digging into the top of the wall. My feet dangle in a darkness that covers the bottom. If there is a bottom.

"Where is it? Where did it go?"

Silence falls heavily above me and I bite my lip. Did anyone see? What will be said? There is no place for me to go but down. Dust layers my mouth. Maybe it would be better to let them take me.

No one says anything.

"Someone must have seen something. Speak up. Quick now."

More quiet, then a master's voice. "That way. I thought I saw a hunched figure scurry down there."

"So did I." "Me too." "That's what I saw." Many voices speak out now, overlapping each other.

"You heard them. That way." Footsteps pound by and fade.

I shift my grip, my paws aching. Is it safe to go up? It sounds so quiet still.

"Bold move, little one." The master's voice rings out above me, and a smiling face peers down at me. "But I figured anyone running from those ruffians is on the same side as me." He grabs one of my arms. A second man grabs the other one and together they lift me onto solid ground.

My eyes widen as I look around the crowd. They knew. They saw where I went and said nothing. They sent the men the wrong way. My mouth longs for words, but words do not belong to me. So I face the master and lean forward until my face touches the ground. I do the same for the one who helped him pull me out.

The master's face reddens. "Go on, before those men come back."

He doesn't need to say more. I bound back to Tracker, this time checking each corner before going forward.

Tracker doesn't even look up when I come out of the shadows. "I take it you found something." He neatly folds the last blanket and sets it on the pile. "About Lord Avery?"

I shake my head as I pull out my cap and stuff my hair under it again.

"Then Princess Tabitha."

I jerk a nod.

He picks up a bag and frowns at it "This would be so much quicker if you'd speak."

My head dips. Is he wishing I hadn't come?

"We'll have to make do. Hmm . . ." He overturns the bag; potatoes spill at my feet. "Sort them. Potato here," he taps the ground, "if the answer is yes. But in the sack if no. Got it?"

I put a potato on the ground.

"Good." He turns to rearrange pots. "Is Princess Tabitha alive?"

Potato for the ground.

"Do you know where she is?"

A third joins the other two.

"Hmm . . ." He stares at the small pile for a breath. "Is she close?"

I dump one into the sack.

"At the northern fortress or the castle in Melek?"

A potato for the sack and a potato on the ground.

"The castle?" An edge of excitement creeps into his voice. "Do you know where in the castle?"

Two more for the pile. It shifts, and potatoes roll every which way. I reach for them. So does Tracker. We bump into each other. I yelp and spring back, rubbing my head.

At the edge of the square, men in red and black prowl from seller to seller. My insides crumple on themselves, like wood that has burned too long. They hunt for me still.

Tracker glances over his shoulder. "Princess Sarah, please tell me you did not meet up with them."

I hang my head.

"I was afraid of that. We had better get you out of sight before—"

"There it is." The men march our way.

"Whatever happens, don't panic." His voice is low and his mouth unmoving. Then he straightens up and steps forward to meet them. "Is there a problem, gentlemen?"

"Why are you hiding this fugitive?"

"John's a fugitive?"

I keep my head down and put the potatoes in two piles; if I sit only, the wish to run will push me too far.

"John?"

Tracker sighs. "As I explained at the border, John's a stray. He's been with me about a year. No, I don't know his real name. That's why I call him John. However, he's a hard worker, and being a deaf-mute, he never talks back. Is there anything else you'd like to know?"

The leader squints at me. "Tell him to bring me that potato." He points to one that ran away from the pile beyond my reach.

"If you wish to see it, I can—"

"I said, tell *him*."

"Fine, fine." Tracker lifts his hands and backs up a step. "Don't let your horse carry you off." He kneels before me and waves his hand before my face.

I lift my eyes to him. Don't panic. Don't run. Yet.

"Po-ta-to." Tracker points to the runaway and then to the leader. "Him."

I point as he did: potato, leader. Anything to give me time. How can I do this? They'll know what I am as soon as I press my paws to the ground.

Or are they hands?

Tabby's words from the cellar return to me. *"One thumb. Four fingers. Palm. Knuckles. Fingernails. Don't you see? You're a person, just like me."* Can I act like a Sarah to make them think I am not Beast? Tabby seemed to think I could. I tug on Tracker's sleeve and point to a short pole nearby.

"Yes, yes. Your . . . stick. I see I've pushed it away again." He offers it to me.

Digging the tip into the ground, I reach as high on the pole as I can with both hands. My insides twist and whirl, a leaf caught in rushing water. If this doesn't work, I must be ready to run. Fast. My eyes squeeze shut and I pull myself up.

My good leg shifts, but I do not fall. My eyes slowly open. I'm standing!

Tracker's face is blank, but his eyes look wetter than usual. He picks up the potato and holds it out to me.

I take it and turn toward the leader. A few paces. That is all I have to do. Swinging the pole forward, I dig it into the ground, lean against it, and jump. My leg wobbles, but I stay up. Three more times brings me to the man. My grin spreads bigger than the potato I offer him. I walked!

The man throws it down and marches away, growling and grumbling.

Tracker dips his head toward me. "Like a true princess."

CHAPTER 20

~

PLANS

The room is ten hops long. Most of the time. Sometimes I swing the pole farther, making my jumps longer, and the room is only nine hops long. Other times, especially as I tire, my jumps are shorter. Then I need eleven hops to go from end to end. But nine, ten, or eleven—the room is the right size.

Thump, hop. Thump, hop. I pass by a fire warming the cool evening, past a bed pushed against a wall, past Tracker leaning over a map on a table. Tracker's friend was good to offer us this room after our day of selling.

"Must Princess Tabitha be in the north tower? One way in, one way out, and no good way to reach it." Tracker scowls at the black squiggles before him. "About our only advantage is the armory halfway up—if Lord Avery hasn't moved it."

I turn and start back toward the bed. Thump, hop. Thump, hop—my aching leg gives away, and I fall. Again. At least this time the bed catches me, which is much softer than the floor. I growl and pull myself back up. I will keep going. Because maybe if I work hard enough, I will someday become a Sarah.

Tracker rises and pours himself a drink from a pitcher. "After my last excursion, I suppose I should be grateful Lord Avery feels secure enough to still hold her there." He drains his cup with one gulp and then stares into its emptiness. "We'll need a diversion, something else to occupy them."

I reach the other end of the room. Give them other prey to hunt? My scarred hands twist the pole they clutch.

"No, Princess. I'll leave you here before using you as bait." Tracker jerks back his chair and sits. "There must be another solution. Maybe another way in."

He isn't leaving me here. Because of me, Two-Eyes has Tabby. I must help her get away from him. My hands tighten around the pole. Must be ready. I start back across the room. Thump, hop. Thump, hop.

Tracker growls as he looks up at me. "I'm delighted at your discovery, Princess Sarah, but I can't think with you constantly pacing!"

I drop to a crouch, my head drooping. I thought my work would please him. My hand rubs my aching leg.

"Princess Sarah . . ."

My shoulders hunch forward, as if that will protect me from the sting of angry words.

Tracker sighs. "I've done it again." The chair scrapes against the floor as he rises.

I shuffle back against the bed, hands clutching the pole at his approach. He has never struck me, but he has threatened it often enough.

He kneels in front of me. "I beg your pardon, Princess. I had no right to be angry with you. You should be rejoicing this day. Do not let me take that from you." Leaning forward, he touches his head to the floor—before me!

Why does he do this? I am Beast. That is my position—to him, to Majesty, to everyone.

Tracker waits. I lift a hand and touch his shoulder.

"Thank you for your understanding, Princess." He lifts his face. "Now may I carry you to the table so we may determine the best way to help Princess Tabitha? Or do you wish to continue your walking?"

I lay aside the pole.

Tracker gathers me in his arms, shaking his head. "Your trust, even after all I've done to you, amazes me."

I curl in on myself.

"That was a compliment, Princess, not a criticism."

He thinks I did well? I lift my head. Tracker thought I did well.

A door bangs in the other room, prickling my fur. Who comes here this late at night? Tracker looks at me. I look at him. We both know this isn't good. Then shouting breaks out. I twist out of Tracker's arms and he grabs his sword. "Back, quick."

I dart under the table as our door bangs open. Fang blocks our way out. How did Two-Eyes know we were here? Tracker swings his sword and backs up. Fang presses toward him, clearing a path for me out the door.

"Run, Sarah. Run!" Tracker lunges, pushing Fang toward the corner.

I dart out the door and sprint into the dark streets.

Darkness closes its fist around me. On the outside. On the inside. Ever endless. Stupid, stupid, *stupid* Beast. The one thing that should never be done, I did. I abandoned my pack. I ran.

I drag myself through the town. All is quiet. What kind of animal am I that I desert even my pack? Maybe the whispers were right. Maybe I am something lower than a beast.

My feet bring me back to the shadows across from the house belonging to Tracker's friend. Coldness ripples through me, shivers close behind each other. Rivers flow down my face. I am weak, and that weakness has weakened the strength of those around me. Majesty. Tabby. Now Tracker. He could have run too. But he didn't—because he was protecting me.

The door opens; light leaks across the stone. A man is thrust out. Tracker.

He stumbles, drops to his knees, hands pulled behind his back. His head sags forward. On the side glistens a splotch darker and wetter than his skin. Blood. I want to go to him. I want to run from him. I can do neither. My paws stick to the stone, have become the stone. This is the pain I bring.

"Move along." Fang, his wide grin once more showing all his teeth, pulls Tracker to his feet and pushes him ahead into the blackness. A second man follows with Tracker's friend. Their footsteps fade.

Follow them, stupid Beast! But my legs refuse to move. They know better than my insides that there is nothing I can do. I only make trouble. In my desire to help get Tabby back, I put Tracker in a snare instead. If I try to help him now, what greater hurt will I bring?

Shadows fade to gray; the light is coming. I stumble to my feet. My back aches. My legs are stiff. I plant my forepaws and swing my good hind leg forward. The useless one scrapes along behind. I walk down roads and up paths, but I go nowhere.

The wind gusts. A leaf, shriveled and brown, tumbles in front of me in the road, still empty. But it will not be that way for long. Thumps come from houses and fire-smoke grows strong. The man-pack is busy on the inside while I walk on the outside, where I belong.

I have destroyed Majesty and his pack for all days.

Doors open. People move among the houses. A hole gnaws at my insides, growing bigger and bigger, a hole that many meat bones can never fill. It is time to go back to the forest, the only home fitting for me. I leave the town.

Horse feet clop against the ground—men wearing red and black head my way. I dive into the tall grasses along the road's edge and squirm under a bush. I push a branch to one side. Fang ties a bag to his horse and climbs onto the prancing animal. A second horse tied to the first bears a slumped rider. Tracker? He is doubled over, as if his insides hurt, and his face is so puffy and scratched, I almost cannot tell that it is him.

"I wish the king success with this one." The second man walks to the other side of the horse. "He's quite stubborn."

Fang's grin only widens. "Oh, don't worry. His Majesty will break him. He's good with a whip."

Good with a whip. My paws dig into the ground, grasping for the dirt and grass I stand on as the words send me back to the cellar, back to the hovering darkness, the sound of Tabby's sobs, my burning skin, the whip's hiss-thwack.

Fang kicks his horse and takes off down the road, Tracker's horse pulled along behind. The other man walks back into the town. This can't happen. I bolt out of the bushes and down the road, the way Tracker and Fang went. Two-Eyes is not *good* with a whip. He is a master.

And this time Tracker will be on the whip's other end.

I stretch out my legs. *Faster, faster, faster!* My paws grab at the road. But no matter how hard I push myself, horses run faster than me. Much faster. Light grows strong and fades. Night overtakes me. Then when it seems the shadow time has no end, the light comes back.

Light, darkness, light, darkness. One passes to the other again and again, until I do not know how long it has been since Tracker was taken away. But I know where they went. They went to where Tabby is: Majesty's castle in Melek. So I go on still, sneaking onto a wagon for a ride when I can, walking when my feet are all I have.

Days grow warm. Why am I doing this? Tracker would have reached the castle long ago. Two-Eyes has already beaten him, whipped him, maybe even silenced him forever. As for Tabby—is she alive? Two-Eyes has had her for so long, so very long. Maybe I walk on for nothing. But I do not know, and I must know.

I limp to the top of a hill. My paws feel every rock on the road. My insides pinch each other from a long time with little food.

A cloth snaps in the wind; above the trees waves the red-and-black flag of Two-Eyes. Not as nice as Majesty's blue and silver, but a good sight anyway. I am almost to the castle. I keep my pace slow until I reach the edge of the trees. Familiar towers jut up among the tumbling waters of the river, and the roofs of Melek beyond peek around the wall like a cub hiding behind its mother.

I can hold back no longer. I bound forward with more strength than I have known in many days.

"Did you just see what I just saw?" A man's voice hits me from behind like a stone.

My head twists to look back over my shoulder. Two men in red and black, near the forest's edge, scramble to their feet. Is there no place his pack doesn't roam yet?

Wiping their mouths with the back of their hands, they toss aside what's left of a midday meal and reach for the bows at their feet. I race back for the shelter of trees, cutting across open ground away from the road.

"Hurry. It's getting away."

Back and forth I dart around trees. I leap over a boulder, roll under a fallen log. A bush whacks me in the face. I tumble down a dirt hill, landing at the edge of the river. Never have I seen water move so fast. It foams white with rage, roaring much like Master when he beat me. But I have to get across, and I have to cross now.

I sprint along the edge. My face burns. I pant. The shouts of the men, which had faded, grow stronger. They will reach me before a startled bird can take flight. An old tree leans into the water. It doesn't go all the way to the other side, but it is all I have. I climb onto the trunk. One leap should get me to the other side. Should.

"There it is!"

I sprint down the slick trunk. Water sprays my face. The soft, wet wood bends under me.

"It's gone mad."

I jump. Splash! I don't quite reach the other side. The cool water latches onto me and tries to drag me farther in. I kick. My forepaws grab stones and pull. The water releases me. I spill onto land—dry, solid land.

"Don't just stand there. Shoot!"

I scramble up the dirt hill and lurch to the side. An arrow buries itself into the ground where I was a moment before. I climb over the top and scurry into the woods.

"We lost it, you stupid . . ."

The trees swallow the words. I collapse against a trunk. But I do not rest long. The men will return to Two-Eyes. They will tell him what they saw. I push myself to my feet and hurry on.

Still, when I see the castle, I must stop and stare at the gray walls taller than two trees. Somewhere on the other side of those stones are Tabby and Tracker, neither knowing I'm here, that I'm coming for them.

And somewhere on the other side is Two-Eyes, preparing for my arrival.

CHAPTER 21

PENETRATION

Reaching the castle was a problem. Entering it without Two-Eyes knowing—that is bigger than a problem.

High above where I crouch among the tangled bushes, Two-Eyes has men pacing along the wall. Back and forth, back and forth. And this is at the back of the castle where the stone wall is solid and nothing crosses the moat. How many more men with bows and swords march on the front side?

But I must get in somehow.

My paws pluck at the grass, and I toss some into the river. The green strands twirl around and then float on by the castle. Why did I not think of this when I was coming? Tracker would have planned something. But not me. So what if I watched him trace a path through the black squiggles, seeking another way in?

I frown at the dark, churning water. Another way in? Something lurks beyond. Something I should know. What am I missing? I cannot fly over the wall, for wings are not mine. I cannot climb up it, for my paws cannot cling to the straight-up stones. I cannot go under—that is it! Under the wall. Through the water. Tabby talked about an underground lake fed by water on the outside. If the water can go there, I might be able to too. Then I can go up the tunnel to the cellar and . . .

I choke. The tunnel. Cold. Dark. Made of stone. My body twists into knots so tight that even air can barely squeeze inside me. I cannot do this. I cannot go back to a place like that. Yet I must. For Majesty. For Tracker. For Tabby.

For me.

My teeth clamp together, and I look up. The men on the wall have their backs to me. I dive into the river.

The cold water grabs me and pulls me down toward the river's bottom. I kick my legs, claw at the water. *Don't fight it. Work with it.* The Keeper's words come back to me. Pull, kick, pull, kick. I blow air out. Pull, kick, pull, kick. My legs stretch out for the rocks around the castle. Kick, pull, kick, pull. My paw brushes stone. Grabbing onto a rock, I shoot up and gulp air. How can it look farther across the water from here than from the other side?

A bird screeches above me. My eyes go up, up, up. The wall. It's so . . . tall. And solid. A cliff of stone blocks, leaning, tipping, ready to fall on me.

The man marches along the top, a speck against the blueness. A circling predator bird. I sink into the water. He goes by without seeing me. He searches so hard for a far-off prey that he misses the one at his feet. But how long will that last? I must find the way into the underground lake soon.

I bob and swim among the rocks poking partway out of the river. My eyes search above the water for a hole while my paws feel below the surface for an opening. My hind leg scrapes a stone. I cut the back of my forepaw on a sharp edge. I stop and sink deeper into the water as a man on the wall's top goes by.

Maybe there is no hole through the rock. Maybe the hole is not big enough for me. Maybe there is no underground lake at all. I work my way across the back of the castle and partway down the side. Why do I keep on? I cannot get in, and even if I could, what good will it do?

I squeeze around a big rock and dive again. Nothing here but . . . My right paw flails. No stone. I push it in farther and wave it around. A hole. Not big, but large enough for me. I float to the surface. My legs feel the tug of water rushing into the hole. This has to be it.

I suck in all the air my insides can hold and slip into the hole. My legs kick. I pull at the water. My shoulder bumps rock. I release a bubble of air. *Faster, faster!* The Keeper's favorite word pushes me. Kick, pull, kick-pull, kick-pull. My insides burn. How much farther can I go on? Should I turn back? Can I turn back?

My head breaks out of water—air. I twist onto my back and suck in. The air tastes like it has been still too long, but the burning eases.

What to do now? My paw says this is only a small, open spot with a low ceiling before the tunnel slips under water again. How far have I come? How far to the lake? What if I do not have enough air? My eyes close. I see Majesty, the sadness in his eyes. I failed once. I will not, cannot, fail again. One more deep breath and I flip over, diving below water again.

The tunnel dives too, going down as much as it goes forward. My back scrapes the top—or is it now a side?—as I swim deeper. My legs ache. My kicks weaken. I thrust myself forward. The stone walls pressing around me vanish, and I float freely in water. The lake? I claw at the water and burst through the surface.

Into darkness.

Cold fingers squeeze my middle, and I twist my head around. Not a speck of light. My eyes cannot even tell me where water ends and air begins. Darkness wraps around me, goes into me. My feet feel like heavy stones, pulling me down, down, down into the black lake.

Water splashes up my nose. I flail upward, sputtering, coughing, choking. My paws claw at the water. But the water only gives way before them and closes behind them. There is no escape. Not from the water. Not from the darkness. This is all there is. All there will be.

I shake my head, water flying from my fur to plop back into the lake. There must be solid rock to cling to nearby. I came through it. And if I find rock, I can follow it to the tunnel, and the tunnel leads to the cellar, the kitchen, food, warmth, light.

I twist and paddle toward where I came from. Or where I think I came from. With all my thrashing, the tunnel under the water may not be behind me any longer. My insides tighten. But even if I twisted around, I must come to stone *some*time. And now I can leave my head out of the water—water so calm that it doesn't pull or push me.

My paws scrape cold, hard stone. My insides loosen a little. The tunnel is next. Feeling for the rock wall at my left, I swim on. And on. And on. How big is this lake? Am I swimming in circles? What if the tunnel does not come to the water's edge? Maybe it ends above my head, beyond my reach. Maybe I swim in a big hole filled with water. Maybe there is no way out of here.

My feet find a solid place to rest. The water is not so deep here. I stagger forward and out of the lake. Ground. Solid ground. I press my face to the dry stone. I made it.

Water drips and cold coils around me. Shivers splash over me, one on top of the other. I am not out of here yet. I need a dry, warm spot. Soon. I force myself up on my legs and shake off as much water as I can. Clothing and fur stick to me. So tired. Maybe I should rest longer. Just a moment or two.

Later. After I find my way into the kitchen. I plant my forepaws and swing my hind leg after. One more step. Take one more step.

The ground rises steadily. One shoulder brushes stone, and I must change which way I face. Another step. Another step. I bump into a wall. A real one, not of solid rock but cut blocks. Almost there! I fumble with the ropes and latches. My body trembles all over. Finally, stone softly grinds against stone. Light breaks the darkness.

I lean back and breathe. Light. It's real. I soak in the flickering glow. I made it to the underground lake and up the tunnel to the . . .

This isn't right.

My insides lurch and I scoot back into shadow. There should not be this much light in the cellar. I stare, but it stays the same:

the light is not being carried, and this is not the cellar. But if this is not the cellar, where am I?

Big mounds of yellow, prickly grasses—the kind the horses eat—block almost all my door. I push the top of one mound to the side and squeeze out into the room beyond. On one side, heavy wood doors open into stone pen rooms. Dark spots stain the floors. Chains dangle from walls in and outside the rooms.

The dungeon.

My insides churn up my throat and into my mouth. Bitter, sharp, burning. I swallow them back down. I am not trapped. I can go back. The place by the lake sounded big. There are probably more tunnels. One of them leads to the cellar.

But I do not move. Water drips off me and creeps along the cracks in the stone floor. This may be the dungeon. It may remind me of where the Keeper kept me. But the light is here. Down there—only darkness. I stare at the bowl lamp hanging between two open doors. If I could get it down, I could slide it ahead of me for light.

The lamp is high. My tongue sweeps around my mouth, trying to moisten its dustiness. I should have drunk from the lake before coming here. Too late now. I'll catch a drink going back. I press my forepaws against the wall and pull myself up on my hind leg.

Clanging shatters the quiet, and my ears catch a jingle of keys. Someone's coming! I drop to the floor and dart into the nearest open door.

"Give in yet?" Two-Eyes says as his steady step approaches.

I slink back, cowering in the shadows. If he finds me here now . . . I swallow. I should have stayed with the darkness.

"Answer me."

A man of night's blackness stumbles into my sight and falls to his knees, clutching his middle with one hand. Tracker. His shirt is gone; his back is a shredded mass of skin and blood. Some of the blood is old and dried. Some is not. He lifts his face toward me. One eye has swelled closed. The other looks at me, glazed with dullness, emptiness. Does he even see me?

"What is that?" Two-Eyes steps toward the grass piles and rubs his toe across the puddle I left behind.

The tunnel! I left the door open. Although the yellow hill still hides most of the door, Two-Eyes will not miss it when he lifts his head. Bad Beast. What have I done now? A whimper escapes my mouth.

Two-Eyes whirls back around toward Tracker, his whip tightly clutched in his hand. His eyes narrow on the smaller pen rooms. "Who's there?"

Tracker pushes up. "No one." Tracker croaks a whisper. "Except a few of your rat relatives."

"Enough!" Two-Eyes uncoils his whip, and it bites into Tracker's back, forcing a moan from him.

I bite my paw to keep in my own cry. I can't let him do this. Not for me. I creep forward. Tracker looks at me. He doesn't say a word. His lips don't move. But inside I hear his order from the night the men took him. *"Run, Sarah, run!"* My paws stick to the stones under them. What should I do?

Two-Eyes lifts his whip again. Tracker can't take much more. I start forward.

"Wait!" Tracker holds up a shaking hand over his head.

"What?"

"I'll talk. I'll talk." The words that start as a cry sink into a whisper that even my ears can barely hear. His hand drops and his head slumps, a prey tired of the chase, waiting for the predator's final strike. Why is he doing this?

Two-Eyes coils the whip around his hand. "I'm waiting."

"I—no." Tracker slides sideways and looks beyond Two-Eyes to me. "First, Princess Tabitha. Make sure. She's. Safe." His words come in gasps, but I know. He speaks to me.

"You're hardly in a position to bargain." Two-Eyes drops the coils of the whip, his fingers tightening over the handle. "Then again . . ." He nods to himself. "I'm not an unreasonable man. Request granted. Guard!"

I bite back a growl. If Two-Eyes does this, it is not for Tracker's or Tabby's good.

A man with many keys enters. "Yes, Your Majesty?"

I cringe. That name belongs only to one, and Two-Eyes isn't him.

"Fetch the girl immediately."

"As you wish." Many-Keys bows and backs out.

This is it. If I want to leave, now is the time. I slide against the wall and climb over the prickly mounds.

Boots clomp against stone; Two-Eyes edges nearer to Tracker. "How about a foretaste? To show your good faith. Who are you? What's your relationship to Elroy?"

"Name's Mason." Tracker wheezes. "I serve—served as protector. For the royal children."

I push the stones back, and with a click, they lock into place. I hold very still. No noise from the other side comes to me. Here all is quiet and dark. Maybe Two-Eyes did not hear.

And my head be stuffed with feathers, as the Keeper would say, if I think that. Two-Eyes heard. He will try to find the door, and when he cannot, he will be angry. Whipping angry.

I stumble through the dark tunnel. If I don't hurry, Tracker will be surrounded by darkness too—for all days.

CHAPTER 22

INTERCEPTION

limb and listen. That is how to go forward. Slowly. Quietly. One step at a time, even though my insides push me to go fast. I cannot help Tabby or Tracker if Two-Eyes catches me.

Crouching low, I crawl onto the next wood step leading up into the kitchen. The second tunnel, the one to the cellar, hid from me for a while, but I found it, and now no more doors are *locked* between the castle halls and me. But some are still closed, like the one above my head. What lies on the other side?

My ears strain to hear. A pan clanks. Footsteps shuffle. There's one . . . no, two in the kitchen. Perhaps three, if one is not walking around. And I have to get by them all. None can know I'm here.

I start to push up the door in the kitchen floor.

"Hurry up!"

At the loud voice of a master, I drop back down on the step. Boots pound across the floor above my head, and a door bangs—the one leading outside if the sound comes from where I think it does.

"What do you think—"

"Quiet, woman. His Majesty requires a dog now. An intruder is suspected in the castle."

A dog? The bird pounding inside me stills. So Two-Eyes did hear the door click.

The next breath claws scratch against the wood floor. A short shriek pierces the air. "I don't care if this is the shortest way. Get that animal out of my kitchen—or it'll be your head when His Majesty's dinner is ruined!"

The claws circle around me . . . and stop near the door I hide under. Snuffling follows—the dog has picked up my scent. I scoot down another step. Should I run back to the tunnel?

"Come on, you."

The dog whines and paws at the door.

"Probably smells the food down there." A second man whistles.

The scratching stops, and finally the claws click across the floor away from me. Slowly the air I hold inside spills out.

A mate grunts. "Humph. Intruders indeed. Probably looking for an excuse to raid the food. You—what are you standing around for? Back to work."

Feet patter across the floor again. I listen to the shuffling above me for a little longer before sliding back to the top step. *An intruder in the castle.* Two-Eyes knows I'm here. And he suspects there is a way out of the dungeon. That is why he called for the dog. To help him find the door.

My paws clench. Now I must move faster. If Two-Eyes can't open the door, he will try to whip it out of Tracker. He may also send the dog to search the castle for me.

I push the door open a crack and blink in the light. Warmth from a fire noses my face. My insides growl at the scents of meat and bread. I press a paw against my underside. Tabby and Tracker first. Then food.

A mate turns and walks to the fire. "Give me a hand with this." The second joins her. Both backs are to me.

I could wait long and not have a better time than this. I squirm out, my underside scraping the floor and the door pushing down on my back.

Something thumps to the side. My head jerks. I missed one.

A third. A not-quite-a-mate she-cub with wide eyes, a potato in her hands. Gwen. My body tenses, not sure whether to pull back or bound ahead. Will she tell the others about me?

Gwen rises, putting herself between the mate and me. Her head nods toward the open door. I pull out from under the floor door quickly. Too quickly. The door thuds behind me. The younger mate jumps with a screech. "Intruder!"

I flatten myself on the floor behind a barrel. Gwen nudges her pile of potatoes with her foot, and they roll across the floor. "Not an intruder. Potatoes. I knocked them over." She crouches and grabs for the nearest two.

"Probably on purpose, trying to scare the spirit out of—"

"Enough." The growl in the older mate's voice easily cuts through the younger's words. "I don't want to hear any more talk about intruders or ambushes or any of this other foolishness going around. Do you hear me?"

"Yes, ma'am."

"Now both of you back to work."

Gwen grabs for the scattered potatoes. Reaching for the one nearest me, she whispers, "Go." She has done all she can for me. I bound through the open door into the hall.

Shadows and quiet close around me. Not like when I was here last. Then light filled every place; laughter and footsteps rang out. Now, emptiness. What has happened to everyone? Not another person walks here, it seems. I shiver, coldness wrapping itself around me, even though the halls are warmer than the tunnels below. At least I'm no longer dripping water.

I hurry toward the north tower and Tabby. Each step brings me closer. Each step is time lost. The north tower stairs curve up before me. Will I find her before she is taken to Two-Eyes?

Only one way to know.

I press my forepaws to the first step and climb up. And up. And up. Past lamps and twisting shadows. Past dark doors with heavy bars. My legs tremble. I pant. How much longer can I keep going? I already walked to the castle, outran arrows, swam to the lake, and climbed tunnels twice. All of me begs to stop and rest. Sleep. But I cannot. Tabby, Tracker—time is too short.

Thump. Thump, thump. Thump-thump-thump. Footsteps. Many of them. Coming down. I scramble back down the way I came. Those behind come nearer, become louder. Time to hide. But where? The halls at the stairs' bottom are too far away. I reach a wide step by a door. A wood bar holds it closed. I push upward. Heavy, so very heavy. Finally it swings up, letting me open the door and slip inside, among swords and spears and other weapons.

"Did you see that?" Men stop near the door.

"See what?" The laughing sneer raises the fur on my neck. Fang is back too.

"Someone went into the armory."

"It's nothing. A servant."

Crouching against the wall, I tip my head to see better. Fang stands outside the door with two other swordsmen, Tabby in the midst of them.

"It didn't look like any servant I've seen."

"The ambush tales getting to you?" Fang jabs the pale swordsman next to him.

"They are not."

"Then check it out. Or not. I don't care. I've a prisoner to deliver." Fang pushes Tabby ahead of him and the other follows, leaving the pale one behind.

I grab a rod from a wood rack near the door, but that won't do much good if he has a sword. Avoiding the weak light from the room's one narrow window, I swing past stacks of arrows, spears, and swords. Shadows are thickest among the shields stacked in a corner between the bows and spears; that will be my best hiding place. I slip behind them.

The pale swordsman pokes his head into the room. "Who's in here? In the name of His Majesty King Avery, I command you to show yourself."

He needs a shadow prey to chase, one that is not. I slip the rod under my shirt across my back. I don't need it now, but I will.

Then I grab a loose bowstring and put the end of a spear leaning against the wall into the loop tied into the bowstring. The man pokes among some crates. I scoot backward as far from the spears as the bowstring will let me.

The man rubs his head, his drawn sword lowering. "I could have sworn . . ."

I yank.

Spear slides against spear, the whole row scraping the wall and crashing to the floor. The man jerks up his sword, swinging it wildly side to side. I easily bound around him and out the door, kicking it closed behind me. The bar drops back across it. The man yells and pounds on the wood.

"Martin? What's going on up there?" A voice—not Fang's—drifts up from the steps below. "Martin, answer me!" The voice trembles.

Fear? Of what? Of me? But there is only one of me . . . except he doesn't know that, does he? I pull out the rod and whack it against the stone again and again, making as much noise as I can. My voice adds screeches and moans and howls. A lamp dangles against the wall. Darkness will help hide me. I thrust my rod up and knock the lamp loose. It clatters against the stone and the light goes out with a hiss.

"Ambush!" Footsteps pound down ahead of me.

I follow, banging my rod and knocking lamps from their places until I am almost to the bottom. Then I go silent, as if tracking prey.

"Ambush!" The alarm brings many feet rushing below. "Up there. Not far behind us. Ten, a dozen men with swords jumped us. They grabbed Martin. I barely escaped."

Ten men with swords? Fear must have been deeper than I thought.

"Ten?" Fang laughs the word. "How did I come to be surrounded by such worms of men? Go, all of you. I can handle the girl."

Feet clomp toward me. I press into a black doorway at the stairs' bottom and grip the rod hard. Men charge by without a glance in my direction, the scent of fear clinging to them like the damp leaves on the forest floor. When the last one disappears around the curve, I slide the rod across my back again. Now to get Tabby. I bound through the halls toward the dungeon.

"Keep moving, *Princess*." Fang's voice curls upward in mockery, ringing harshly against the stone walls.

"Please, I—" A slap cuts off Tabby's words.

Hold on, Tabby! Two halls cross each other, the last corner before the dungeon. I peer around the edge. Fang shoves Tabby toward the door leading down to the dungeon. Darkness colors the skin under her eyes, as if she has not slept in many nights, and scratches cover one cheek. She pulls her cloak tighter around her, letting light touch her arms. They are covered in purple-black and green splotches.

Not the marks of a whip but still the work of Two-Eyes, from his treating Tabby as Master treated me. But Tabby is not a beast. Two-Eyes should not treat her as one, must not treat her as one again. I dart across the hall. My shadow springs up from a lamp and then vanishes as I reach the other side. Tabby gasps.

Fang growls. "Martin, Eved, I've no more time for your pranks today."

I slide my rod out; the end bumps the wall.

Fang narrows his eyes, then breaks into a grin. "So the rebel dogs have come to play with the girl. Show yourselves that I might join the fun. My blade has not tasted blood in many a day." He slides out his knife, tosses it up in the air, and catches it, pointing it high. He thinks I'm a master.

Lowering my head, I spring out into his path. Fang's knife cuts the air above my head, and before he can twist it into a downward thrust, I plunge my pole among his legs, striking his ankles. He sprawls backward, and Tabby leaps from behind, stomping on his wrist. His knife clatters to the floor. I kick it away, swing my rod at him. Tabby tosses her cloak over his head. He snatches it off. I swing the rod with all I have. With an insides-curling thwack, head and rod meet. He drops like a rock in water, his whole body falling still.

"Sarah!" Tabby falls to her knees and wraps her arms around me, only to pull back with her nose wrinkled. "Why are you wet?"

I squirm out of her grasp. Run now. Words later. Already echoes of feet come our way, and Fang moans, starting to rouse. I paw at the door.

"But that goes to the dungeon!"

As if I didn't know. I avoided this place when I lived here with Majesty because it is too much like where the Keeper kept me. But predators think prey will run from danger, not deeper into it. Besides, Tracker's down there. Tabby tugs open the door. I dart down into the gloom. When we near the bottom, I slow and wave for her to stay back.

Many-Keys sits on a chair by the door into the dungeon itself. His eyes are closed, mouth wide open. I nod at the extra keys hanging on a peg near the door. Tabby hesitates. I whine quietly. *Do it. We need them.* Tabby sighs and grabs them. She starts back up the stairs. I snag her skirt with my teeth and tug her behind a stack of crates, thick with the scent of meat left too long in the sun. I wrinkle my nose, and Tabby gags, covering her face with her arm. "What is *in* these things?"

I block her from leaving. I don't like it any more than she does, but it will help hide us from the dog Two-Eyes called for. Now how to get Many-Keys to leave?

Footsteps pound down the stairs. Sleeping Many-Keys snorts and sits up.

"We have a problem," says the newcomer. "The girl's gone, released by an ambush. No one can find her. It's all chaos upstairs."

Many-Keys frowns. "Do we have to tell you-know-who?"

"I don't see a way around it."

"He's not going to be happy." He unlocks the door.

"You're telling me." The message bearer trudges inside.

Voices murmur.

"What!" Two-Eyes roars. "What do you know about this?"

Silence.

A whip cracks. A man cries out. Tabby clings to me, trembling. I grind my teeth. I will *not* bolt. Cannot. Tracker is why we're here. Hiss-crack, hiss-crack. Tabby buries her face into me, shuddering at every strike of the whip.

"I'll deal with you later." Two-Eyes stalks out, a stocky dog at his side and the message bearer in his shadow. The dog sniffs along the floor, searching for prey to track. I press farther back.

"Go summon the other dogs."

"Yes, milord." The message bearer scurries by and up the stairs.

The dog reaches the crates. Lifting its head, it looks at me. I hold its gaze. Will it tell its master we are here?

"Secure the prisoner. I'll be back soon." Two-Eyes throws the words at Many-Keys and marches by. "Lymer!"

The dog glances at Two-Eyes, then back at me. I hold my air in. *Go on.* The dog snorts with a shake of its head, as if to clear the crate's smell from its nose, and trots up after Two-Eyes.

My paws slowly unclench, and beyond the crates, keys clink. Many-Keys is headed inside the dungeon. I follow.

Tabby grabs my shoulder. "We'll get locked in there." Her words are strong, even if whispered. "Then *he* will find us again." She shudders.

She fears Two-Eyes, as she should, but I pull away. I can't leave Tracker here.

"Sarah!"

I keep going. Finally she patters after me.

I slip through one of the open pen doors, Tabby at my heels. Clank! A key locks a door. Many-Keys walks by and the outer door slams shut. We're trapped inside.

Tabby wraps her arms around herself. "I hope you know what you're doing and have some infallible plan to get us out of here. The keys don't work on this side, you know."

Ignoring the sting of words, I swing out and paw at the only closed door among the pen rooms. Tabby sighs and tries her keys until one opens the door.

Tracker lays face down, crumpled, back oozing new blood.
Tabby gasps. "Protector?"

I bound inside. We can't be too late, we can't be. I worked
too hard to get here. I nose an outstretched hand. Tracker groans.
He's alive! I wrap both my paws, dirty and scarred, around his
big, dark hand.

His head turns and eyes blink. "Princess Sarah? Princess
Tabitha? You're both safe?" Only a wisp of sound, but still words.

I nod my head, water flowing down my face. If I had waited
any longer . . .

Tabby kneels down at my side. "We're . . . fine." She lowers
her voice as she glances at the stone wall. "For now." Another
shudder shakes her body.

A corner of Tracker's mouth lifts. "Shall we show her,
Princess?"

I push myself under him, his cheek against my head. He
manages to loop one arm around my neck. I push up; he is almost
too much for me to lift.

"Sarah, where are you going? We're locked in here."

Tracker's chest shakes, though no laughter escapes his
mouth. "She's going . . . to the . . . secret passage."

"What?"

"Show . . . her."

I grind my teeth together and stagger forward. Tracker's
groan whips my insides.

Tabby scurries behind me, and the weight eases as she lifts
his legs. I crawl forward. One step. Two steps. We slowly turn and
shuffle toward the tunnel door. When we reach the yellow grass,
I slip out from under Tracker and paw at the mound until there
is a path to the door. Now how to open the tunnel from this side?
There are no pegs here like in the cellar. But the chains—aren't
they in about the same place? I tug and pull and twist. Latches
click. The wall slides in.

My insides uncurl a little. Almost there. We carry Tracker
inside, and I help him sit while Tabby gets a lamp. Then we push

the mound of yellow grass and the stone wall back into place. I slump onto the floor. We're safe—for the moment.

Tracker, tipped against the wall, raises his hand and drops it heavily on my shoulder. Light ripples across his dark face. "Well done, Princess Sarah. You have done what I thought impossible. His Majesty will be proud of you." His eyes shut. "Very proud."

His hand slips from my shoulder.

CHAPTER 23

GWEN

Plip. Plip. Plop.

Water drips, rippling through my sleep. Plip. Plop. Plop. Plip. Yawning, I stretch my legs and crawl out from under a blanket. All is quiet in the cave. Tracker's chest still rises and drops; he has not yet fallen forever still. Tabby huddles against a wall, a blanket tightly wound around her, but she finally sleeps quietly rather than twisting and moaning, thinking that Two-Eyes chases her. I cannot tell her he is not. While Two-Eyes is not down here, chasing us, he is tearing apart the castle above us, hunting for our scent.

Between Tracker and Tabby, a small fire burns in a pit, the smoke drifting through a hole in the cave's roof, which Tabby thinks leads into one of the other castle chimneys. I add a couple more sticks to it from the pile stacked along one wall. Majesty planned well. This cave next to the underground lake has all we need. Bedding and blankets, swords and bows, pots and pans and plates, buckets to hold water and wood for the fire. With the food from the cellar, a whole pack could live here many days. I don't know what we would have done if Tabby had not found the cave opening that I missed during my wanderings in the dark.

My stomach rumbles. Is it mealtime? I cannot tell for sure.

There is no light here except from the fire, and that burns as long as it has wood to eat. But it could not hurt to get food, right?

I slip a bag onto my back and check the other two again. Neither seems ready to wake. Tabby continues to slumber, as one who has not slept in many days. Tracker twists in his sleep, his breaths short and thin, then calms again. How Tabby and I were able to move him all the way down here I do not know.

I head up the tunnel at a limp. All the swimming, running, climbing, and fighting have stiffened my body. But even a limp is movement forward, and I come to the cellar after a while. Nothing moves inside it, and all noise seems to come from above in the kitchen. I slip inside.

Streaks and spots of light push through the floor, but it is still hard to see. I sigh. I'll have to trust my touch. My paw dips into a barrel and I put six of the wrinkled, round things it holds into the bag. Then I go on to the next crate. Maybe this way we will be able to eat at least one of the things I grab.

When my bag will hold no more, I go back down the tunnel to the cave. Slinging off the bag, I huddle by the fire. Caves are cold. Not as cold as the coldest days of white, but enough to make me shiver. I hold my paws to the flames.

With a cry and gasp, Tabby sits up. I bound to her side. Two-Eyes was chasing her in her sleep again. I know that without her telling me. She hunches over, one arm clutching her middle, panting and shaking hard. I snuggle up against her, and she lays her hand on my shoulder, her fingers clutching my clothing. After a long while, she doesn't pant like one running, and her grip on me loosens. "I'm sorry. I didn't mean to . . . it was so awful I can't . . . how did you ever . . ."

I rest my head on her leg, and her words stop. I know, and she knows that. But Two-Eyes isn't here, and while we must still leave his territory, his whip and his arrows and his fist cannot reach us at this moment.

When Tabby no longer shivers, I pull away from her. A new shudder ripples through her, but she doesn't cry out. Instead she pulls her legs up to her chest and wraps her arms around them. "Will they ever go away, Sarah? Will he ever stop haunting me?"

She still thinks about Two-Eyes; he will hunt her many days, even if she never sees him again. And there is nothing I can do about it. I grab the bag and drag it back to her, bringing her the only thing I can give her. If only I could do more. She opens the bag and pulls out an apple, wrinkled with age. "Food!" She bites into it and then closes her eyes to savor it. A drop of water slips down her cheek. "Thank you, Sarah."

Tracker twists and mumbles in his sleep.

Setting aside her food, Tabby pulls the blanket tighter around her shoulders and pads over to Tracker. "I've wanted to meet the Protector ever since Father told me he existed. Sometimes I would wander off in a crowd and watch who followed, trying to spot him. I never did figure it out." Shaking her head, she kneels at his side. "Not even when the slaver took me, even though I knew he had to be nearby. I never knew how near until . . ." Her words catch and she reaches to tug the blanket over him again. "Why did he have to hurt him? He was only trying to protect me." Another drop of water slides down her face.

I press up against her side, but she doesn't seem to feel me. "This is all my fault."

Tracker stirs. "Princess?" He blinks, his hand reaching for her, trying to find her.

"Here. I'm . . . I'm here." She scoots closer and grabs his hand.

"Princess Tabitha." Grimacing, he lifts his other hand toward her face, but before it gets halfway there, it drops back to his side and his eyes close. "I'm so sorry."

"Sorry? For what?"

"For this." He slides the hand she holds from her grasp and up to the black-green splotches on her arm. "I was . . . I was supposed to . . . protect you." His words come out squeezed, as if he doesn't have enough air to say them.

"It's . . . it's nothing." But Tabby trembles, though she tries to hide it. Being prey for Two-Eyes is never nothing.

Tracker knows it too. He grips her hand, rising up, eyes wide.

"It is not nothing. You have suffered much because I didn't protect as I should have."

"Shh . . . It's fine. I'm fine." Tabby tries to get him to lie back down.

Tracker shakes his head. "Please, Princess, pardon me. Please."

"Of course."

Tracker still stares at her wide-eyed.

Tabby swallows hard. "You are pardoned." Her voice trembles as if the words are almost too heavy for her tongue to lift.

But they seem to make the load Tracker carries lighter. He relaxes back with a sigh. "Th-thank you, Pr-Princess." His words slur together and soon he sleeps again.

Tabby tucks the blanket back around him, and then looks up at me, her face wet. "Sarah—I think he's dying."

<hr />

Waiting. Always waiting. More and more it seems that is all I can do. My legs long to stretch out, to have a reason to run. Instead I must wait.

I sigh and rest my head on my forepaws, staring at the darkness of the cellar, not quite as complete as the stone tunnels. A slice of light pushes between the floorboards above my head, falling on a barrel. Footsteps shuffle and a board creaks. I came back up here soon after Tabby woke, and it won't be long before she will wonder where I am. How much longer can I stay here, waiting for what may not come for a very long time?

Wood scrapes against wood. Light tumbles down the stairs. I press back into the shadows. I must not be seen until I am ready. A foot appears on the top step, followed by a second foot, a brown dress, a firestick, and the face of a girl between a she-cub and mate. Gwen.

My waiting has brought what I want. This time. I slip out from behind the crate and stop before Gwen. I lean down and touch my face to the dirt floor before looking up to her.

She blinks down at me, then dips her head, backing up

one step from me. "Lady Sarah. What do you need from your servant?"

Air whooshes out of me. She will help me, though Two-Eyes must be making everyone upstairs hurt in his anger—anger caused by me. I turn, take a couple of steps, and wait.

"You wish me to follow you?"

I nod but then glance up. Will the others miss her?

She steps closer. "I am not expected back immediately."

Good. I go to the door to the cave and duck inside. Gwen, following me down the tunnel, lifts her firestick high. "Oh. This is amazing."

Racing ahead of her to the cave, I tromp noisily so we don't scare Tabby. Tabby runs out to meet me. Dropping to her knees, she wraps her arms around me. "Sarah." She buries her face in my neck and sighs. Slowly she lifts her head. "I've been so worried. I thought he had—Gwen?" She rises and takes one step forward, only to stop again, body rigid, as if she fears Gwen will turn and bite her.

Instead, Gwen dips in greeting. "Princess Tabitha."

"Princess?" Tabby's shoulders slump with a tiredness that goes deeper than a lack of sleep. "I'm afraid not many people call me that anymore." She lifts a hand to brush hair out of her face, but when she sees her hand in the firelight, smudged with dirt and the nails broken, she grimaces. "I can't blame them."

Gwen steps forward, hesitates, then places a hand on Tabby's shoulder. "Pardon me for saying so, but it doesn't matter what others may say"—her gaze shifts to a dark bruise on Tabby's face—"or do. You're a princess because that is what His Majesty, King *Elroy*, calls you."

Tabby closes her eyes and slowly nods. "A princess, for always and always." She stands straighter than before.

I shake my head. This is getting nothing done. I push past Tabby to Tracker's side and give a short yap.

Tabby's eyes open. "You're a healer." She grabs Gwen's arm and pulls her into the cave. "We need your help. This man . . ." She chokes on her words and waves at Tracker.

Gwen kneels at his side. Maybe she will be able to help, to get Tracker up and walking again. But the frown on her face grows deeper and her forehead wrinkles.

"Well?"

Gwen shakes her head. "I've never dealt with anything like . . . this is beyond what I know. I could make a paste for his back and give you some herbs for tea. But . . ." She rises, brushing off her skirt. "He needs to see a master healer before too long."

"But how?"

"I don't know. Wait. There's a wagon leaving early tomorrow to collect more food. If you can sneak onto it before dawn, I think you can get through the gates. No one ever bothers to check an empty wagon."

"Dawn?" Such words mean nothing in this black hole.

"Don't worry. I'll come and get you."

"But what if he . . ." Tabby chews her lip, and her hands tremble. "If someone catches you, he will . . ." She stares down at Tracker.

"Then I'll take care not to get caught, won't I?"

―――――

A world of gray and black. A world of stone.

Crouched at the door of the kitchen, I wait and listen while Tabby and Gwen struggle to carry Tracker up from the cellar. Right now all is quiet, but my paw clenches around the rod I brought with me. Quiet can become loud fighting very fast.

Tabby grunts. "I don't know how you became so strong, Gwen."

"Water buckets. And pots full of stew." She lets out her own grunt. "That'll do it for you every time."

They rest Tracker on the floor. His eyes don't even flicker open, and his breathing is thin. How much longer will he hold on?

Tabby rolls her shoulders.

"We're almost there, Princess. The wagon is already outside

the stables. We only have to carry him across the courtyard and slide him into the bed under the tarp."

"Only?" Tabby groans, rubbing the back of her neck. "Are you coming too?"

Gwen dips her head. "No. It'll arouse too much suspicion. But I made sure someone is at the other end to meet you." She pulls the door open to the outside.

I go first, listening, smelling, watching. No dogs roam about. No people stride by. I nod at Tabby and Gwen. They lift Tracker and stagger forward. I keep two paces behind them, watching for danger. But there is no shout or pounding of footsteps. Will we actually leave without fighting?

I wait under the wagon as Tabby and Gwen put Tracker inside.

My body quivers as I try to take in everything around me. The smooth, cold stones under my feet. A bell ringing far away. The wind smelling of wet leaves and damp dirt, whistling among the towers. The steady thump-thump-thump of a man marching along a wall. The yip of a dog somewhere at the far side of the castle. A strip of wood smoke drifting upward. The low rumble of the river. Early day twittering. The wagon creaking as Tabby and Gwen move Tracker around.

Gwen hops to the ground. "Ready, Lady Sarah?" She holds up a corner of the scrunched-up canvas, allowing me to crawl under it. "Keep safe. Speed to you all."

The cloth drops and I shift my weight, trying to find a more comfortable spot.

"Halt!" The sharp command rings against the stones.

My insides stutter to a stop and not even my nose dares to twitch.

"What are you doing out here?"

"I . . . I was . . . just . . ." Gwen hunts for words like a berry fallen among many leaves.

"Speak up. Quick!"

"A list. The cook had a new list for the driver."

Quiet. My paw feels around for the rod. Does the man who

stopped Gwen accept her words? Or does he sense there is more? I shift my weight, preparing to spring.

Horse feet clip-clop toward us. "Hey, you. Did this girl bring you a list?"

"No." The wagon shakes and metal jingles; a horse is hooked to it.

Not good. I scoot forward toward the edge.

"Sarah!" Tabby forces my name out between her teeth and grabs my hind leg. She is trembling hard. She doesn't want me to leave. I don't want to either. But too many have felt Two-Eyes's whip for me. Gwen will not be added to that list. I shake Tabby off and raise the edge of the canvas.

A man in red and black grips Gwen's wrist and drags her toward the kitchen door. "I'm taking you to King Avery."

"Please . . ." Gwen, trembling so hard that I can see it, tries to pulls back. He strikes her face with his hand.

I leap from the wagon and bound across the open ground. This must stop and it must stop now. I skid into a crouch between the man and the door and growl. The man shoves Gwen behind him, pulling out a sword. "What are—where did you come from?"

Your darkest dreams, I hope. My paw shifts the rod.

"Away from there." He points the sword's tip at my face.

I snarl and snap my teeth. Tracker cannot protect any more. I must now. The flat part of the sword swings toward my head. I duck, swinging the rod to meet it. Metal smacks against wood, nearly yanking the rod from my paws. I ram the end into his foot.

"You fiend." He side-hops away and thrusts the sword's point at me.

I twist away. The point wedges between two stones. Beyond him, Tabby pulls Gwen into the wagon.

"Belzac! Eved!"

Two men come running, making the fight three against one. That is a fight that cannot be won. I drop my rod and run. Back and forth. Around the castle. Behind the forge. The men chase me for a little bit, then drop farther and farther behind. Time to go back to the wagon. I circle around the stable.

The wagon is gone.

Where is it? My ears catch the clip-clop of horse feet. I spin around. The wagon rolls toward the gate. The driver must be in a hurry to leave. I run after it, trying to stay to the shadows. A corner of the canvas lifts. Tabby's face frowns out, her eyes darting side to side. The driver pulls the wagon to a stop, waiting for the gate to open. I rise up.

Two men with swords step forward. "Do a thorough check."

The driver slouches forward, muttering.

"What is that you say?"

Stiffening, the driver stares ahead. "Only said it's my fervent wish that any lurking rebels might be found soon." He glances at the leader. "Sir."

"Very good." The swordsman nods and joins the second one looking under the wagon and tapping the sides. At the back they reach for the canvas.

They want prey to hunt? I'll give them prey to hunt. I leap into the open and charge for the open gate.

"You there! Halt!" Arrows fly from the wall above.

My insides pull back, wanting me to turn around. I plunge forward. For Gwen. For Tracker. For Tabby.

An arrow grazes my right shoulder. Pain shoots through my leg and spider-webs across my back and neck. I gasp. My feet stumble. I tumble in a heap.

Voices shout. Arrows stop falling. A dog howls. The wood under me shakes from footsteps and the thrashing river.

No. I am not going back. They cannot have me.

Pulling myself to the bridge's edge, I dive into the churning waters below.

CHAPTER 24

CORNERED

Hard, cold, crushing. The water strikes me with one fist after another, as if not happy about my throwing myself into its arms.

Tumbling, tearing, thundering. I try to claw my way up, out. But which way is up? Which way is out? The fist closes around me, squeezing out my air, pulling down my body, nails digging into my skin. I twist and kick and thrash. My shoulder throbs. My head pops out.

Sputtering, coughing, gasping. Houses, people go by. A shadow passes over me. The river tosses water into my mouth and yanks me back under.

Dark. Coiling. Squeezing. My legs stiffen. My paws can no longer feel what they pull against. But the water is tiring from our fight too. Up. One more time. I give a hard kick. Air slaps my face. I gulp it down.

The river pushes me past open ground and into the spotted shadows of a forest. Thick grasses with brown tops gather along the edge, the water slower and smoother now. The river has admitted defeat. I stagger through the grasses and mud onto land.

Where to now? Leaves all around me rustle. On the ground. In the trees. Among the bushes. Part of me wants to join the animals I hear. But I cannot. Not yet. I must go back. Find the healer. Find Tabby, Tracker, and Gwen. I turn my face toward Melek, half limping, half crawling along the river's edge.

But the river carried me farther than I thought. The light grows warm on my back. No sign of any houses. My clothing dries stiff with mud. My fur, pulled back by Tabby into a braid this morning, hangs in tangled clumps. Still the town hides from me.

Only when the shadows are long and one edge of the sky is fire-lit does Melek appear. I do not like that it took me so long to get here, yet this might be better. The pack of Two-Eyes prowls everywhere, and the shadows give me hiding places that would not be mine in the day.

Two swordsmen march by on the main road. I scamper across into the shadows on the other side—or the closest thing to a scamper that I can manage. I have been to the master healer's home only once, after Gwen was taken. He wanted to look at my paw and make sure it was healing right, but he could not leave a cub he was watching. So Majesty brought me down to him.

Darkness covers most of Melek by the time I find the right house. No one lingers nearby, so I slip around the corner and paw the door. Did Tabby and Gwen get Tracker here soon enough?

Someone shuffles around inside. I press against the side of the house. No one is in sight, but how much longer can that last? Latches click and the door creaks. A man, stooped over like a dried leaf curled in on itself, squints out. "Who's there?"

I lope in front of him.

More squinting, then—"Lady Sarah!" He backs up, opening the door wide for me.

I limp into the large, single room. Dried plants hang from the ceiling. Pots and jars line the walls. A low fire burns in the hearth. But no Tabby, Tracker, or Gwen. Where are they? What happened to them? I swing around.

Healer Yakov squints at me again. "What is it you seek, Lady Sarah?"

"It's looking for its so-called friends, but they aren't here, are they, Beast?" A shadow fills the door, and as it steps forward, it becomes Two-Eyes.

I back up, crouching low. How did he know I was here?

"No, your precious princess took the fastest way out, stopping only long enough to let one of the patrols know that I would find an important package here."

I growl. He speaks wrong words. Tabby would not leave me, much less tell Two-Eyes where I would go. Something went wrong with what we planned.

But then how *did* he know to look for me here?

"I guess she finally realized harboring the weak only makes you weak, and she decided to lose the burden slowing her down."

I back up a step. No. Tabby does not see me that way.

Healer Yakov hobbles between us. "Your Majesty, I beg your pardon for interrupting, but I must ask you to leave while I care for the injured."

"And begging your pardon, you're wasting your breath and my time." Two-Eyes shoves the healer aside and stalks toward me. Fang blocks the door behind him.

There must be a way around them, past them. I sidestep to the left. Behind Two-Eyes and Fang, beyond where they can see, Healer Yakov backs up, his head tipping toward the wall. The window! It won't be easy, but it is a way out. And if I can get out, I have a chance. The healer unlatches the boards covering it and edges away again.

I retreat in front of Two-Eyes. My eyes do not stray from his face, but I think about where things were when I came in. The table. A chair. A clay pot filled with powder.

Only a few more steps to go.

Two-Eyes uncoils his short whip. I grab the pot and throw it at him. It shatters; powder flies up. I bound onto a chair and jump for the window. Crack! The whip coils around my middle and jerks me back.

My shoulder slams into the ground. My body rolls back. My head hits a table leg. Pain crackles outward, and I curl into a ball against it.

"Take it."

Hands grab. Ropes bind. More pain. I shake my head, try to

clear it, and open my eyes. A pace away lies the healer, all still, blood around his head like an animal after Master's dogs . . . I crumple over, my insides heaving out before I can stop them.

"We have what we came for. Let's go."

Chuckling, Fang throws me over his shoulder, and I'm carried into the night.

CHAPTER 25

※

A DEMAND

What happened? What went wrong? Where are Tabby and Gwen and Tracker? Why weren't they at the healer's?

How did Two-Eyes know I would be there?

I come up with many answers. Someone saw me in Melek and told him. He tracked me from the woods. He knew I was hurt and would go to the healer's for help. Or perhaps Two-Eyes caught Tabby and Gwen and Tracker, and they told him where to find me. The hiss-crack of the whip rings in my ears, and I shudder. But if Two-Eyes had them, he would have told me to remind me that no prey escapes him. Wouldn't he?

Time, sights, and sounds squish together like mud stomped by too many feet. The wagon's rumblings go through me. The heavy cloth covering my cage flaps against the bars. I curl into a tight ball against the sharp stabs of light. Every wheel creak screeches *gone, gone, gone.* Tabby's gone. Tracker's gone. Gwen is gone. I am alone, left to predators stronger than me.

I squeeze my eyes shut, trying to push those words from me. But they nip at my heels, dogs in pursuit of tiring prey. And I am so tired, so very tired.

The wagon hits a rock, throwing me against the bars of my cage. I cannot stop myself; my paws are bound, hind and fore.

Pain spears my hurt shoulder. Water stings my eyes. Why does Two-Eyes not kill me and end all this? Does he not see that the hunt is over, that I can run no farther?

Instead he pushed me into this cage and sent me off to—does it even matter where? The place may be different, but my end will be the same. Bars, ropes, chains. Whips and fists. Darkness. Stillness. Kept for all days in a deep lair of Two-Eyes, never to be found again.

My pack has abandoned me anyway.

No, no, no! I beat my head against the cage's floor. Tabby and Tracker and Gwen would not do that. Something went wrong. Two-Eyes must have learned what happened somehow. They had to run; Two-Eyes got between us. But they will come for me, take me from his hand as I took Tabby and Tracker from him.

Yet how far could they run? Tracker could not even walk. He needed to see the healer. Gwen said so. And Tabby needs him to lead her to Majesty. So they would not make him walk now, hurting him more, to find a safe place away from Two-Eyes sooner . . . would they?

I twist, and my forepaws yank against the ropes binding them behind my back. I want to cover my ears, want to keep the words out. But they are deep inside me already.

———◦◦◦———

We're here.

Where "here" is I do not know. My cage is still covered and I cannot see anything. But we have come to where we were going. The wagon has stopped and a gate has clanked shut behind us.

The need to fight and flee pounces on me. Must get out. Must get away. I thrash and kick my hind legs and fling myself against the bars.

Growling laughter from Fang pelts me from beyond the cloth. "The sleeping beast is finally awake. Too bad it doesn't know it's too late."

The cage scrapes across boards and drops to the ground. My

head bangs against the top. Pain shoots through my legs. I slump to the bottom.

"You know the orders. Do it. But remember—he wants this one alive."

The cloth snaps away. Light pierces. Too bright, much too bright. My eyes squeeze shut, my head tucking against my body. Then the cage is overturned, tumbling the world. The sky lands below me, the stone ground above me. Or is it the other way around?

But before I can put the sky and ground back where they belong, hands grab me, lift me high, and throw me against a wall. My chest and back crash inward, trying to meet. Darkness spots the light. I collapse, everything a smear of hard, gray stone—the ground, the walls, the nearby buildings. Even the sky above and the men around look hard and gray.

Boots slam into my left side. I gasp and crumple into a ball. Protect my underside. Hide my face. Keep predators out. A hand digs into my fur, yanks my head back. Rock-hard fists pound against me again and again. I try to turn my face away. I cannot.

I'm tossed to the side. My good hind leg twists under me; arrow pain shoots through it. I roll over, try to move it. It doesn't move right. No! I have to be able to walk. If I can't walk, then I can do nothing. I cannot even think of running away from all this. Then I know. That is what Two-Eyes wants. For me to crawl before him for all days, like the Beast I am.

Fang laughs loud and long. "Run, Beast, run." He laughs harder.

Men grab me again. More fists, more kicks—pain after pain attacks. Arrow pain, spear pain, bone-gnawing pain, shattering pain. I want to beg them to stop, but words belong to men, not to me. Not to a beast. I can only whimper, and predators don't listen to whimpers.

"Enough!"

It stops. The hitting, the kicking, the beating. Only the pain stays. I curl into a tight, shivering ball, face to the ground.

"Open it."

Something wood scuffs and clatters against stone a pace away. I do not raise my head. I do not want to see. I do not want to know. It will not stop it from coming anyway.

Feet half push, half kick me backward. The stone ground drops away behind me. My eyes open; I teeter at the edge of a dark, muddy pit as deep as a man is high.

A whimper rises up. My throat chokes it.

I'm pushed over the edge.

Pictures flit through my mind. Chasing Tabby through castle halls. Majesty's smile over a food feast for two in the middle of a night. The darkness under Tabby's eyes from too little sleep. The hunched shoulders of Majesty. The writhing crowd before the selling block, rising up, twisting into red flames eating Master's house, Two-Eyes coming out of the flames, covered in black, whip in hand. I try to run. The bushes turn against me, hold me in place. Two-Eyes raises his whip.

I jerk awake, shivers rattling my body, plastered with cold mud. The pit. The pictures were only that—pictures inside my head.

I blink—only one eye opens as it should—and start to roll over. Pain squeezes and releases me many times. My shoulders burn, my hind legs throb, my head aches, my insides twist together. I try to breathe slowly. A sharp shard slices through my side where too many boots hit. I tuck my knees to my chest and rock forward.

Why did Master have to be no more? Even in his worst rage, he never did all this to me. And that was when he could find me. Often I could hide until he was only a little angry; his rages always went away with time.

But there are no trees or bushes here. I cannot hide from Two-Eyes, and I cannot wait for his rage to go away. He whips when he scowls; he strikes when he is smiling.

My head drops, my cheek pressing against the mud. It is as

he said. There is no escaping, not from here, not from him. So why even try?

———⁂———

Fingers press against my neck, pulling me out of pain's muddy depths. "It's alive."

I should fight. I should flee. But what I *should* do can no longer wrestle me into doing it. I turn my face away, not bothering to open my eyes. *Go away. Leave me alone.*

But the man at my side does not hear my silent wish or does not listen. I am picked up and lifted high. "Here you go."

Other hands grab me and pull me higher, out of the pit, before tossing me onto the stone ground. Light and warmth tingles my skin. But it reaches no deeper. Coldness covers my insides, and I feel nothing but the throbbing, stinging, burning pain of the outside.

"Look at me." Two-Eyes. He's back.

I open my one good eye and slightly tip my head up. Black boots and the dangling tip of a whip are as high as I can go. The rest of him is too far away. My head drops back, waiting for whatever he will do.

"Give it some water."

A hand turns my face and something cool and wet dribbles against my cheek. I shouldn't, but—I roll my head farther that way, opening my mouth wide. Water. Real, fresh water. I swallow all I can. Why is he giving me this? He never does something unless he gains from it. But I have water. Clean water.

The trickle slows to a dribble and then single drops. No. Don't stop now. I lift my head, trying to catch every little bit. Two-Eyes crouches at my side. "Still thirsty?"

I tilt my head. The water bucket sits only two paces away. There must be a way to reach it.

"Then perhaps you won't mind answering a question for me first." He brings his face close to mine, forcing me to look into his two-colored eyes. "Where is Elroy?"

A chill puddles inside me. He wants me to show him where Majesty is? Betray the only pack to claim me? The chill hardens into cold stone. No. I have scattered the pack, weakened their strength, even abandoned it under attack. But I will not betray them. Not to anyone.

Never to Two-Eyes. I bare my teeth with a snarl and spit in his face.

His hand crushes my throat to the ground, cutting off air to my insides.

I arch my back and twist. It does no good. I am too weak. There will be no fighting a predator as strong as Two-Eyes. Darkness prepares to pounce. I sink against the ground.

Two-Eyes thrusts me aside. Air rushes back into me. I suck more in, all I can get. Darkness retreats.

"Throw it back. Give it nothing until I say." He wipes off his cheek with his sleeve. "We have time to work on this one."

His words strike deep, deeper than fist or whip ever could. He doesn't think anyone will come for me. He thinks my pack has abandoned me.

He strides away and hands fling me back into the pit. Pain shatters my body. My head sags forward. I was right after all. No one risks their pack for a beast.

No one.

CHAPTER 26

NEGOTIATIONS

In the pack, the master's words are everything. What he says, his pack does. Two-Eyes is a master. So when he told his pack to give me nothing, they gave nothing. No food. No water. No anything. My insides are left to gnaw on themselves.

It is not a new feeling. When Master became very angry or was thinking of other things, I could go many days without seeing a lump of bread. But many days have passed by since then, and under Majesty, I had much food and had it whenever I wanted. It would still be that way, but I left. Why did I not stay with him instead of going after Tabby?

Long days drag on, followed by longer nights. Water falls from above and pools in the bottom of the pit, giving me a little to drink. I watch the sky and cling to the twig that Majesty is planning how to get me. He said he wanted to make me like Tabby, or did once. Does that not mean he'll come for me?

Yet light and darkness change places as they always have. Birds circle above during the day, and at night I make pictures from the milk flecking the black sky, like Tabby showed me once. Sometimes footsteps pass by, but no one peers down at me. Maybe even Two-Eyes has left me behind.

I squirm and pull and somehow get my bound forepaws around my hind legs to my front. The rope's knot is covered in mud. I chew on it anyway, trying to loosen it. The rope will not let me go.

A shadow falls across me—a man leans over my pit, hands clutching the wood bars. My insides jump. Has Majesty sent someone for me?

Then the man grins, the wide mouth of teeth all too familiar. My shoulders slump forward. Fang jumps down beside me, boots splattering mud. "Rest well, Beast?"

I scoot back, pressing against the dirt wall behind me. A water bag does not hang at Fang's side, and my nose does not smell meat or bread. Whatever he does bring then, I will not want.

But what I want is not what Fang cares about. He listens only to Two-Eyes. He slings me over his shoulder as if I were an old, wet blanket. The pit twists and tips, and I cannot tell which way is up and which way is down. I squeeze my eyes shut. *Please, let it all go away.*

The world settles, and a breeze nuzzles my cheek as if it has missed me. This is much better than the thick air at the hole's bottom. And the smells! Many of them I knew well once, but it has been so long, I am slow to name them all. Berries. Warm earth. Fresh water. Many green things at their best time. Wood smoke. Roasting meat. My insides lurch. I snort and shake my head. But the smell of food stays.

A door creaks open, and darkness wraps a smoky fist around me. I blink, trying to see through the shadows, barely broken by flickering lamps and firesticks. Thick stone walls stand tall on either side as Fang carries me through hall after hall, past wood doors with heavy bars. Then food smells strike again, much stronger than before. Roasted meat. Boiled potatoes. Warm bread. Wine. My insides twist and writhe, wanting out, wanting at the things I smell.

Fang drops me on the floor by a table filled with food. I want to lunge for it, but Two-Eyes stands between it and me. So

I crouch, forepaws pressed to my middle. Maybe if I don't look, the food won't pull so hard.

A bone drops in front of me.

Do I see what is not? I nose it, then pounce. Meat! I bend over it, gnawing for the scraps left. My insides beg for more. Can I eat the bone itself somehow?

Fang laughs and Two-Eyes joins in. "You brought this on yourself, you know."

My head jerks up and I clutch the bone to my chest. He won't take it from me now, will he?

"All this could be yours." He waves at the table of food. "And so much more. A dry place to sleep. Fresh water. A healer for your crippled body. All you have to do is one thing."

One thing? I lean forward. I'll do it! Anything.

"Show me where Elroy is."

I jerk back. Anything but that.

He plucks a big chunk of bread off the table and waves it before me. "Choose wisely, Beast."

My insides rumble. But I can't. I must. I have to have food. I can't keep going without it. But to betray my pack, to betray Majesty . . . I rock back and forth, my head nearly hitting the floor. Majesty will send someone for me, just like Tracker went after Tabby. I only have to hold on. Only a little longer. Hold on a little longer and he will be here.

Only . . . what if he doesn't come?

There's a knock on the door. Two-Eyes whirls around, crushing the bread in his fist. "What!"

The door opens only a little, and a pale, sharp-edged face that looks like old bones pokes in. "Pardon me for interrupting, Your Majesty, but—"

"I left strict orders not to be disturbed."

"I . . . I know. I mean, a man is here, and orders were, that is, you said if anyone came in with information . . ." Bone-Face stumbles over his words and then plunges all the way. "We know where they are."

"Detain him and I'll be . . ." Two-Eyes drops his gaze to me and his eyes brighten like a predator that has caught the scent of prey again.

I coil back, pressing the bone to my chest.

"Wait. Did they . . ."

"Yes, Your Majesty."

"Bring him in."

"As you wish, Your Majesty." He bows and disappears.

My body quivers. With that glint in his eyes, this will not be good for me. I scoot back a half pace.

The door opens again, and a man shuffles in. He twists a hat in his hands and jerks a bow toward Two-Eyes, his too-big clothing flopping around his twig body. Two-Eyes takes a seat behind the table. "I'm told you bring news concerning the former royal family."

"Yes, Your Majesty." Another bow, clothing flapping.

"Well?"

"It happened this way: I live down toward Bending, and one day I found I was needing some extra supplies. Well, the crops aren't quite ready, so I didn't see I had any choice but to head up onto Calby. But my wagon is old and—"

"I assume this all has a point?" Two-Eyes picks up a knife lying by the meat and presses the tip into his finger. A small dot of red appears.

The man's eyes widen, and he bows quickly again. "No, Your Majesty. I mean yes, Your Majesty. Because my wagon broke I had to walk through the woods, and, well, there they were."

"Who? Where?"

The man twists his hat into a ball that fits into his hand. "His Majesty. I mean His Former Majesty. King Elroy. And his daughter. A couple of others too—a dark man and another girl."

Majesty, Tabby, Tracker, Gwen. I sigh. They were all there. Even Tracker. Two-Eyes did not get one of them. Because of me?

"But where? Where are they?" Half rising, Two-Eyes slams the knife against the table.

The flopping-clothes man skitters backward, ready to flee

the bite of the predator. "About a day's hard ride from here. Your Majesty." He bows again.

Two-Eyes settles back into his chair. "How do you know it was them? What were they doing? Where were they headed?"

"The dark man kept calling them 'Your Majesty' and 'Princess.' They were arguing. About where to go next, I think. I'm not sure. I didn't stay long."

"Surely you can remember something more." Two-Eyes rests his hand on the knife again.

The man's neck bobs. "The princess—she was all upset-like. About going somewhere or not going somewhere or something like that. The dark man said they couldn't wait. The princess got very angry then. She yelled"—the man twists up his face—"'I don't care. We can't go back. There's no time,' I think. It was something like that. And His Majesty—I mean His Former Majesty—agreed."

Wait. Can't go back? Go back where? I swipe at the words, but they dart away beyond my grasp. Is the man saying Majesty and Tabby aren't coming back for me? No. Tabby called me a sister. Majesty risked his pack for me. They will not leave me here. Cannot.

Two-Eyes rises. "Thank you for your excellent work." He half pushes the man out the door. "Provide my man with directions to where you saw them, and he'll grant you your reward." He closes the door on him and strides back to me, planting his boots before my face. "Still believe the girl hasn't seen what a burden you are? Still believe she hasn't left you to me?"

I hunch forward, paws clenching. This isn't right. It can't be. Two-Eyes lies. Flopping-clothes man lies. They all lie.

Don't they?

⚬•⚬

I toss and turn in the pit, where Two-Eyes soon sent me back "to think about what I heard." My whole body aches, inside and out, and I cannot make it go away no matter how or where I lie, any more than I can make the words go away. *We can't go back. There's no time.*

Above me wind howls, the sky growls, and jagged streaks of light leap from place to place. Water pours like a bucket tipped on my head, cutting gorges into the wall, filling the bottom of the pit.

I shiver and huddle against one side. The Others did not like me to join them, but on nights like these, the need for warmth would end our fighting. But tonight I am all alone.

No! That is what Two-Eyes wants me to think. Tabby comes for me. Or Majesty will send someone. Maybe even Tracker, if he is now strong. Those other words about not coming back— Two-Eyes told the man to say them and maybe even gave him some of those shiny, yellow pebbles to do so. That is why the man said that.

Finally I sleep, but it is not good sleep. Two-Eyes chases me with his whip through the woods. I leap behind a log and huddle there, shivering. *Go away!* But as he walks by, someone shouts, "Here she is." I whirl around. Tabby stands over me, pointing. Two-Eyes grabs me and flings me aside.

But when I look up it is not Two-Eyes but Majesty who raises the whip.

CHAPTER 27

SURVIVAL

A heavy blanket hangs over the sky and covers everything in gray quiet. Even the birds do not make their usual morning noise or fly over. It is as if all have left because they know a hungry predator prowls here.

I drink some of the water pooled at the pit's bottom and wait. Wait for Two-Eyes and his pack to hunt down Majesty. Wait for him to plan his next move. What else is there for me to do?

The mud shifts near me. A worm crawls out. I pounce. I caught it! It wiggles across my paw, wet and slimy, but it is prey. And prey caught means food. I swallow it whole, and my face twists. Ugh. Give me a bone of meat, even an old one left long in the sun. But I have no such bones, and worms are still better than nothing. I dig through the mud and find five more of the dirt crawlers.

Shifting to another spot to hunt the wiggly prey, I see me in the water and stop. Wet, matted fur; a face scarred and smeared with mud; emptiness where eyes should be. The face of Beast, not Sarah.

I splash the water to make it go away. Beast or Sarah, it doesn't matter. Majesty will come for me.

But what if he doesn't? What if he *can't*? I curl over on myself, but nothing helps the pain gnawing through my insides. Will the darkness take me forever?

Horse feet clatter against stone above.

My face lifts up and I cock my head. I can see only the gray sky-blanket, but my ears strain to hear. This should be the first news about the pack's hunt, about whether they found Majesty and Tabby and the others.

A few footsteps stride by. A horse snorts. Muffled voices toss words back and forth that I cannot hear well enough to know. But this is not the noise of a whole pack returning with prey. Majesty and Tabby must have escaped Two-Eyes again. So maybe, just maybe, they will come for me after all.

The quiet takes hold again. What would it take to lure something bigger than worms into my hole? There must be a way, and I must stay strong until Majesty and Tabby return for me. I stare up at the sky. It is changing, losing its grayness. Other colors gather, the colors of pain—blue, black, green. Not the colors the sky should be.

Two times I've seen the sky that way. Rage soon followed: winds I could not stand against; water so thick I could not see Master's house from the pen; great growlings and day-bright light that made the air sizzle as if on fire; falling white balls sometimes as big as a man's fist, shredding leaves and breaking branches. Everything ran then, and Master even brought the Others and me into his house.

If this sky drops white balls, would Two-Eyes even remember I am out here?

The wood bars covering the hole are shoved out of the way, and Fang, his lip curling, jumps down beside me. I scoot back. He is not here to take me inside because of the white balls.

Fang's grin spreads even wider, showing off his many teeth. "Does the beast want to play?" With a flick of his hand he flips out his knife. It embeds into the mud next to my head.

I shudder and roll away. Fang grabs my foreleg. I kick the water and thrash and push my feet deep into the mud. But the worms have not given me much strength. With one yank, Fang dumps me into the water at his feet, my head diving into its coldness. I push up, coughing and sputtering.

"Now that you've bathed . . ." He hooks his arm under my middle, grabs his knife, and hoists us out of the pit. I fall limp, too weak to fight any longer. Why does it matter? Tabby and Majesty will not reach me soon enough—if they come at all.

Wind whips around us and then stops all at once as Fang carries me inside. He twists and turns through many halls. I cannot tell where we are or how to get out again, even if I could slip from his grasp. Up some stairs. Down others. Through halls, and up more steps. Fang goes into a small, dark room and drops me by a heavy hanging cloth, like the kind that would cover the walls in Majesty's castle.

"Please begin again." The voice of Two-Eyes booms beyond the cloth.

I edge forward. The room beyond the cloth is open, holding only a table and stool, but the two people in it make it seem full. Two-Eyes stands by a window, his back to a tall slouching man wearing clothing held together with many strips and squares of cloth.

"If you want, Your Majesty." Patches does not even bother to bow.

"I want." Two-Eyes turns from the window toward the man, a flash of light outside twisting odd shadows across his face. "Very much." His eyes do not shift toward me, but I know. These words are for me.

I pull back, burying my face between my forelegs, my bound paws behind my head. I will not sit here and listen to these words. Fang yanks my forelegs away and pins them to my side. I squirm, but that only makes Fang chuckle. Lowering his mouth to my ear, he whispers, "You'll want to hear this, Beast." He shoves me close to the cloth where I cannot escape the story already being told.

"There were three—no, four people around a fire, yelling." The words are flat, as if the teller did not care that there were four people or that they were yelling. "A couple of girls. A couple of men. One looked strange." Patches shrugs, hands in pockets.

I swallow hard. More news about Tabby and Majesty.

"Strange how?" asks Two-Eyes. "Dark-skinned perhaps?"

Patches only shrugs. "That might have been it. Don't really know. Don't care. Anyway, they were yelling, so I figured that was as good as any time to grab some food and go."

I frown. The other man said all this before. Why did Two-Eyes want me to hear it again?

"Don't remember much else but . . ." Patches leans back and squints at the ceiling. "One of the girls—the young, pretty one—was upset about something or other. She yanked something from around her neck and threw it away." He pulls out a small, green cloth. "Shiny things are a weakness of mine. So when it caught the light, I knew I had to find it." He unfolds the cloth and offers it to Two-Eyes. On it lays the gold bird from Tabby's necklace.

The floor spins away toward the ceiling, and darkness takes me.

Water splashes across my face. Coughing, I roll onto my side. What happened—Tabby's necklace. The one that went with mine, that she promised to always keep, always wear.

And she threw it away.

My head slumps to the cold, hard floor. Tabby no longer wants me in her pack. Or she does not want me enough to fight Two-Eyes for me. She now knows what he can do, has felt the strike of his fist, heard the crack of his whip. I would not want to come back either, not for a burden that only slows the pack down.

A pair of boots strides before me. "So you've decided to rejoin us."

I do not raise my eyes or turn my face to Two-Eyes. My pack has left me behind. There is no one left to fight off the strong predators circling me, predators who can do with me what they want until I fall forever still.

Unless I give them what they want: Majesty's hiding place.

Water stings my eyes. How can I lead Two-Eyes to Majesty?

How can I not? I have no pack left to help me. If I want to keep seeing new days, I have to give Two-Eyes what he wants. I twist myself onto my knees, my insides feeling like a pack of dogs are tearing them apart.

"You've come to a decision." A sneer twists across his face. "You've chosen to help me."

I've chosen to see more days. But first I must get out of here. Two-Eyes must let me beyond these walls and gates to show him where Majesty hides. He must let me walk through the forest. In the forest I escaped from Two-Eyes once before. Maybe I can again. But what if I can't? I must be sure I will walk away from all this. I tip my head toward the table.

"You want something in return." Thick silence. He rests his hand on the end of his knife, his fingers tightening around it. "Why should I? Why should I give you anything? I could kill you now if I wanted."

Could, but won't. He wants Majesty's hiding place, and he wants it more than he wants to kill me or I wouldn't be sitting here. I wait.

Two-Eyes picks up from the table a thin, creamy square, empty of any writing. "What did you have in mind? Food? Drink? A dry place to sleep? No beatings for a week?" A threat rumbles under his words.

I do not let myself even blink. All these will last only a little time. I want more. I want to go back and live among the trees in the place I know best. And I want to go without needing to look over my shoulder for him the whole way.

"You want something more."

I lift my bound forepaws.

"Freedom? You want your freedom?" He barks a laugh. "That's easy enough." He pulls the knife from his belt.

My paws jerk back against my body.

He stares down at me and then nods to himself. "You want me to release you completely."

He understands now. I wait.

"But if I let you go, how will you lead me to Elroy?"

175

I stare at the creamy square Two-Eyes holds. If a few black scribbles can give Two-Eyes Majesty's kingdom, then they must be able to clear a way to the forest for me.

"Ah, a certificate of release. Very well. I can do that." He takes a seat and adds a few black marks across the cream square. When he finishes, he rises, waving for me to take his seat.

I climb up and stare at the black lines. They mean nothing to me. But I stare at them and then start to take it. Something blue peeks out underneath. I nudge the other parchments aside. Majesty's seal. Why would Two-Eyes have Majesty's seal on something, unless . . . the wager?

I glance up. Two-Eyes has his back to me as he whispers to Fang. I roll the page with Majesty's seal around the one Two-Eyes made me and turn to climb down. A green cloth on the corner stops me.

Two-Eyes sees. "You want the necklace? Here. Have it. As a token of my good faith."

His words are not true—he wants to remind me why I do this—but I take it anyway. Now there is no going back. If I cannot run from Two-Eyes in the forest, I will have to give him my pack for my life. And should Majesty come now . . .

My paw tightens around the necklace.

They aren't my pack any longer.

CHAPTER 28

BETRAYAL

ighting with the Others for food was hard. They bit. Blood flowed. I often limped away tired, hungry, and hurting. Many of the ridges on my face and forelegs came from those fights. But that is nothing like fighting myself, and locked in an empty room high in a tower of the stone building, I have no one else to fight.

I try to sleep, but Majesty and days now gone pursue my steps. I try to pace the room, but even after a healer looked at my hurt leg, it is slow to grow strong again and I must stop often to let it rest. I eat, but food comes at odd times and the little given cannot keep me busy long. So I am always tired, always hungry, always hurting, and if I could look inside me, many ridges would be forming there too.

But I did what I had to. All those words Tabby said, all the things Majesty did—they mean nothing to them. *I* mean nothing to them. Hard times came to the pack, and the weak were left behind. So I do now whatever I must to see more days.

Still, my insides are not as sure as my head—or is it the other way? I do not know. Not about that, not about anything. All of it is too big for me. What do I know?

I have escaped from Two-Eyes too many times.

As we travel toward the border that Tracker and I crossed many days ago, I hunt for any chance to slip away. But the rope tying me to the wagon is thick and the knot strong. At all times I am watched, day and night, by two men with their hands on their swords. And even if I could break free from both rope and men, I could not run far or fast; the little food from Two-Eyes is for keeping me alive, not for making me strong.

We pass the town where the men took Tracker. We enter the woods, and the wagon pulls to a stop where the road splits into two. My insides shake. I wanted to leave Two-Eyes behind long ago.

"Off, now!"

The rope around my neck is yanked, and I jump to the ground. Pain bites into my hind legs; my good one that was hurt still aches often. Two-Eyes and the many men he brought watch me, waiting for me to lead them to Majesty. Majesty, who took me into his home. Majesty who fed me. Who gave me warm blankets and a place by the fire. Cared for me when I was hurt. Held me in his arms and protected me. That Majesty.

I stare down the left side of the road. I could take Two-Eyes away from Majesty. He does not know where we must go to find Majesty. He would not know I led him the wrong way. Until we do not find Majesty. And then he will be angry. Whipping angry. I shudder.

A horse snorts and sidesteps. Two-Eyes narrows his eyes. I am taking too long. My paw slips into my pocket, touches the rolled parchments, the cloth holding Tabby's necklace. Nothing in me stirs. The inside ridges have hardened so that, like the bottom of my paws, I feel little. I am packless now. I must escape the predator anyway I can.

I turn down the road I came on with Tracker.

———

The forest is warm and filled with wetness from storms. Panting, I limp forward down the path I can barely find among the damp leaves. I want to stop. I want a drink. I want to go back and say that I would never show Two-Eyes to Majesty's hiding place. But Two-Eyes pushes me on, snapping his whip at me. It does not touch my back, but the sound alone makes me wince. I hurry on, legs trembling under me.

Why did I do this? The words Two-Eyes wrote saying that he'd let me go are nothing. He will not let me go when we reach Majesty. He is a predator. He knows that without a pack I am not strong enough to fight him. He will tear me to pieces, not release me. My head droops, and a single water drop slips down my cheek. Majesty was right to leave me behind. Only the lowest of beasts hunts its own pack for food. If only there was another path to lead Two-Eyes down! But it is too late. The trees stop, and the bridge points out the way we should go.

Below, the river growls and roars; we do not belong here. But Two-Eyes cracks his whip and drives me forward to the clearing around Tracker's house, a place that should have been safe from Two-Eyes. Except I betrayed the pack. I slump to the ground. Let the horses behind walk over me. I should have that and much, much more done to me.

But Two-Eyes leads them aside. No, crushing by horse feet is too good for me. Too fast, too painless. Instead he orders a man to tie me to a nearby tree and strides toward the house, both sword and whip in hand, making me wait even longer for the end—after seeing Majesty.

Crashing and yelling and breaking splinter the air. I bury my head under my foreleg, eyes squeezed shut. I do not want to know. Yet my ears strain to hear, listening for that scream, for the shout that Two-Eyes has found Majesty and Tabby and the others, for the sound of harm coming to those who did me no harm. Instead, one pair of feet stalks toward me, twigs snapping a warning. Two-Eyes grabs me and thrusts me against the tree trunk, his hand coiling around my neck.

My paws curl in on themselves. I . . . will . . . not . . . fight. Let the darkness take me for always and always. Then I will never hurt the pack again.

Come on, Sarah. Fight.

The words Majesty spoke over me when Tracker first brought me here slam into me. I don't want to fight. I must fight. I don't want the darkness to take me for always and always. My back arches, and I claw at the hand crushing my throat. *Let me go!*

Two-Eyes catches both of my forepaws with his free hand and crushes them against me as he leans in, his nose nearly touching mine. His two-colored eyes burn, blue cold fire and unearthly green fire, with the wildness of a predator that smells blood but can't get to it. "Where. Are. They?" His teeth, kept from the expected bone, crunch words.

I shake my head. Majesty isn't here?

His hand tightens, darkness sputters across my sight. "No more lies. Where are they?"

I don't know! They're supposed to here. A wheeze of a whimper squeezes past his hand, my insides pounding, aching, burning, ready to push out any way they can. Two-Eyes drops me. I crumple to the ground and curl into a ball on my side, gasping for sweet, fresh air.

He paces away from me and back again. His hand strokes the coils of the whip hanging at his side. "Lorcan, tie it up. Now."

Grinning, Fang slinks toward me, ready to provide the teeth for his master's bite. "With pleasure, milord."

Coldness turns my insides to stone. Two-Eyes asked me to show him Majesty's hiding place. I did that. He can't, wouldn't . . . I shove myself back and claw the rope at my neck. I'm not going through that again. He barely left me alive last time. I won't walk away from it again. Not with him in this kind of rage.

Fang and several of the men reach for me. I growl at them, snapping at hands, kicking at legs. But there are too many. They latch onto all four of my legs. I arch my back and twist and thrash. *Let go! Let me go! I did what Two-Eyes asked. I brought him here. I brought him to Majesty's hiding place. I didn't know he wouldn't be here. I didn't know!*

They shove me over a half-fallen log, the bushes around it slapping my face. They do not care what I did or did not do.

Two-Eyes is their master. They do what he says, like any good pack. My forepaws are tied together; rope binds me to the tree. My whole back is open, ready for the whip. *Please, please, please. Don't do this.* Water blurs my sight and I twist and pull on the rope. It does not loosen, not even a little.

"Will you or will you not show me where Elroy is, Beast? This is your last chance." Two-Eyes stands in front of me, bushes to his knees. His fingers clench around his whip.

How can I lead him to Majesty when I don't know where Majesty is anymore? I whimper.

"Have it your way." Two-Eyes steps around behind me and tests his whip on the air. Crack!

My body jerks and I yank on the ropes. I have to break free, have to! The ropes bite into my skin; my breaths come in shorts bursts. *Please! Let me go, like you said you would. I did what you asked. I could not know Majesty had left.*

A twig snaps as Two-Eyes sets his feet. Then I understand. He knows that I have told him everything, but he does not care. He has wanted to do this for a long time. Now he has a reason and the anger to drive him.

The whip hisses. My eyes snap shut. Crack! The whip bites into my back. I yelp, my head rearing. Crack! Fire burns across my back and shoulder. Crack. Crack. A howl squeezes out of me. I can't do this. I can't. It hurts too much. *Let me go. I'll do anything. Just let me go.* Crack. Crack. Water flows down my face and I choke on air. Stupid beast. Should have run long ago. Never should have turned back to the healers. Never should have turned back to Majesty that day on the hill. Crack! My paws curl into tight balls, their claws digging in deep, but they cannot match the searing pain of my back.

"Lord Avery, I command you to stop." The strong voice of a master's master rings out.

My head jerks up. Half of my insides leap forward; the other half curl into a trembling ball. I did not think I could shake harder than when I knew what Two-Eyes intended to do, but I shake harder now.

Majesty has returned.

He steps out from among the trees a few paces in front of me, still dressed in simple brown clothes. But the heaviness, the slumped shoulders are gone. Sword in hand, Majesty holds his head high, shoulders back, eyes alight. And I know. He would never leave me to Two-Eyes for all days. He would have come for me, always planned to come, maybe had been on his way.

And I betrayed him.

CHAPTER 29

FORGIVENESS

My head slumps against the log. I cannot look at Majesty any longer. The whip hurts, but it is not what hurts most. I know that now, seeing Majesty standing there. For Majesty's wrath can shred places no whip can touch.

"You *command* me to stop?" Two-Eyes barks a laugh and, with a hiss, the whip swings back to strike again. "Have you forgotten so quickly? *I* now rule this country. You no longer have the power to command anyone." He snorts. "Well, no one except perhaps this pitiful beast."

"Stop—or you will forfeit your life."

"*My* life? I'm the one with a dozen men at my command. They'll stop that flimsy excuse for a blade long before it could ever reach me."

Four men step over the log, headed for Majesty, as if to show that their master's words are true. Majesty's face does not flinch, nor does his sword waver. "You speak truly of that. But what about my arrows?"

Leaves rustle, and there is a thud, not of one arrow hitting dirt, but of three so close together their sound is almost one. The men stop, and Two-Eyes hisses. The hidden bowmen wanted to miss—this time.

"Release Sarah, Avery." Majesty steps forward.

I cringe. I am trapped between two powerful masters with no way out. They will fight. One will win. But I will be shredded to pieces before the winner is decided. Fought-over prey always is.

Two-Eyes snorts. "The beast? I thought you'd want to be rid of it. After all, it led me here to you."

"I know."

Two words, little more than a whisper. But they bury themselves deep inside me. Majesty knows I betrayed him. A shudder ripples through me.

"Then allow me to save you the trouble of killing it. I know how much you dislike blood." Crack! The whip chomps into me.

A whimper escapes, but I no longer fight. Seeing Majesty . . . I cannot hide from what I did any longer. I betrayed the pack, and by the laws of the pack, I must die. Whether Two-Eyes kills me with his whip or Majesty with his sword does not matter. The end has come.

"Last chance, Avery."

The whip hisses. I clench my paws, waiting for the next strike.

"Don't say I didn't warn you."

Three new arrows whiz from the trees above. The two men closest to Majesty crash to the ground, and an enraged howl erupts behind me. Two-Eyes? An arrow hit Two-Eyes? I jerk back, twist around trying to see. The other men are backing up, staring at the trees, jumping at the slightest rustle of leaves. But I cannot find Two-Eyes. What is going on? What is happening?

Majesty bounds forward and over the log. Metal grinds against metal.

I yank on the ropes, but they hold firm. I cannot see what goes on behind me. Only flashes of color and movement. Is Two-Eyes alive? Wounded? Attacking?

The men still on their feet turn back. Several more arrows—I hear at least six—are shot. Grunts and cries say some find their mark.

I yank again. I need to see. Need to get away. Need to hide.

A dark form darts toward me without a sound. My head whips forward. Tracker kneels in front of me. He's alive. Walking around.

"Good day, Princess." Keeping his eyes down, he pulls out a knife.

I recoil, a whimper squeezing out of my mouth. What does he plan to do now?

Tracker grabs my foreleg and holds it still. "You did some foolhardy stunts back at the castle, I hear. Stunts that no one in their right mind should ever attempt." He cuts the ropes binding me. "Thank you. It saved my life." Sliding his knife away, he dips his head to the log between us. Then he sits back again and offers me his big, dark hand. To him, I am still part of the pack.

I put my paw in his hand.

He pulls me up and into his arms. Holding me close to his chest, he charges into the woods, away from the fighting.

A cry rises above the shouting. "It's gone. How, where did . . . there! Get them!"

I shudder, and clinging to Tracker's neck, bury my face in his shoulder. He tightens his grip on me and makes his stride longer. Twigs snap. Leaves slap. Tracker skids to a stop.

My head pops up. Fang stands before us, the tip of a sword pointed our way. Tracker glances back at the two chasing us and then down at me. I'm holding him back. I twist out of his arms onto the ground.

He nods and turns without a word, pulling out his sword.

I lurch for the cover of the forest. Ducking under a leaning tree, I splash through a mud puddle and stagger through some bushes. My back burns, my chest heaves, arrow pain shoots up my good hind leg. I will not be able to do this for long. Too many days without food. Too many days trapped in small spaces. Too many days traveling and too many strikes of the whip. I stumble around a big rock and collapse.

Behind me a man hacks at the bushes. I flatten myself to the ground. Maybe enough dirt covers me that I will blend in and he will pass by without seeing me—if I can stop panting so hard.

"Sarah!"

The whisper yanks on me and lifts my head. Tabby? Above me trees tower, and beside me light splatters the ground, but nowhere do I see her.

"Over here." A hand pokes out of a hole by an old tree, covered over with a tangle of vines and roots.

The man's back is turned. I limp over and crawl in next to Tabby.

She's dressed in brown he-cub clothing much like me, but the darkness around her eyes is gone and so are the splotches on her arms. Instead, she smiles as she smiled before the time she spent with Two-Eyes, the marks he left on her insides now healed. She wraps her arms around me. Me, who brought all this trouble. I squirm away, and a soft lump in my pocket bounces against my leg. Her necklace.

I pull out the green cloth and look at it. What really happened that day? I offer it to her.

She gasps at the gold bird within. "My necklace." She touches its wings lightly.

Footsteps tromp nearer. Tabby tightens a hand around the necklace while reaching for the bow at her side with the other. I dig my hind feet into the dirt, my body ready to spring. One breath passes. Then two. The footsteps fade away. My body relaxes. Tabby releases the bow and opens her hand to look at the necklace again.

"When he took this, I never thought I would . . . where did you find it?"

My shoulders hunch. So Two-Eyes did take the necklace from Tabby long before she ever left his grasp. That story about her throwing the necklace away was just that—a story.

And I betrayed her too, along with Majesty.

Tabby crouches beside me. "I know, Sarah. But you did it, it's done, you're sorry, and in my book it never happened." She opens her other hand to me. My feather necklace now rests in her palm. "Will you please come home now?"

Somewhere nearby a man is hacking leaves, hunting for me, and I can only stare at the necklace I left behind when I sneaked out to join Tracker. So many days have passed. So much has happened. Maybe Tabby can say it never was, but she's not the pack leader. Will Majesty be able to say the same—knowing it could hurt his whole pack?

No. I turn my face away. I can't take the necklace. Not yet. Maybe if Majesty could, then maybe I can . . . but no. He will never want me back.

"I understand. I'll wait." She wraps up the necklaces together and tucks them into a pocket. She cocks her head. "I think he's gone." Grabbing a bow lying to the side, she climbs out, looks around, and waves for me to follow.

I chase after her, but I am tired and weak and Tabby gets farther and farther ahead. Once I almost lose sight of her. Twice she must wait for me to catch up. She urges me on, but I do not have much left to give, even for her.

A distant rumbling grows and grows. We break free from the forest. The bridge across the roaring river stretches before us. Tracker and his mate, bows in hand, already stand on the far side. Majesty is over halfway across.

"Come on, Sarah. We're almost there!" Tabby bounds toward the bridge.

A man steps out of the trees five paces to my right. Tracker shoots an arrow. It buries itself in the man's chest.

"Don't stop now!" Tabby sprints across, braids flying.

I hobble after. Almost there. Almost there. But my feet slow.

The bridge moans and shudders. Suddenly the whole thing shifts and twists. Some boards ahead of me stand up instead of lying flat. The ones under me tip into a hill. I slide toward the edge; I grab for the railing. The river snarls below me. Tabby, almost to the other side, leaps for the ground and lands on it with a tumbling roll.

Majesty pushes Tabby toward Tracker before whirling back to me. He shouts something. I can't hear it. Water and terror roar in my ears.

He clambers down the cliff to the rocks along the river's edge. He stretches out his arms. "Jump, Sarah! I'll catch you."

"Catch you? Why would he catch you, Beast?"

My head swings toward the river's other edge. Two-Eyes stands at the end of the bridge, three men at his side, including Fang.

"You betrayed him. Why would he *want* to catch you?"

His words smash against my insides harder than any boot, and I almost lose my grip on the bridge. Is he right? Am I only changing one master's whip for another's sword?

"He's not there to help you. He's leading you to your death."

My gaze drops back to the river's edge. The rocks around Majesty—they're so hard, so jagged. If Majesty pulls away, rocks will crush my body and the water will sweep away my life.

"Please, Sarah. Trust me." Majesty leans forward until he is in danger of falling into the river himself. "I love you."

He *loves* me? My paws tighten around the wood railing. If only he still could after . . . No. I am a monster, a betrayer. Not even Majesty could love someone like that.

A board splinters and a rope snaps. The bridge bucks, nearly throwing me into the writhing, white river. I wrap my forelegs around the post I cling to, shivering. I won't make it. It will all fall into the river the next time I move. The voices of Majesty and Two-Eyes pound at me.

"I know you think you're a beast, Sarah, and that no one could love you, especially after all you've done—"

"Hurry, Beast!"

"—but you already have my love. You don't have to earn it or explain it or even understand it."

"The bridge won't last much longer."

"You only need to know that it is."

Two-Eyes shouts something, but I can't hear him. My eyes have locked with Majesty's, so deep, so strong, so tender. *Don't have to earn it. Don't have to explain it. Don't have to understand it. Know that it is.*

The bridge kicks and twists, tearing loose from the ground holding it. I close my eyes and jump.

"Oof." Arms wrap around me, sending a fresh burst of pain across my whipped back. "I've got you."

Despite the pain, my eyes pop open. Majesty smiles down at me.

He caught me.

He loves me.

A groan and a splintering of wood jerk my head around. The bridge vanishes into the white clutches of the river. I shiver.

Majesty hugs me to his chest and turns back to the cliff. "You're safe, Sarah. I love you. For always and always."

I feel his words more than hear them, but they wrap around me like a warm blanket. Safe, protected, loved, a part of the pack for always and always. Majesty lifts me up to Tracker, who leans over the cliff.

"Don't just stand there. Shoot them!" The roar from Two-Eyes carries easily over the river's growling.

Tracker hesitates. Majesty waves him on. "I'll be fine. Get the girls to safety."

Tracker clutches me closer, backing away. An arrow thuds into the ground. Majesty grunts, his face twisting in pain. The black feathers of an arrow peek over his shoulder.

No! I try to leap from Tracker's arms. He holds me tight.

"Now." Majesty throws the word at Tracker, but his eyes he locks on me. Then he lets go.

CHAPTER 30

PROPOSITION

Plip, plop, plop. Water patters on the leaves and drips into puddles. Plip, plop, plop. For three days the sky has cried. For three days its big drops have soaked everything beneath it. Majesty is gone, for always and always.

Because of me.

Those words pound themselves deeper into my head with every step I take, the wet ground squishing around my paws, as if it is trying to suck me down into it. But Tracker cuts a path through the forest, dragging us all forward—his mate, Gwen, Tabby, and me. We cannot stop. Two-Eyes tracks us still.

Because of me.

My head hangs lower. My steps slow, as if rocks were tied to my back when I wasn't looking. Why don't they turn on me and end it all? Instead, they plod on ahead—a tight-lipped Gwen behind Tracker, his mate with her hand on a stoop-shouldered Tabby. No one looks at me. No one speaks. I may be traveling with a pack, but I am as alone as when Two-Eyes caught me.

Because I am nothing without Majesty.

"Princess Sarah."

I raise my face. The others have stopped walking, and Tracker now stands in front of me. He crouches down. "I know you're tired, Princess, but I need you to keep up."

190

His words aren't hard, but they still whip my insides. We're going too slow. Because of me.

Tracker sighs and straightens up. "Evie, will you take the rear for a while?"

His mate glances at Tabby, who stares at the ground, her cloak pulled tightly around her. She doesn't even twitch when Evie slides her arm from her shoulders. Evie adjusts her own pack and circles behind me. "As you wish, Mason."

Tracker tromps to the front, and his mate herds me closer to Tabby. We begin walking again, going on and on and on.

Ahead of me, Tabby's foot hooks a tree root. She stumbles, then crashes to the ground with a cry. Rolling over, she pulls her knee to her chest and clutches her lower leg. I bound forward to help her.

"Get away from me!" She kicks out her unhurt leg, catching me in the shoulder.

With a yelp, I spring back. Tabby struck me. She has never struck me before.

"Princess Tabitha." Tracker's words slice the air on a knife's edge.

Tabby's shoulders slump.

Kneeling at her side, he pulls her hands away and checks her leg. "A few scratches, nothing broken or sprained. Bruised at worst." His words are softer now. "It'll be fine."

"No, it won't be." Tabby's hands clench. "It'll never be fine again. Because he's gone. For always and always." She chokes on her words, and water spills down her cheeks.

"Oh, Princess." Evie wraps her arms around Tabby, stroking her hair, rocking her as if she were a very young cub.

Her insides are all torn up. I want to go to her, help her, but the sting in my shoulder remains. *Get away from me.* I slink back until the leaves of the bushes hide me, just as they used to do when Master got angry. But what if Tabby's anger doesn't go away?

"Where's Princess Sarah?"

I wince at Tracker's sharp words, and I curl into a ball. Is he now angry with me too?

"Does anyone see Princess Sarah?"

Silence follows his question. I should go to him before he gets angrier. My body refuses to move.

"Evie." Tracker's voice calls his mate nearer. Steps tread closer to me. "There's a clearing a short distance ahead; we'll stay the night there. Take Princess Tabitha and Gwen, and I'll follow when I can." He sighs. "But don't expect me too early. This could take a while."

"What about Lord Avery?"

"Be on your guard, but I think we've thrown him off our trail for now."

There's quiet, and then, "Be gentle, Mason." Steps retreat, and after a few more mumbled words, feet plod away.

Tracker's footsteps pace back and forth. Is he going to leave me behind too? Leaves squish; Tracker settles on the ground next to a nearby tree, his legs stretching in front of me. If I move, he'll know where I am.

A soft scratching rubs against the air, and curls of wood fall to the ground; Tracker is working on another arrow. Which means he won't be going anywhere soon. My legs ache from staying curled up for so long after walking for even longer. Water slides off a leaf and plops on my head. A dirt crawler wiggles by, like the ones in the pit. Why didn't I stay there?

"Was King Elroy a liar, Princess?"

Tracker's words crush my insides. He knows I'm here? I shake my head. Of course he knows. He's Tracker. I've never been able to hide from him. I roll over and crawl partway out, staying as close to the ground as I can. It's all I can do to show that I know he is better, higher in the pack than me.

Tracker keeps his eyes on his knife, his hands never pausing in their work. "You didn't answer me. Was King Elroy a liar?"

I push my paws into the mud, then shake my head. Majesty never told that kind of story.

"Then why do you act as if he were?" Tracker tucks his knife and unfinished arrow away, before turning his face to me. Dark shadows cover his eyes. "He called you a princess, yet here you cower like a common street dog."

Water flows down my face. He is right. But I cannot be everything Majesty called me, no matter what I do. My paws clench, ragged claws digging into the soft underside. I am only Beast, can only be a beast. I know nothing else.

"Listen to me, Princess Sarah." Tracker slides down onto his belly, placing his face on the same level as mine. "You are what King Elroy declares you to be. If he said you're his daughter, you are his daughter. If he said you're a princess, you are a princess. And nothing—not failure, not betrayal, not others' treatment of you, not even his death—can ever change that."

You're a princess because that is what His Majesty calls you. Isn't that what Gwen told Tabby in the cave too? Even though she didn't look like a princess, and even though Two-Eyes had treated her like a beast, Tabby was still a princess—because Majesty loved her and called her a princess. Just like he had me. My head lifts.

Tracker sits back on his knees. "I bet Evie has food ready by now. Shall we go see what she's put together tonight?" He offers me his hand. One thumb, four fingers, palm.

I place my hand on top of his.

As Tracker said, the clearing is only a short way down the path. Still, by the time we reach it, Evie not only has food ready, but she also has set up a shelter of a heavy cloth held up by a few branches. Wrapping his arms around her, Tracker smiles, a rare sight since we left the river. "You never cease to amaze me."

"They're small things, Mason, very small, in light of everything else." She tips her head toward the far side of the shelter. There Tabby sits hunched over on a log, her back to the rest of us.

"Small things go a long way in hard times." Tracker presses his mouth to her head and lets go of her.

She shakes her head and crouches by a bundle. "At least you found Princess Sarah." Lightening her voice, she offers me a small smile and holds out a lump of bread. "Would you like something to eat?"

My insides rumble *yes*, but my gaze is drawn back to Tabby. I shake my head and lope past Evie.

"Princess Sarah?"

"Wait." Tracker holds his mate back.

I reach the log Tabby sits on, and I stop, pain again pricking the shoulder she struck. *Get away from me!* Her words whip me again. Can I do this? My hands clench. Should I do this?

She's vulnerable, very vulnerable. Majesty's words from the inn, before Two-Eyes won the wager, whisper in my ear. *She's hurting, confused, and scared. She doesn't know what to do.* If only Majesty were here! He would know what to do. *Keep her safe, Sarah.*

I swallow and awkwardly pull myself up to sit on the log just like Tabby. She doesn't look at me, as if I am not here at all.

"Mason, look—"

"Shh, my love. I know."

Now what? If I were Majesty, I could hold her. If I were Tracker, I could talk to her. But I am not Tracker and I am not Majesty. So I wait instead.

Darkness creeps in. Water falls less and less from the sky until nothing more comes down. Silver light pokes through holes in the shadows. A wind causes the shelter's cloth to flap and snap. Tabby shudders. "This is all your fault, you know."

I wince at her words, thick and muffled, yet with a sharp point to them. Because she is right. I brought all this upon us. I didn't mean to, but I did.

"Father would still be here if it weren't for you."

My insides recoil as if she had kicked me. I wrap my arms around my middle but stay where I am.

She sits up straighter, her hands clenching. "I wish he were here instead of you." Her words, clearer now, strike the air with bruising strength, but as soon as she says them, she crumples back on herself, as if her insides hurt the same way mine do. "But Father wouldn't wish that." Her head sinks lower, her hands falling limp in her lap.

A water drop rolls down my cheek. If only I could make her hurt go away. But I can't. I can only sit here and hurt with her. I slide toward her, hesitate, and then wrap my hand around hers. I wish Majesty was here too, instead of me.

Tabby stiffens, staring at our hands. Two, three breaths pass. Did I do something wrong? I start to pull back.

Tabby's fingers close, locking our hands together. "We're very alike, the two of us. Both lonely, neither fitting in with the rest," she murmurs before lifting her face to me. The night's silver light glints off wetness on her cheeks. "Sisters for always and always."

"Hold still please! This is difficult enough without you twisting around every other moment, Princess Sarah." Gwen pushes me back down on the rock and wraps a torn cloth around my chest.

Every day she's asked to look at my back. Every day I have refused, until I tired of pacing around her. I would let her look, and she would stop asking about it. But when she saw what the whip had done, talk ended: she was putting on a paste and a wrapping even if Two-Eyes and his whole pack threatened us.

My good leg bounces. I should have refused again. Pacing would be easier than sitting here. Tracker left for a nearby town early yesterday to find out what Two-Eyes was doing. I wanted to go with him, but he said he would travel faster alone. He was right; I would only slow him down. But staying behind left me restless.

Gwen huffs. "You're worse than the groom's son."

Tabby stifles a giggle at us from where she turns meat over a fire. A good sound, one I haven't heard in many days. I twist around to see her better. A darkness still lurks in her eyes, but not as much as before.

"Princess!" Gwen turns me back to the way I was. "There. One more wrap and we're done." Gwen pulls the cloth around me again.

A twig snaps.

My head jerks up. Someone is coming. Tracker? I cock my head at the rustle of leaves. The steps sound like his, but why so much noise? He's a hunter. He doesn't like being heard before he is seen. If he runs so that I hear him coming, he runs very fast. He bursts out from among the trees.

"Mason!" His mate steps between him and me.

Gwen grabs my shirt and pulls it over my head. I growl and try to see past it. What has happened? Has Two-Eyes found us?

"She's decent again." Gwen steps back from me. I drop into a crouch and swing over to Tabby's side.

Panting, Tracker drops to one knee before us and bows his head, hiding his face. "Princess Tabitha, Princess Sarah."

His odd approach, the way he says our names, makes my skin tie in knots, despite the day's warmth. This is about more than Two-Eyes being on the way. Tabby and I look at each other. She pulls herself up to sit taller. "What news do you bring, Protector?"

"Lord Avery . . ." Tracker's voice breaks, and his hand clenches. "Lord Avery has His Majesty and plans to kill him in seven days' time."

Tabby gasps, her hand flying to her mouth. I shake my head; Tracker's words are all tangled together.

"For shame, Mason." His mate stomps forward, her arms folded across her chest. "To distress the princesses so. Lord Avery may have His Majesty's body, but you can't kill a man who is already dead."

Tracker lifts his head, wetness sparkling on his cheeks. "I have no desire to distress the princesses, my love, but my words fly true. His Majesty, King Elroy, lives. I saw him with my very own eyes."

Majesty lives? Can that be true? I edge nearer to Tracker. I want to grasp his words with all of me. But I saw the arrow hit Majesty. I saw him fall.

Tracker rests a hand on my shoulder. "The arrow only wounded him, and he was able to drop to a safe spot at the bottom of the cliff. So he lives . . . for now." He bows his head again.

My fingers dig into the dirt. That can't be. We have to stop Two-Eyes.

"There must be something we can do." Tabby leans toward Tracker. "Please. I . . . I can't lose him again."

"I understand, Princess. I'll do what I can, but . . ." Tracker shakes his head, hand tightening on my shoulder.

He does not need to say more. I know what will happen. I've fought packs all my days. One against a whole pack? He'll be shredded. I rip myself out of his grasp and bound away from him, away from the shelter, away from everything. I run until I cannot run any more, legs aching, insides burning. I collapse panting under a tree.

The wind rustles the leaves. A squirrel scolds me. I curl into a ball. This can't happen again. There must be another way. But what? We cannot buy Majesty; there's no money. Nor is our pack big enough to threaten Two-Eyes. But what else is—

Another wager.

I sit up. Could it work? It would put one against one. Weak against strong, yes, but the weak will live longer against one than against a whole pack. And Two-Eyes might do a wager again: his eyes brighten at even the word of a hunt. My hand slips into my pocket and rubs the corner of the rolled parchment. I also have one thing he wants. Could it be enough?

I walk back toward the camp and pause on the edge of the trees' shelter. Gwen and Evie huddle around Tabby. Near the fire, Tracker sits on a log, sharpening his knife. Every few strokes he lifts his head and scans the trees. His gaze sweeps past without ever seeing me.

This can work, but I will need his help—help he won't want to give. But it's the only way. He will see that. Planting my hands on the ground, I swing into the clearing. Tracker's head jerks up, and when he sees me, his shoulders relax. He nods to me and returns to his knife sharpening. I stop at his side.

"May I help you, Princess Sarah?"

Gwen, Tabby, and Evie all whirl toward us; they did not see or hear me approach. Everyone watches me. If I am to do this, now is the time. I offer the parchments to Tracker.

Resting his knife across his knees, he unrolls them. "'I hereby authorize the immediate death of this paper's carrier—His Majesty, King Avery."

What? That is not what it is supposed to say. I peer over Tracker's arm, but the black squiggles mean nothing more to me than when Two-Eyes made them. He planned for my death from the beginning.

"Somehow I suspect that was not what you were told this was." Tracker tosses the parchment into the fire before his eyes fall back to the other page. "What is . . ." He lifts it closer. "This can't be. Princess Sarah, how did you ever get a hold of *this*?"

"What is it, Mason?" Tracker's mate steps to the edge of the shelter.

"The wager contract. Do you know what this means?"

His mate, Gwen, and Tabby look at each other.

"We can finally prove Lord Avery unrightfully claimed the throne—that he had to win fairly, not merely win." Tracker turns back to me. "Who else knows you have this?"

I shake my head. If Two-Eyes had known, I wouldn't be standing here.

"I can only imagine what he would give to . . . That's the idea, isn't it? You think he would trade His Majesty for this."

I shake my head. It is strong but not enough. I point at me and then at the top of the parchment. I hope the word I want is there.

Tracker frowns as he puts together what I mean. "No." Ramming his knife into the log, he pushes to his feet, walking away from me.

I fold my arms and wait.

"I won't—can't let you do that, Princess Sarah."

"What's wrong?" Tabby edges forward, her fingers twisting around themselves. "What does she want?"

"A wager."

Tabby rubs her head. "A game of Catteran? We did fine together, Sarah, playing against Father, but this . . ."

I shake my head. Not that.

Tracker's eyes narrow. "What do you have in mind, Princess?"

He knows. I know he does. He has tracked me too long not to. But he wants to be wrong. I pick up a bow and act like I'm shooting it.

"An archery match?" asks Evie.

"No, not archery. She wants a hunt." Tracker scowls. "With herself as the prey."

My insides quiver, and I want to run. Tracker looks much like when I refused to move with the rest of the slaves and he threatened to whip Tabby if I didn't walk. But Majesty's life hangs on this. I will not back down.

Tracker steps before me, using all his height to make me feel small. "Princess Sarah, with the authority given to me from His Majesty King Elroy, I forbid you, as your protector, from any such foolish attempts."

I fold my arms. This is the only way. He just doesn't want to say so.

"But the idea is perfect."

All heads turn toward Gwen, and she steps forward. "Pardon me for saying so, but Lord Avery sees himself as a master hunter from whom nothing escapes. Yet Princess Sarah has. Many times, if all you say is true. He would risk much to prove his superiority and regain his reputation as inescapable."

Tracker's mate wraps an arm around Gwen. "One against one. You must admit, Mason, that strategy is sounder and more likely to work than your taking on a dozen armed men by yourself. And as Gwen pointed out, the princess has done this before. Perhaps she can do it again."

Tracker turns away, staring at the knife buried in the log. I need his help, but I cannot make him give it. Tracker yanks the knife out. "Fine. I will go to town and . . ."

I growl. My wager. I will be there.

"*We* will go to town and make Lord Avery the offer. We'll start before daybreak. That should give us a little time to prepare for our meeting—if you are absolutely sure this is what you want to do, Princess."

I nod, never surer of anything. I will take my stand at Majesty's side—even if it is my last.

CHAPTER 31

PREPARATION

The wager seemed like a good plan while we were in the forest. It would be hard to do; Tracker said so many times. But sheltered by trees and far from Two-Eyes, I knew the plan could work and Majesty would live.

But now . . . Tracker, Gwen, and I trudge down a hot road for the sixth day. Crowds of people—mates, masters, cubs—press around us, kicking dust up into my face. My feet ache. I'm tired. My insides crave food and water. The wager still seems like our only way to help Majesty, but good or planned? More like a scuffle over a bone with a much bigger dog. I rub the ridges on my face, the only thing I gained from my last fight like that.

I dodge around legs and bump against others. My low, swinging crouch draws eyes. Tracker sees it too. "Up you go." He lifts me onto his back, and I cling to his neck.

Now heads bob up and down before me, and beyond that, I glimpse humped houses hunkered into a small valley with a river. We're almost to where I must face Two-Eyes, the master predator who has hunted me so many days. I never thought I would ever seek him out for anything. Now for Majesty I must stand before Two-Eyes, not as a beast but as a princess. But can I do all I must? My mouth tries to form the words in my head, but like every other time I've tried, nothing comes out. I growl, my grip on Tracker tightening.

"Easy, Pri—Sarah." Tracker shifts how he holds me. "I would prefer not to be strangled."

I duck my head and force myself to loosen my hold on him.

Another road joins ours, and more people jostle for the best places. Tracker, caught in the middle, slows his stride, and Gwen, who came to help make me *Princess*, presses against him.

"Spectators come to see the death of the king." Tracker shakes his head with a growl. "Word spread far and fast." He swims against the flow of people, and as we enter the town, he squeezes into an empty path between houses, finally breaking free from the crowd's pull. We all breathe deeper. Tracker knocks at a door.

A mate opens it and her eyes widen. She waves us inside, locking the door behind us. "Mason! Have you a death wish? Rats have overrun our town, if you didn't notice."

"Aim your arrows elsewhere, Merriam. I'm here to pry His Majesty—may the throne be his again soon!—from the rats' jaws." He sets me on a bed in the corner of the single room. "Now if I may, let me introduce you to His Majesty's daughter, Princess Sarah, and our helper Gwen, a fine cook and one gifted in healing. Princess, this is Merriam Ferrier."

The woman eyes Gwen and me. "I beg the pardon of the princess and Healer Gwen, but these rats have pointed teeth and sharp claws. Don't we need something more . . . deadly to blunt their bite?"

"Not if we plan to give them their own tails to chew." He unlocks the door. "Now please provide the princess and Healer Gwen with whatever they need. I will return shortly."

"And if you don't?"

"Find a cat, the bigger the better." He leaves before she can say more.

"Mason, Mason." She shakes her head.

Gwen steps forward. "Mistress Ferrier, I require a tub of water, somewhat warm if possible, a brush, an extra blanket if you have one, and a drink for the princess. Her journey has been long and arduous." Then she pulls a curtain to cut off the area by the bed from the rest of the room.

I slump against the end of the bed. We still have so far to go, so much to do, and many things could go so very wrong.

"Princess?" Gwen lays a hand on my shoulder. "Are you feeling ill?"

Yes, but not in a way that she could help me with. I push myself up and shake my head.

Missus Ferrier hands Gwen the brush, blanket, and cup. "The water is heating, and it will be done as soon as possible. Is there anything else I can get you in the meanwhile?" Missus Ferrier's voice has lost its hard edge of demand, and her eyes dart between Gwen and me, as if she stands near a mighty predator that she first thought was a harmless grass eater.

"No." Gwen shakes her head, softening her own voice. "That will be all. Thank you."

Missus Ferrier bobs her head. "Call me if you need anything else." She backs behind the curtain.

I sigh. Time to get moving again. Two-Eyes will stop for no one. So I can't stop either. I motion for the walking stick Gwen has carried. I wrap my hands around the rod. Every day since Tracker reminded me I was a princess because Majesty said so, I have worked at walking when no one could see. I wanted to walk in on Tabby someday to make her smile. But I cannot wait. I must walk now, not let Tracker carry me like he planned. That would show weakness. I must look strong. I must act like the princess Majesty says I am. Besides, if I walk, Tracker's hands will be free to hold knife, bow, or sword.

Pulling myself to my feet, I cling to the rod, shoulders hunched. All of me hurts from my feet to my head. No good. Head up. Shoulders back. I belong to Majesty.

Gwen covers her mouth with a hand. "You're . . . standing."

I am, but that is not enough. Two-Eyes will not care that I stand. I want—*need* him to look twice. I shuffle-hop along the bed's edge. My legs wobble much, but I stay up on my two feet.

The second time goes better, and so does the time after that and the one after that.

Then my water is ready, and Gwen helps me to wash. My back is still tender. My matted hair causes her much trouble. But we finish soon after Tracker comes back, and I put on what he brings me: an ankle-length dress of cream with blue stitching and a blue sash. Clothes for a princess, my first she-cub clothes. My hands brush the soft cloth again and again as Gwen twists my damp hair into a single braid down my back.

Tracker also brought shoes for my feet, but I toss them aside. They will only make my walking harder. Gwen offers me the rod. "Ready?"

Standing, I nod. She pushes aside the curtain, and I take two steps forward.

Tracker stops his pacing and stares. He opens his mouth to speak, snaps it shut, and drops into a deep bow. "Princess Sarah."

A small smile lifts the corner of my mouth. Maybe this will work.

Gwen wraps a dark cloak around my shoulders, and I motion for Tracker to carry me. I need to save my strength. This will be hard enough as it is.

Missus Ferrier shakes her head. "Hot water, a pretty dress— what kind of bait are you laying anyway, Mason?" She dips her head toward me. "If I may be so bold to ask."

"We are making an offer that Lord Avery cannot refuse. We hope." And with that, he carries me outside, leaving Gwen behind to explain.

Tracker's legs eat the ground with long strides through street and crowd. I clutch my pole with both hands. Will this work? What if Two-Eyes only laughs and tells his pack to take us where we stand? Yet to see Majesty and stand beside him again as one of his pack—for that I will face Two-Eyes and all his men, even if they devour us in the end.

Tracker slows and growls. I strain upward to see over the heads of the people crushing us. Only a little way separates us from the open square, but no path goes from us to it. We are trapped, too far away for our plan to work.

"If I make a path, can you walk the rest of the way?"

I eye how far we are and nod. I *will* make it there, one way or another.

He sets me down, and when my feet rest firm on the ground, he pulls out his knife. "Step apart, or in parts you'll fall." His words are not loud, but the threat rumbling underneath makes *me* shudder, and the words are not even for me.

Heads whip toward us, and at the sight of his sharp blade, people back away. Tracker plunges ahead, calling the same thing again, louder. I follow him, keeping my head down and pulling the cloak tight around me, as if that'll protect me from the many eyes turned toward me.

When we are a few paces from the front, Tracker slips his knife away. But his hand rests on the handle of his sword, ready to pull it out at the first danger. I lean my head against his arm, my legs already tiring. My gaze roams past the line of swordsmen in red and black to the wood platform in the open square. It is like the place where Two-Eyes bought me. Here though, no wood block stands in the middle, but a gold chair with red cushions.

A wagon rumbles through the crowd and past the line of swordsmen. Majesty is shoved onto the platform. His hands are bound and his clothing is torn and dirty, but he holds his head high. He is not prey for Two-Eyes. He is Majesty. My face burns. How could I ever think *I* could help *him*? He does not need me or Tracker or the people in the crowd who might help us if Two-Eyes tries to stop us. If Majesty wanted to walk away now, no one, not even Two-Eyes and his whole pack, could stop him.

No, Majesty stays because he wants to, because what happens here will bring about something else he desires. Or so it seems as he faces the crowd. From person to person he looks, surprise never wrinkling his face, and several times he nods to himself; this is what he knew he would see. Then his eyes find mine and he smiles, as if standing on two legs and wearing a dress is the way he has always seen me.

A carriage stops behind the wagon, and Two-Eyes steps out. Dressed in black and red, he wears Majesty's crown. I snort. The crown sits tilted, too big for his head. Two-Eyes is not and never will be Majesty.

Two-Eyes settles on the chair, and Majesty is roughly pulled forward. Tracker tenses. I grit my teeth, biting back a snarl. We both know Majesty should be the one on the chair, not Two-Eyes. We both want to stop this now, but we cannot. We must wait for Two-Eyes to make his next move before we act. Will he follow the path Tracker told me about, the way others have done this before? Or will he be the master predator, sinking his teeth in the neck, not caring about days now gone?

The crowd quiets, and Fang steps forward. Unrolling a scroll, he calls, "This man, Elroy Aven, former king of Ahavel, has been found guilty of treason and other unlawful activity, as listed here."

So Two-Eyes has chosen the way of days past. My hands tighten on my rod. That means my time will come soon. Very soon. What if I cannot do this? Tracker will speak the words, but Two-Eyes will laugh, seeing only a weak beast. I need him to see me as more, stronger, more dangerous—the greatest prey he has ever hunted. My mouth must make the words I hear in my head.

"Because of these things, Elroy Aven has been found worthy of immediate death. Will anyone speak on the behalf of this prisoner? Let him do so now."

High above, a whirling bird caws. It is the only sound. The crowd does not whisper even a breath.

"Again I ask: Will anyone speak on behalf of this prisoner?" calls Fang.

It is time. Tracker steps forward to answer for me, but I must do this myself. Pushing past him, I straighten my shoulders and let the cloak slide from me.

"I will."

CHAPTER 32

❧

A King's Ransom

Two simple words. That is all that leaves my mouth. Yet long after I speak them, they hang in the air.

Behind me, murmurs rustle through the crowd like wind in the trees. I have challenged the power of the ruling pack. In front of me, swordsmen look at each other and Two-Eyes grips the arms of the chair, none making a move because no one knows what move to make; attack has come in a way they did not expect. Beside me, Tracker simply stares at me, one of the few who understands what has really happened: I have claimed the words of men as mine. My silence is over.

My rod strikes the stone with a loud clack, and I walk forward. Rules say I can now speak without harm before the throne for Majesty, but rules don't always go the right way when Two-Eyes is around.

The line of swordsmen between Two-Eyes and me shifts, and Tracker presses close beside me. His hand grips his sword handle hard. Two-Eyes waves to let us through.

I step into the open space around the platform, my insides beating to be let out. If anything goes wrong now . . . My gaze slips to Majesty, though I do not want it to. His face is damp and the love in his eyes—it is more than I can bear. I dip my face away from him, even as I want to soak in what I thought I would never see again.

Two-Eyes leans forward, nose flaring. Much like the first day we met, we lock stares, battling for the leader's position. His eyes narrow. He knows there is more here, that we don't come to only speak for Majesty. I lift my chin; he notices the ridges across my cheek. "So the beast has returned to its master like a pig to its mud pit." He sits back, a smile slinking across his face. "What is it you seek today? A bone perhaps?"

My teeth clench. No flinching. No looking away.

Growling, Tracker steps forward, partly pulling out his sword. "Speak to the princess with respect, you . . ."

I put out my hand to stop him. Never provoke a predator. Rage makes him strike sooner, and Two-Eyes will be angry enough before long.

At my stopping of Tracker, Two-Eyes widens his grin; he thinks we cower before him. "And you brought your oh-so-faithful protector with you today. How practical. So what is the oddity going for on the market today, Master Mason?"

Tracker mutters something I cannot hear and steps in front of me, as if he can take the sting of words for me—words meant to hurt him as much as me. And they did sting him. His whole body ripples with anger. He wants to attack now.

I lay a hand on his arm. Two-Eyes is baiting him. Tracker takes a deep breath, rolls his shoulders back, and lifts his head. "Princess Sarah, daughter of His Majesty King Elroy, has come to offer you a wager for His Majesty's life."

"A wager?" Two-Eyes curls his lip in a sneer. "With this creature, this beast? That is a jest worthy of a royal jester. Why, what could this dressed-up animal possibly have that I should even consider stooping to such a bargain?"

Tracker lifts up the parchment I took from Two-Eyes. "She wishes to wager this document—"

Two-Eyes leans forward, his whole face flattening. "How did you come by that?"

"—and her life against the life of His Majesty, King Elroy."

"Is that all? You might as well ask for the whole kingdom," he growls.

Tracker looks at me. I shrug. Why not? We have nothing left to lose.

"It would be only reasonable that the crown be restored to His Majesty along with his life."

Two-Eyes glances over our heads. "And what if I refuse? For you've given me very little reason not to. Shall you attack me with your—what is it? One puny sword?" He raises one finger. "Unless the beast hides something more than claws and teeth behind that ridiculous garment."

I frown, letting my eyes close. Wrong. All wrong. The words are too many. Like he hides something from us. My ears catch a thin, stretching sound.

My eyes open again, and I force my tongue into the strange twistings needed for the words of men. "If we . . . no danger, why . . . ar—arrows?"

"Arrows?" Yanking out his sword, Tracker whirls around.

A murmur arises in the crowd. "Did she say arrows? From where? Does anyone see—there!"

I keep my face to Two-Eyes. Never turn your back to the master of a pack. A single arrow shoots way over our heads, burying itself in the wood a pace to the right of Two-Eyes. He glares at those beyond me.

The cries quiet behind me. The bowmen are stopped. Whether by the few who still follow Majesty or by some sign from Two-Eyes, I do not know. But the bowmen will not be shooting again soon. The crowd doesn't want arrows flying over them any more than I want them aimed at me, and a pack stirred by fear to attack is hard to stop.

Tracker, rock-faced, backs up to my side. "Well done, Princess," he whispers. He slides his sword away. "Despite this latest act of treachery in a long line of treacheries, the princess still offers the wager. The winner shall take all."

"And just out of curiosity—I still see no reason to even consider this foolish offer—what kind of wager is it that you're proposing, Beast?" Slumped in his chair, he spits the last word at me. Like I could ever forget what I have been all my life.

But a smile twists my mouth. If we made it this far, we might reach the end. "A hunt."

Two-Eyes remains slumped, but his head lifts. He has caught the smell of prey. "A hunt? And what shall we be hunting? Beasts?"

He jabs that last word at me, not knowing how true his aim is. "No. Me."

Another murmur, like a rush of water, passes through the crowd. Off to the side, Majesty bows his head, as if he knew this would come but does not like it.

Two-Eyes rises. "Maybe this would be best discussed inside. Shall we adjourn to a nearby house?"

He took the bait. I dip my head to hide my growing smile and wave for him to lead. He strides off the platform and marches inside a house, followed by four of his men, including Fang.

Tracker bends his head to my ear. "Do you wish me to carry you, Princess?"

I shake my head. Too many eyes watch here. If Tracker carried me now, I would show a weakness I must hide as long as I can. My hand grips the rod and I walk toward the house Two-Eyes went into. Tracker stays at my elbow, steadying me at every wobble. At the door, I stop. There is not much light here, and I squint to make out the dark shapes.

The room is simple and open. A bed. A fire pit. A few pots and plants hanging from above. And in the middle Two-Eyes already sits at the wood table, Fang behind him. His fingers are pressed together, and over these he watches my every move. The prey has surprised him. But beast or not, I am still below him.

"You offer me a wager, yet little incentive to accept it. A document? I could have it taken from you with little trouble."

One of his men steps nearer, sword raised.

"And your life? Even if it meant anything to me, you—and this poor excuse for protector—already rest in my palm. All I have to do is say two little words."

A second man on our other side raises his sword.

I lift my head, even as a rock sinks my insides. "You won't." At least, that's what I am planning on.

"And what makes you so certain?"

Besides that we are still talking at all? Tracker rests a hand on my shoulder. "Princess Sarah knows that you delight in the hunt and would relish another opportunity to prove once and for all your untouchable superiority. After all, you boast that nothing ever escapes you. Yet the princess has again and again. But if you could catch her in a fair hunt, rumors would be silenced and your throne would be assured for the rest of your days."

"For the smallest crack can crumble an entire castle—is that it?" Two-Eyes half closes his eyes, as if bored. Yet a tension coils around his body; he is anything but bored. "And what, may I ask, are the parameters of this said hunt?"

I frown. Parame—what?

Tracker leans down to whisper. "He's asking what the rules are."

Oh. Leave it to Two-Eyes to make the simple hard. "You ch-choose." Those are danger words that can make me much trouble. But what else can I say? I did not think of that before.

A smile slithers across his face. "We are two days from Melek. Put Elroy on the throne in those two days."

"Wh-what?"

"We'll start tomorrow, at sunset on Eagle Hill, just outside of town here. I'll send Elroy to the town keeper's home at Calby. You must take him from there north to Melek and place him on the throne there before the sunset of the second day. If you do, he may keep his life, the kingdom, the throne. But if not . . ." He shrugs.

Why did I let him choose? Too late now. I lift my face to Tracker. Is there anything we can do?

He steps up. "You must hunt the princess without the aid of dogs, and you must be the one to take her."

"I wouldn't have it any other way. And like any good prey, she cannot use horses, wagons, or weapons of any kind—only what nature has given her."

"Even animals have rocks and holes in the ground. Dogs learn how to steal from a house. If she can find it or take it, she should be allowed to use it."

Two-Eyes could not argue that. "And I suppose I'm to let Elroy walk free when it shows up at the door?"

"Of course."

"I cannot be everywhere at once. My men must be allowed to report to me."

"Report, yes. Capture or restrain, no."

More words are batted back and forth, Two-Eyes and Tracker fighting over the same bone. It makes my head hurt. He can't do that. I can do this—if I do it in one way.

Finally their words stop. But they did not talk about one thing. "I go be—fore you."

Tracker nods. "Yes, she's right. She must be allowed to start at least two hours ahead of you."

"Forget it," growls Two-Eyes. "It can have five minutes."

"One hour."

"Fifteen minutes."

"A half hour."

Two-Eyes press his fingers together, then nods. "A half hour." He rises. "And that finishes negotiations, don't you think?"

I step into his way. "Write."

My sound is more like the growls I have always made than the words of men, and Two-Eyes bats it away like a buzzing bug. "A useless formality, I assure you."

I don't move.

Two-Eyes sighs. "Fine." Sitting again, he calls for ink and parchment. After putting down many scribbles, he offers it to me.

It is nothing to me but black worms wiggling across smooth ground. But I look at them until some time has passed and give it to Tracker. He will make sure Two-Eyes does not change words from mouth to page. He nods. "It appears to be in order. Anything else you wish to add, Princess?"

I start to shake my head and then stop. Rules do not bind Two-Eyes. He takes the path that loses him nothing. I tug Tracker down to whisper in his ear. "If he does not, I win."

Tracker straightens up. "Princess Sarah asks that if anyone violates these terms, the wager will immediately be forfeited to the other side."

"Simple enough." Two-Eyes adds those words and signs his name at the bottom. He then offers me the pen.

I curl my fingers around it. Back at the camp, Tabby insisted on teaching me my "name," and we practiced many times with a stick and dirt to form the right-twisting worms. But my hands are made for fighting, not writing. Biting my lip, I slowly form

Princess Sarah

Then, like Tabby told me, I add a swirl under it so Two-Eyes cannot add anything to it.

Next to his name, mine looks like a twisted tree, with splotches of ink and some parts too big and others too small. Not at all like the one Tabby did. But it's there.

My name written by my hand.

Two-Eyes peers at it, nods, and leaves with his men. I follow with Tracker at my side.

Outside, Majesty is being prodded back into the wagon. My insides clench. What if Two-Eyes kills him despite the wager? No, he will wait. Majesty must be alive at Calby or I'll win the wager—and the kingdom.

I turn away from the platform and walk back the way we came. The crowd opens a path for me, but I am tired. Turning into an empty road, I lurch forward, nearly falling.

Tracker carries me the rest of the way.

CHAPTER 33

THE HUNT

The day's fight has almost ended. Darkness gathers at my back. Black trees spear the sky before me, spilling redness across the edge like blood from a gash. Above, purple-green bruises cluster together. The light is dying and nothing can stop it. Otherwise I would.

But I cannot, and each breath brings me nearer to a run like no other. My hands dig into the stone beneath me. In days before, the hunt was for me and me only. But now a whole pack will live or die because of me. Because of a Beast.

To my right, Two-Eyes leads a tall horse. A strong, powerful animal to carry a strong and very powerful master. My insides bounce from front to back, from side to side, like a trapped bird. My few minutes will not be long enough; he will follow too soon on an animal faster than I. I should have asked him to be on foot too. There can be no going back now. I have what I have, and what I don't, I don't.

Many of his pack swarm around him, and he gathers from them his whip, sword, knife, bow, and arrows. A net and rope coil are tied to the horse. Two-Eyes acts as if I seek to change the rules on him. But with only Tracker and Gwen at my side, what could I be planning? My brown he-cub clothing could not hide even a knife from him. No, if someone has planned anything, it is Two-Eyes.

Feet shuffle behind me and whispers thicken the wind. A crowd has come to watch me leave, and the closer the time comes, the bigger the crowd grows. A few give me half smiles. Many carry stone scowls like Two-Eyes and his pack. But most watch because it is something to watch, and they will follow whoever wins. Spectators, Tracker called them.

Tracker crouches beside me. He does not look at me but keeps his face to the forest. A strong man who could help me so much, one I must soon leave behind. "Ready, Princess?"

Can anyone be ready for this? Yet everything I have done, all the fights I fought with the Others, the life I lived under Master, even the training the Keeper made me do—these have given me what I need. If someone had prepared me specifically for this, that training would be no different than what I have done. I nod. I am as ready as anyone can be.

"Remember. You can trust His Majesty. His ways may be mysterious, but they'll always be true." Tracker backs up to Gwen's side. "I'll be waiting at Melek."

My hands press flat against the rock still warm from day's light, and I lean forward. Soon the horn will sound. Soon I will run.

The black trees eat the last of the light's ball. A man blows a loud blast. I spring forward. Stones skitter under me and bounce down the hill ahead of me. I half run, half slide behind them, keeping as near as I can without plunging nose first to the bottom.

Two-Eyes laughs, the sound of it bellowing behind me. "Run, Beast, run! Enjoy the lead. It will not be yours for long."

His words latch onto me like burrs to fur. I shake my head to loosen them and race past the fields of tall grass. Run. Get to the forest. Hide. Wait for him to pass. Out here I am in his territory. Among the trees I'll be in mine. As I reach the edge of the forest, I glance back. Two-Eyes rides the horse in circles. It won't be long before the hunting starts.

Already in more shadow than light, I charge down the road. Among the trees, it narrows to two packed dips in the dirt with much grass between. Far away, a bird calls its night greeting, "Whip-o-will, whip-o-will," while a low buzz drones beneath it. Darkness deepens. I turn from the road to the trees, leaves slapping my face. A light would help, and yet it is good I don't have one. Two-Eyes would come to it like a moth to fire.

A mouse scurries across my path. A moment later, a dark shadow-breeze whooshes above my head, followed by a small squeak: a predator bird has caught the mouse. I shudder. If Two-Eyes sneaks up on me like that, the mouse and I will be the same—dead. Time to climb. Finding a tree tipped over in the storms, I crawl and swing up into the branches and jump from tree to tree, only a few strides from the road.

The light fades from stone gray to a blackness that makes the sky and leaves look the same. I test every step. A fall could hurt me so I cannot run, but I must stay up as long as I can. I creep forward, so slow now.

Clip-clop. Clip-clop. A horse—Two-Eyes will be here soon.

Half smiling, I hunker down on a limb near the tree trunk. Two-Eyes will have to be quieter than that if he wants to catch me. And he thought the horse would help him because it can run faster than me. He did not think of the noise. Maybe it is good I did not ask that he walk on his own feet.

A skulking shadow pulls away from the rest. Leading the horse, Two-Eyes wanders from edge to edge. He peers under every bush and around every tree within two paces of the road. But his head is always tipped down. I hold myself very still, keeping even my breath in. If he does not know I can walk among the branches, he can stay in darkness a little longer.

Finally he moves on, out of sight and hearing. I push away from the trunk and creep again along the branches. A yawn stretches my mouth. My body says it's sleeping time. But I cannot stop. Not yet.

The hunt has only begun.

Where is Calby? Why haven't I reached it yet? I should have been at the town by now. Needed to be there by now. Even if Majesty is strong, able to run long and fast, it will take us more than a day to walk from Calby to Melek. And I must get him out of the town and into the castle, both of which could eat more time than I have.

I push myself to the fastest lope my body will give. Plant hands, swing leg forward. Plant hands, swing forward. I shouldn't have walked among the branches so long. I should have returned to the ground sooner. I should have done so many things differently.

My hand brushes over my face, shooing away the words. My fingers come away wet. My whole face is damp. When the light returned, it returned hot and strong. My thick tongue licks my lips. I long for water, a cool breeze, time to rest. But the day is nearly half gone, the air stands so still that not a leaf twitches, and the only water around drips down my face and back.

I lower my head and push on. One day—two at the most— is all I have to do. I can live with anything for that long. Then Majesty will sit on his throne, and Two-Eyes will have to leave. He must. The pack belongs with Majesty. Tabby belongs at her home. With or without me.

The trees become farther apart and the path widens. Almost there. I must be. My swings grow longer, and soon a walled town on a hill peeks between the trees. Calby, at last.

Now to find Majesty and get us out of here.

A cloud of dust rises between the town and me. I squint against the glaring light. A rider, alone. I can't see more than that, but I know. It's Two-Eyes. He knows I've not reached the town and is coming back to search the woods for me. I dive through the bushes and search for a tree to climb. All the branches hang above my head, beyond my reach.

Leaves shuffle behind me. Two-Eyes steps off the road. He must have spotted me.

I squirm along an old fallen tree, under a thin blanket of vines. It covers me, but will it be enough? I hold my air inside, ready to spring if his gaze catches me. Not that I can outrun an arrow.

Two-Eyes steps into the open area I left. "I know you're here, Beast. I saw you come this way." He turns in a slow circle, pulling out an arrow. "You might as well give yourself to me now."

My hands curl tightly. Should I run while his back is turned?

"Why do you make this so difficult on yourself? You'll never win. You can't. You have too far to go. Even if you leave for Melek now, you won't get there in time."

He's right. It can't be done by anyone. Why should I even keep going?

"Come on out, and I promise I'll let you live."

No! My eyes snap shut. If he will let me live, it would be only to live a life worse than dying. Giving into him cannot happen. Not now. Not ever.

Leaves rustle beyond me. Two-Eyes swings around, raising his bow. When the leaves rustle again, he releases an arrow.

A growl rumbles into a roar, and a brown bear charges into the clearing.

Two-Eyes spews words that Majesty would never want me to say and yanks out his sword. I turn my face away, unable to watch the attack. The roars and howls are bad enough; they wrench shivers through my back. But after a few minutes, it's over. Quiet rests on the forest again except for some heavy breathing. Human breathing. Two-Eyes still stands, master over the bear.

My insides lurch at the brown fur stained red. That could have been me. Could still be me.

Grumbling, Two-Eyes wipes off his blade. "Stupid animal. Should have known it wouldn't be that easy. That beast isn't even halfway here yet, I wager. Probably wandering lost in the forest." His muttering fades as he stomps back the way he came. A slap of reins, and horse hooves pound away deeper into the woods.

That's it? He went away just like that? Or is this a trap to lure me into the open? I lie still, waiting. Birds call to each other. Still not a whisper of air from Two-Eyes. Maybe he did leave. If so, what am I doing still here?

Wiggling forward, I poke my head out. Nothing changes. I am alone. I bound forward and soon the trees are behind, and Calby sits on a hill before me. Calby is not large as far as towns go. Big enough to have a wall, it does not have so many houses that every tree is squeezed out. Rather, their leafy green heads bob and sway among well-kept thatched roofs. The man-pack that lives here lives well.

I circle around to the town's far side. A wall means there are only two ways in, a gate at each end. Both will be watched. But the men think they will see me go in the first gate, not the second.

Two men are by the far gate. They both wear the red and black of Two-Eyes, but they watch the wood blocks they throw more than those who go in their gate. Good. If I can pass by without their knowing who I am, they cannot stop me or send someone after Two-Eyes.

I sneak back along the road where they will not see me, find a strong stick, and walk back toward Calby on two feet. This is slower than when I walk with both hands and feet, but it will help hide me. Then he will not know where to look for me, and I can run faster and straighter. Or so I tell myself. After all, he cannot be everywhere at the same time . . . right?

A wagon rumbles from behind me. Two-Eyes has his men looking for a single person. If I can ride, I might slip by without even a question. I wave my hand at the driver.

He pulls to a stop, eyes widening. "Princess Sarah?"

My mouth drops open, all words gone. I cannot even force out a stutter.

"I knew it!" The man slaps his knee with his cap. "You are her! I thought so, as I came up from behind. Wait until the missus hears this one. She'll be thinking I'm telling stories. That or I've been at a bottle too long." He grins at me. "So what can I do to be helping you, Princess?"

"A r-ride." My tongue trips over the words I push out.

"On my wagon? You want to ride with *me*? Oh, if only the missus could see this! Maybe she'd think twice before giving Old Thaddeus one of her tongue lashings—and those lashings can be getting mighty strong, I tell you. But here I ramble on, like the old man I am. Please, climb aboard, Princess! Anything I can do to help." He offers me a big, grimy hand and pulls me up onto the seat next to him.

I dip my head, not sure how to act around this man. "How— how you . . ." Stupid words. They just won't come out right.

"Know who you were? That was easy enough. I'd heard of the wager—I 'spect most everyone has by now. That was mighty brave of you, if you don't mind my saying, stepping in front of that double-faced imposter—or should I say doubled-eyed?" He chuckles. "So anyway, when I see you standing there, a girl in boy's clothes, I says to myself, 'Thaddeus old boy, what do you make of that?' And I says, 'I'm a-betting that be the Princess Sarah everybody has been talking about.' It just figured." He clucked at the ox and the wagon jerked forward.

"Oh." This is not good. If he knew me so easily, how will I ever get past the men at the gate?

"Speaking of which, you might want to get that braid of yours out of sight, if you don't mind taking advice from a foolish old man. At least, that's what told me about you."

I fingered my hair. "H-how?"

He pulls off his hat and offers it to me.

I shrink back. "I . . . I can't."

"It's not much, and a princess like yourself deserves better, but . . ." He shrugs.

I finger the edge. All this help was far more than I deserved. "Thank you." I take it and stuff my hair up under it.

"Just doing my part. Me and a lot of other people would be more than happy to see King Elroy back on his throne." He looks at me sideways and shakes his head. "The Princess Sarah, riding in my wagon. Wait until I tell the missus."

We near the gate, and my fingers curl around the stick on my lap. Will they stop us? What if they know me? Will the driver get into trouble? Maybe I shouldn't have done this.

We slow, but the swordsman is shaking those wood blocks in his hand, and he waves us on without lifting his head. "Move along."

I'm in!

We pull onto a side street, away from the crowd, and I hop down. I cannot let this man get into trouble because of me, and every step now leads to more danger. I pull off the cap, but I cannot make myself hand it to him. "May I . . . ?" I hold it tight. Will he understand what I am asking?

"Of course, of course, you can keep it! My cap, worn by a princess. The missus will never believe it when I tell her." He grins as if I had given *him* the kingdom. But maybe in a way I have.

I take a deep breath. I know what I want to say to him, but can I get it all out? "Tell your . . . missus I would not . . . be this far . . . without you." The words are tree-trunk stiff, but I make it. I get them all out. Smiling, I bow to him and then turn away, leaving him gaping after me. Time to find Majesty.

"A princess, a real flesh-and-blood princess. Wait until I tell the missus!"

CHAPTER 34

MAJESTY

Walk in, ask for Majesty, walk out. A simple thing, easy enough that even a beast can do it without trouble. At least, that's what the rules say.

Rules don't matter to Two-Eyes.

I slouch against a wall and tug the cap down farther on my head. Across the street stands the town keeper's house. At two levels, it is the tallest house in Calby and one of the biggest. A small pack of men could hide inside.

A man steps out. Another enters. Each time the open door frames darkness, telling me nothing about how many hide within. I cannot know what is inside until I go in, but I cannot go in until I know what is inside. Two-Eyes is too much of a predator. He knows lures and snares, those things not for killing but holding prey until the hunter arrives. This could be a trap with Majesty as bait.

Another man leaves.

I clench my teeth, a growl rumbling in my throat. This is not bringing me to Majesty, and the longer I wait, the closer Two-Eyes comes to returning. Why can't the whole pack just leave the house so I can go in the back door and get Majesty?

Wait. If I can draw out the pack, I would know what is inside. What would bring a whole pack outside? Another pack attacking would, but I am one. I have no pack to help me. A dog with matted fur ambles by and sniffs in my direction. Or do I? I push away from the wall and hobble back toward the square I'd passed earlier. Like the one I worked with Tracker, many people fill it. People buying. People selling. People looking, people passing through. And like where I worked with Tracker, many things are being sold, animals among them. Birds in cages. Larger four-footed animals in pens. Horses tied along the side.

I walk from cage to pen, pen to cage. The birds must wait. But the others . . . I pull the metal pegs holding the pen doors closed. One I pocket, one I drop in a pot, and a third slides well under a pile of blankets. The horses' reins loosen easily too. They can run when they want to. Now I must make them want to.

Turning from the square, I head toward the edge of Calby. An empty, low-roofed house sits near the town's wall but within hearing of the square. The streets nearest me are empty. Time to find out if I learned anything from Master's dogs. I climb on the low roof, suck in much air, and release a screeching howl.

Calby snaps awake, listening, waiting. A nearby horse snorts and sidesteps, shaking its head.

I howl, yip twice, and howl long again. A howl answers me and a second calls to the first. It's working. It sounds like a pack gathers for an attack. One more cry, and I drop back to the ground.

The nearby horse rears and bolts. From the shadows, a dog bursts forth and races after it. Mates scream, cubs wail, and masters shout, adding to the growing noise. By the time I reach the square, the buying and selling is no longer being done. Masters fight rearing horses. He-cubs chase pigs and sheep. Mates call for their cubs. People run here and there and everywhere. No one sees me. I hobble through, opening the last cages. The birds fly up and away with squawks and a flutter of wings. Once on the square's far side, I slip into the shadows and howl again, though not as loud as before.

A horse screams. So does a mate. "They're getting closer."

"It came from there."

"No, over there."

"Are you sure it's just one?" People point in different directions.

Good. If this noise does not bring out Two-Eyes's pack, nothing will.

Three men, one with a rod, one with a short whip, and one with a knife, run toward me. "It's not here."

"Are you sure it was this way?"

"I'm not sure of anything." The man with the knife spots me. "Hey you, boy, did you see that dog—"

"That didn't sound like no dog I've ever heard," growls the rod man.

Knife-Man scowls at him. "The dog that was making all that racket?"

Dog? I force my mouth flat as I shake my head. "But th-there . . ." I point to where I stood only moments before.

"I told you it was this way. Come on. It can't have gone too far." Knife-Man rushes by me, the two others close behind.

The smile I had hidden now creeps out, and I weave between buildings, back toward the town keeper's house. When I come to it, many men are outside. Maybe I will make it in and out unseen. I circle around to the back door. No one lingers in the kitchen.

Dropping to all fours, I lay my stick next to the door. There is no need for it here. Inside I must go fast, and if anyone catches me, they will know who I am, whether standing on two feet or walking on four.

I poke around the kitchen and cellar. I do not find Majesty, although some bread finds its way into my mouth and pockets. The front room is empty too, except for two men in red and black. They stand in the doorway, crowds rushing outside. Majesty must be upstairs.

One of the swordsmen leans out farther into the street. "Hey, you. What is going on down there? What is all the racket about?"

If I want to climb to the floor above, now is the time. I sprint along the room's edges toward the stairs.

"Let me go!" The older he-cub thrashes against the swordsman. "I don't know nothing, nothing except there's something out there and it's coming this way. But ghost, devil, or monster who can say?"

Ghosts, devils, and monsters? Is that what they say I stirred up? Smiling, I climb the stairs and creep down the hall. There are two rooms. The first has a snoring man in a bed—how can he sleep through all that noise?—but no Majesty. I creep to the second door and nudge it open.

Hot air rolls into my face, dust and sweat thick on it. There is no breeze and little light, every window closed tight against the outside. This room has been made a cage. Majesty must be here.

I push the door open wider. It creaks. A man at the table looks up. "You." He half rises, grabbing his helmet off the table. "How did you get by everyone downstairs?"

Uh-oh. I slink back a step, but before I can do more, a black shadow rises up behind him. Crack! Wood splinters; the man slumps to the floor.

What was that?

Tossing broken wood away, the shadow man steps over the body and drops to his knees. "Sarah."

Majesty. In one bound I'm in his arms, nearly knocking him over backward.

"Careful there. Try not to restrain yourself so much." Majesty chuckles and his chin drops against my head. "You started quite a howling ruckus out there."

How did he know—it doesn't matter. I'm here. In his arms. My head rests against his chest and I can hear the steady thump-thump inside. Protected, loved, but not safe yet. We still have to leave Calby and get to Melek. And the first day will be gone too soon. I wiggle away from him. We have to get out. Now. I pace the room, looking for ways out and cocking my head to catch any steps coming our way. I stop by the door. All seems quiet below. But for how much longer? We made enough noise up here.

"What is wrong, Sarah?"

"Go. Now."

Majesty does not spring up. "You're talking, really talking." He leans back with a broad grin. "Do you know how long I've waited for you to do that?"

I growl. Doesn't he get it? We need to leave. Now. We can't let the men find us together up here.

"Don't worry. I know these types of men." He rises, unlatches the boards covering the window, and pushes them open, filling the room with light. "They'll be enthralled with all that chaos you stirred up for a little longer." He knots a thin blanket around a splintered piece of wood. Throwing the blanket out the window, he wedges the wood against the wall. "Not the strongest, but it'll hold for as long as we need." He straps on the sword from the fallen man and boosts me onto his back.

Steps thump up the stairs.

"Ready?"

My insides squirm. The ground is far away enough that, if we fell, I might not walk for many days. I nod anyway. Two-Eyes and his men will do worse if they catch us.

Majesty crawls out the window and climbs down the wall, holding onto the thin blanket. He runs out of blanket before wall. "Hold on."

I cling to him tightly. He drops the rest of the way to the ground. We land hard but safely. I hop off his back and grab my stick by the back door, stuffing it under my shirt across my back. Majesty dusts off his pants. "That wasn't so bad."

Before I can say anything or even shake my head, yelling bursts out above us. "He's gone!"

We look at each other.

"It's time to go, wouldn't you say?"

What would make him think that? I bound down the street on my hands and feet, darting from shadow to shadow, heading toward the gate I did not come in. Majesty limps behind, and when we stop in the crowd near the gate, he rubs his leg. "I think that last drop reminded my knee too much of that fall from the cliff."

I frown. We don't need that. Planting the end of my rod in

the dirt, I pull myself onto my feet. We cannot do anything about it now. I lead the way to the gate, keeping my head down. We are so close to getting out.

The swordsman here plays with no wood blocks, and his eyes narrow as I try to join the back of another group readying to leave. Majesty steps up behind me, resting a hand on my shoulder.

The swordsman spins around. "Martin! Hart! He's out. The prisoner has escaped! And that beast-child is with him. You. Detain them. You, get King Avery."

The man Hart runs for a horse.

A horse? Majesty looks at me. My insides crunch. I never wanted to sit on one, but horses do run faster. I nod to Majesty. Let's take it.

I hop onto his back, and he charges down the street. People scatter before us. Majesty lengthens his stride and gains speed. Hart still reaches the horse first. He grabs the reins and swings up. No. He can't have it. I let go of Majesty's neck, and with both hands I slam my stick into his middle.

Hart, his leg not yet over the horse's back, tips backwards. He grabs at my stick. I let go. He crashes to the ground.

"Good job." Majesty vaults onto the horse with me still on his back. "Now let's get out of here." He slaps the reins, and the animal bolts forward.

I squeeze my eyes shut. It's one thing to walk on firm branches above the ground. But to sit on an animal that could do anything . . . I cling to Majesty's neck.

"Breathing is a favorite activity of mine, if you don't mind, Sarah."

My eyes pop open, and Majesty laughs. Laughs! As if he likes this. I growl but slide my arms around his chest.

People yell and shake fists at us as they scramble out of our way. Three men in red and black step into the gate, swords out. "In the name of King Avery, we command you to stop!"

Majesty only leans forward and urges the horse on.

"Stop!" But even as the soldier commands, his sword wavers;

he knows Majesty will not stop. He and the other two men dive from in front of us. We're out . . . and going the wrong way.

I yank on Majesty's sleeve and point behind us.

"Don't worry, Sarah. I haven't forgotten about the wager." Majesty pulls the horse around. "Onward to Melek!"

CHAPTER 35

THE GORGE

Hills cluster together, and soon they swallow Calby so it can be seen no more. Yet no dust rises from the road behind us; no shouts or pounding steps pursue us. All is still except for the wind rustling the hill grasses on both sides of us. Still I watch and listen. A predator unseen does not make him less dangerous. Two-Eyes has not given up the hunt. His pack will tell him what we did, and he will come. But will he chase us from behind or circle around and cut in front of us? A horse can go only a few ways to Melek. We must watch our path ahead as well as behind.

Finally, when no one from Calby chases us, Majesty allows our horse to slow. Then he lifts me over to sit in front of him, his strong arms wrapping around me. I need to watch for Two-Eyes. I need to listen for his pack. I . . . I lean back against Majesty, Two-Eyes seeming far away. Can I stay here, at this moment, for always and always? The time past hurts so much. The wager and the threat at Melek darken the time ahead. But here, everything is . . . right.

Majesty cocks his head to see my face. "Comfortable?"

I smile and nod.

We ride on, passing through a small town and following a

forest's edge. I don't say any words. Majesty doesn't either. There is no need to.

As shadows lengthen across the road, we meet a small stream. "Easy does it." Majesty pulls on the reins and the horse halts. "We're all due for a break, don't you think?" He lifts me down to the ground and then peers up at the sky. "We'll have to stop for the night soon, but thanks to this one"—he pats the horse on the neck—"that won't be a problem."

We can't stay long, so I bound up and down the road to stretch my legs. Ah. Much better. Walking from Calby would have made me hurt much, so it is good we rode. But most days I do not sit that long without walking. My legs wanted this break very much.

Legs now happy, I circle back to the stream and crouch at the edge to drink. The water cools my mouth and laps against my hot cheek, as if asking me to jump in.

Why not? Stuffing the cap into my pocket, I dunk my whole head into the water. Oh cold, so very cold! But in a good way. I slowly let out my air and come back up only when I have no more.

The water runs down my neck and back, sweeping the heat away. My body loosens in a sigh. Just what I needed. I shake my head a couple of times, flinging the extra water from my hair. Behind me, Majesty coughs to hide laughter. "Oh Sarah, what will I do with you?"

What did I do now? Resting on my good leg, I eye him. Should I be happy I made him laugh? Or should I duck my head for whatever I did that made him laugh?

Majesty grabs the reins of the horse. "If we are to reach Melek tomorrow, we probably should keep going."

My shoulders hunch. The wager. For a few breaths, I'd forgotten. If only it was already past.

Majesty leans down and nudges my face up. "Don't worry, Sarah. I promised to protect you, and that's what I'm going to do."

Leaves rustle in the night.

Go away. I shift in my sleep and curl into a tighter ball. So tired, so very tired. I don't want to wake up, don't want to check out noises that are nothing. It's late, and I just found a nice spot among the roots and rocks.

Whispers—the wind?—drift past my ear. I roll over, grasping at the sleep slipping away. It's time to rest after being awake a night and a day and part of another night. All of me aches: my legs hurt from running, my hands from climbing, and my back from riding so long into the darkness. *Please let me sleep.*

Something changes in the air. My eyes pop open, my body tight and a breath caught inside me.

A branch scrapes another in the breeze. Majesty breathes deeply near me. A night bird calls, "Who? Who-who!" All things that I should hear. So why do I feel ready to run? Two-Eyes has not found me, and we have time to sleep—by riding we will reach the castle by midday. I yawn and close my eyes.

An extra rustle, more than the wind makes, yanks me back. I roll onto all fours and edge around a tree. Something, someone, is out there. A wild animal? The wind shifts and I sniff the air. Smoke, as from a fire now gone. But wild animals don't make smoke or fires. Something more hunts us.

With two silent bounds, I'm at Majesty's side and shaking his shoulder. He moans and rolls toward me. "What . . . ?" He sees me and knows. Reaching for his sword, he stands. He looks at the horse. No, it cannot help us now. We need to go where only feet can walk. He rubs its nose and lets it go. I swing forward deeper into the forest, away from the smell and noise. Go. Faster. But Majesty limps already. How long do we have before the predator catches up to us?

A snarling yell tells me what I want to know. "They're gone!"

Two-Eyes. I shiver.

"They're close; the ground's still warm. Spread out and find them *now.*"

I bolt, zigzagging between trees, under branches, over fallen logs, and around boulders. Majesty stumbles after me. I wince at the noise he makes. Twice I circle around to let him catch up. Each circle also lets the predators come close behind. I can hear their baying in the night.

I jump off a ledge and wait for Majesty. Darkness crouches under the rock behind thick vines. A hiding place, one I would have never seen if I hadn't had to wait on Majesty. I scramble underneath.

Majesty jumps down and stops. I growl softly from my hiding place. He whirls around, nods, and joins me in the deep darkness under the stone. Twigs snap above; Two-Eyes and his men are almost on us. Majesty kneels beside me and wraps an arm around my shoulders. Will this be enough to hide us? Too late to change directions now. Men leap off the ledge, boots thudding into the dirt at a run. Two, three, seven, ten sprint away, down the hill, rock crunching against rock underfoot, the strong stride of Two-Eyes among them.

Then stillness. We've eluded them for now. Majesty squeezes my shoulder. "Well done, Sarah."

His words barely reach me. Danger is not gone yet, time is short, and we are back on foot. I head deeper into the forest.

We have a long walk ahead of us.

I have lived in the forest most of my days. I have hunted with Master's dogs among the trees, slept among their roots, and hidden myself in their shadow when Master was angry. When food was little, Master would let me roam the woods to hunt for my own food, sometimes for many days. I can find a path through them, even in woods I've not been to, better than most man-packs can find their way through a town they know. But as the light grows strong, chasing the night's shadows away, I stand on a flat stone, the trees around me hiding the right path. I do not know where I am or which way to go.

Majesty sits on the stone beside me and rests a hand on my back. "Are you feeling well, Sarah?"

I nod but cannot look him in the eye. I need food and water and rest. Much rest. All of me, inside and out, is weary. My body tires from too much running and not enough sleeping. My head tires from trying to know how to go around Two-Eyes. Even my deepest insides are tired from clinging to the thought that Majesty will once more be seen as master and I will someday be safe from Two-Eyes.

"We probably should keep moving." Majesty rises.

I know, I know! But I cannot choose the wrong path. We must be at Melek, inside the castle, before this day's light goes away.

"Sarah?"

I dip my head, my face hot. "I do not know . . . the way."

"Is that all that's bothering you?"

All? It is everything! We have to get to the castle. Soon.

"Sarah." Majesty kneels before me and, with a finger under my chin, raises my face to him. He is smiling. "I know where we are. I know the way."

He knows? This whole time he knew where to go?

His eyes glint with laughter held inside him at my silent question. "You didn't ask."

Oh. I dip my head again. *You can trust His Majesty.* How could I have forgotten Tracker's words so soon? "Would you . . ." I nod at the trees.

"It would be my pleasure." He strides forward toward the way the light always comes from.

I jump off the rock and follow close at his side.

Two-Eyes has not broken any rules, but he gets as close to the edges as he can.

Perched on a hilltop, I scowl at the land below. We are close, so very close, almost within sight of the castle. But what do we find? Two-Eyes, a small pack of men with bows and swords pacing around him, and no way to go around without taking a long time.

He planned it that way too. I didn't see that before, but I do now. All those men we went around last night weren't trying to capture Majesty and me—only Two-Eyes can do that. No, they were there to push us into this spot, into the trap.

I climb back down to Majesty, who has stopped partway up to rest his leg.

"What's wrong, Sarah?"

"He's here." The words come out with a growl I cannot hide even if I wanted to. But I do not want to. I've had enough of Two-Eyes and his tricks and traps.

"He? Lord Avery?"

I nod. "And more."

Majesty stretches his legs and stands. "So what would you like to do?"

I cock my head. What can we do? The sun has started for the land's edge, and Two-Eyes stands in our way.

"We could turn back and follow the river through the gorge."

That would take much time. We would have to walk fast to reach the castle before darkness comes. But we could make it—if we do not have any other problems. When we first passed there, Majesty told stories of the cliffs' many holes and how predator men sometimes hide among them.

"Or we can fight our way past there." Majesty nods to the top of the hill, which hides Two-Eyes and his pack.

I wrinkle my nose. Take on a whole pack led by Two-Eyes? No. We made the wager so one *wouldn't* have to fight a pack. I swing downhill.

"The gorge it is." Majesty matches me stride for stride.

Did I do right? Maybe it would be better if we fought it out here. Yet if we can move through the gorge fast, we might reach the castle before Two-Eyes knows we went around him.

Twigs snap to my left. Two swordsmen in red and black appear.

Oh bad, bad, bad. I lengthen my legs. Majesty stays at my side—we cannot let the men turn me one way and Majesty another—and his fingers tighten around his sword. "We'll have to run for it."

I nod. We dodge trees, scramble up boulders, and down the cliff into the gorge. The water splashes around our legs as we cross the river.

The men stop at the edge, as if getting wet will harm them. The first one pulls out an arrow. "Go. Let His Majesty know they've been spotted and are headed through the gorge. I'll stay here and keep an eye on them."

"Yes, sir." The second man heads back the way he came. So much for Two-Eyes not knowing where we are. How far can we get before he hears the news?

Majesty slows his steps. "Sarah, ease up. They aren't pursuing, only watching to make sure we don't turn around."

I still want to run, but his forehead is wrinkled and the limp is stronger than before. He can't keep this pace. I make my feet walk fast instead of run, and soon it doesn't matter. I couldn't run if I wanted to. The gorge is narrow and rocky. The river thrashes in growing rage at being squeezed between two walls of stone. Grasses push between piles of rocks, and splintered wood is scattered across the flatter places. A few trees twist out of the ground here and there. The tall clifftops, so far above, glower down at us. A predator could easily see us from there without our seeing him.

"We'll be fine, Sarah. There's a gap with a rock slide farther down on this side of the river. We'll get out, no problem."

So says Majesty. But Two-Eyes will not wait for us to show up at the castle. He will try to stop us here somehow.

I climb over another boulder, water snapping at my feet. A lone tree leans over the river, and scraggy bushes cluster together at the cliff's bottom. Majesty rubs a hand over his forehead and breathes hard, but he keeps moving ahead, not saying a word.

We near a bend in the gorge and wind swirls around us. I stop, then retreat a step. Something is not right. I cock my head, sniffing the air. It almost smells like . . .

Fire.

Black smoke darkens the air farther downriver, beyond the

part of the gorge I can see. But I do not need to see jumping flames to know. This is not a campfire or a firestick. This is a big fire, like the one that ate the homes of Master and his pack. Maybe even bigger.

I run back past Majesty. The wind gusts behind me. Snapping and popping bounces off the stone walls. No time. The fire moves fast, faster than I can run on flat ground, much less here. It will be on us before we are even halfway to the gorge's beginning. We need to hide somewhere that the fire cannot grab us.

Water? Fire does not like that. The river thrashes white. Too fast. It would pull us far downriver, farther than we want to go—if Majesty and I can keep our heads above its watery fist at all. But what else can we do?

Smoke thickens, burning my mouth and nose and insides. A red glow lights the rock walls behind us. A mouse scurries in front of me, nearly running over my hand in its rush, and dives into a hole in the ground. That's it! The holes in the cliffs, big enough to hold people.

Smoke gathers, clouding the air and hiding some of the cliff. But behind some boulders is a black slit of a hole. I point. Majesty nods and squeezes inside. I push in after him. A stone sits inside. I shove it over the opening. The rock doesn't quite cover it, but it's better than nothing. I huddle down beside Majesty.

Wind roars, heat grows, redness glows. The fire pops and crackles like the harsh laugh of the Keeper. Then it is gone.

I wait a little longer and push the stone aside. The wood on the ground leaks smoke. One side of a tree, the side the fire came from, is black. But the leaves still wave green, spots of grass stand tall where the fire jumped, and water drips from the sky, cooling the stones. I crawl out. The ground is warm but not too hot. We can walk again.

Majesty squeezes out after me. "Well, that was an adventure. Of the best kind too." He grins down at me. "We both came out of it alive." He is trying to make me smile, but I cannot.

We're alive now. But we still have a throne to reach if we want to stay that way.

CHAPTER 36

FORCED ENTRY

We are being watched.

I stop and squint at the cliff tops. All of me is tight. Listening. Smelling. Watching. Straining to find what does not want to be found. Majesty pants behind me. The air tastes of smoke. The tree branches on the cliffs shiver in the wind. No sign of a hunter. A chill seeps through me anyway.

Majesty reaches me, his face white and his limp seen more with every step. His leg is hurting much, even if he doesn't say so. And we still have a long way to go and little time to do the going.

He leans against a tree. The fire burned part of the trunk, and the black rubs off on his clothing. "You feel it too, don't you?" He lifts his face toward the far cliff. "It won't be long now."

It won't be long? Until what? I cock my head, waiting for him to say more. But he moves ahead, his words left at a few.

Light starts to fade in the gorge. Shadows stretch from the tall cliffs across the ground, making our hard path harder. Then Majesty points. A pile of stone and dirt leads up to a hole in the cliff on our side. Our way out.

I bound ahead. A few more paces, a few more minutes, and the gorge will be behind us. And maybe with smoother land and more light we'll be able to go faster. I climb the hill toward the top.

The hair on my neck stands straight up.

For a breath I can't move. Trouble's here. Big trouble. And I know without looking what form it will take. Two-Eyes. I whirl around. On the other cliff he sits on a dark horse, stiff as the tree trunks around him.

Suddenly I see what I missed in my hurry to leave: the fire's trail ends here. Or rather, begins here. The fire was *created* to kill Majesty and me. Now Two-Eyes knows his fire did not catch us and we live. He swings his bow off his back and sets an arrow in the string, aiming for Majesty below me.

I fling myself down the rockslide. Dust and pebbles fly before my feet. Jagged edges cut into my hands and legs. Two-Eyes releases the arrow. I slam into Majesty, pushing him to the side. The wind gusts. The arrow bounces off the stones to my left.

I shove Majesty ahead of me. Two-Eyes reaches for another arrow. But he is still one. None of his pack shows to help him. He must have sent them to the gorge's other end, to the place where we should have come out, chased by fire.

An arrow flies from the cliff above me and across the gorge, diving into the ground just in front of Two-Eyes. His horse rears, and he barely stays on.

My head jerks around. Tracker crouches near the rock pile's top, preparing a second arrow. Help has come! And not too soon. I clamber up toward him. *Toward* him. I almost laugh. Not long ago the sight of him sent me running the other way.

Tracker shoots at Two-Eyes again. Two-Eyes sends two more arrows our way. Both land far from us. Majesty and I reach the top, untouched by Two-Eyes. A few more steps bring us into the trees' protection. Now Two-Eyes can only scowl at us. Putting his bow away, he kicks his horse and rides away as fast as he can go. He must go far around the gorge to find a place to cross, while we have a straight path to the castle.

Majesty grabs Tracker's hand. "Mason, old friend, your timing is impeccable as always."

Tracker bows to him. "Thank you, Your Majesty. I try to make it so."

I cock my head. Tracker was to wait at Melek for us. How did he know to come here, now?

Tracker reaches down to squeeze my shoulder. "Hang around town long enough, Princess, buy the right men drinks, and you can learn much." He walks ahead of us. "And once I knew the what, the where wasn't too hard. But if you'll pardon my boldness, we must hurry. Our time is short and our work great." He leads us into an open spot where two horses are tied.

I hang back.

Majesty, reaching for one, frowns at me. "What's wrong, Sarah?"

I shake my head. Riding horses would help, but using them could lose us the wager.

Tracker nods his head, knowing. "The rules. She cannot use anything except what she finds or takes, or else Lord Avery will win." He steps closer to Majesty, putting his back to the horses. "So I am compelled to confess, Your Majesty, I have been terribly careless and not watched these animals as carefully as I ought to have. I mean anyone, even now, could sneak in and steal them from me."

What? I glance around. Does he think men have crossed the gorge already? Then I understand. Circling around, I untie the horses and bring them back to Majesty.

"See? The princess has taken them right from behind me."

Majesty struggles not to smile. "This is a grave crime indeed, but considering the extenuating circumstances, you have my complete pardon."

"Thank you, Your Majesty." Tracker bows slightly to Majesty and turns to me. "Ready to ride, Princess?"

No. But time is too short to walk. While we have more light up here than in the gorge, the shadows are still growing fast. So I nod. I rode once before and I can do it again now.

He lifts me up and climbs on behind me. Majesty takes the other horse. "Let us be done with this for once and for all."

Blackness oozes across the sky. Jagged arrows of light shoot through it. Rumblings growl at our approach. But we cannot turn back. We are too close.

The wind beats at me, and I huddle among the homes on the edge of Melek nearest the castle. But the buildings offer little protection against either the wind or the glowering stone wall. We have arrived before Two-Eyes, but we still must get inside—through the front gate. There is not time for anything else; the sun almost touches the land.

Two shadows swim across the moat toward the castle. A spider skitters around my insides. It won't be long now. I tuck my hair up under my cap again and grip my walking stick tighter. The tip of a sword peeks out from under the bridge and waves twice.

My turn. I hobble forward. If this works, Majesty will sit on his throne soon. If it doesn't . . . but I don't want to think about that.

The moving blackness swallows the last slice of the sun, and the strong wind gusts against me. I press a hand to my cap and shiver. The heat is going away very fast, and so is my courage. Everything in me says to run. But I must keep on. The end is in sight, and what I must do is little. Act like a wounded animal, draw out the predator, and Majesty and Tracker will do the rest. How hard can that be? My stick thumps against the wood bridge.

"Halt!" A man at the wall's top yells down at me. "Who are you and what's your business?"

More rumblings and flashes. The wind tugs at my cap. The storm has almost caught us.

"Urgent . . . message . . . from the king!" The words Tracker gave me come out choppy. Not good. But maybe the man will think the bumpy words are from shouting.

"You may advance."

One thing done, the easiest one. A fist pounds my insides flat. I can't do this. I must. I limp toward the iron bars between me and the castle—a few paces but a journey of many hours if the gate doesn't open.

A man waits in the gate's shadow. "Your message?"

The voice chills me from the inside out. Fang. Now I see the glint of metal spinning up and down; he throws his knife. I want to run. I cannot. Not now. "I sp-speak to . . ." The name hides from me. Who is it? Who did Tracker think was leading here?

"To whom?" Fang flips his knife again, still not looking my way. I will not be able to hide who I am from him much longer.

"To . . ." I am in trouble. Big trouble. And when in trouble, act dead.

I tip and let my legs fold. My stick clatters away. My shoulder strikes stone. Ow! I grimace, pain spearing my body. This better work or I will wish very much that I had not fallen so hard.

Fang catches his knife and tucks it away, moving toward me. "Open the gate!"

I close my eyes, the ground shuddering beneath me. The gate rises; its creakings and moanings warn of what is coming. Steps stride toward me; a hand rolls me over. "Well, now, what have we here?" My cap is ripped from my head, and Fang chuckles deep in his throat. "The beast has come home."

His words raise the hair on my neck, but I force my body to lay still and loose, as if I am in a darkness where his voice cannot reach me.

Cool metal presses against my neck. "Should I cut its throat now or allow His Majesty the pleasure? That's the question now."

Air in. Air out. I feel and hear nothing. That is what I tell myself. Still coldness weighs down my insides and spreads toward my hands and feet.

The sharp edge cuts in, then pulls away as Fang sighs. "Patience, patience. There's a greater prize, and besides, it's no fun when they aren't awake." He slings me over his shoulder.

"Patience is a great virtue indeed." Low words chill the air—Tracker.

Fang stiffens, and I dare open my eyes a slit, enough to see but not to let anyone else know I am watching.

"That's right. Take it easy." Tracker, dripping wet, stands

behind Fang and presses a long knife to Fang's neck. "No reason to lose your head over this, don't you agree?"

Typical Tracker words. I want to smile, but bite it back—my insides tell me to hold still a little longer.

"Go on." Tracker turns his head. "I'll handle things here."

Wet footsteps squish by. Majesty. He is on his way. Fang shifts, but doesn't say anything.

"See? That wasn't too hard." The light lift, with an undercurrent of threat, returns to Tracker's voice. "Now put her down gently and take a step back."

I am lowered to the ground, the stones cold beneath my back. Breathe in once, twice. Nothing else happens. I let my head roll to the side and open an eye. My stick lies a hand's width in front of my nose. Beyond that, two pairs of boots and a puddle of water fill my sight. Fang still bends over slightly from laying me down. A grin spreads across his face. He swings a hand to his boot—and a knife.

Throwing an elbow at Tracker, Fang spins upward, knife blade flashing. "Intruders! Close the gate! The castle has been breached!" He lunges. Tracker dodges to the side.

I flip onto my knees and grab my walking stick. Whack! I swing the stick into Fang's legs. He stumbles forward. Tracker grabs his shoulder, plunging his knife upward under the arm.

Fang's eyes widen; his grin fades. He crashes to the ground and lies all still, like an animal in the teeth of Master's dogs. Tracker wipes off his knife and tucks it away. "Sarah! Princess Sarah. We must go. Now."

I blink and shake my head. All around me shouting and clanging and barking and running steps compete against the sky's growing growls. Then one cry rises above the others. "The king! The king's coming."

Hooves pound the ground; Two-Eyes bends over a horse, his whip cracking. I grab my stick and race after Tracker, who sprints for the front door, sword now in hand. He yanks the door open, away from a man trying to bar it on the inside. Tracker points his sword at him and growls. The man runs.

That is fine with me. I don't want to leave another man like Fang. We charge through empty halls to the throne room. Majesty meets us at the doors. Almost there.

"Ready, Your Majesty?" Tracker holds his sword in one hand and rests his other on the door's handle.

Majesty grips his sword with both hands. None of us know what waits on the other side. A trap? A pack of men? Nothing? Majesty nods. Tracker pulls on the door.

Nothing happens.

He tries again, harder. The door rattles but refuses to open. Two-Eyes has locked us out.

Tracker lowers his sword. "What now?"

Majesty points upward. "The balconies, northeast side."

"I'll get the rope." He runs down the hall.

"Come on, Sarah. This way." Majesty limps away from the hall that Tracker took.

I bound after him, staying close behind. The halls are so quiet, so still, so . . . empty. Water spots mark the floor where Majesty walks, leaving a clear trail behind us. We reach the stairs, winding and narrow. We must go one at a time. Majesty is first, with me after. My legs ache. I fall behind, and Majesty must wait for me at the top.

Boots thud against the steps.

I look up at Majesty. He looks at me. He wants me to go ahead, let him deal with our stalker. I flatten my mouth and shake my head. I won't leave. I'm done with running. "Go. If time wins, I'm dead."

Majesty slowly nods, his face like when I offered the wager, as if he knew this too would come, that it had to be this way, but he still hated it. "Stay safe, Sarah." Stooping down, he brushes his hand across my cheek—the scarred one—and even though he does not say it, I hear it. *I love you, for always and always.*

With a deep sigh he disappears around the corner, and I swing around to face the man with the stride I know too well.

Time to end this now.

ᴍETAMORPHOSIS

The footsteps climb up the stairs, up toward me. They are not fast. They are not slow. They just come nearer and nearer, never a breath more or less between the soft clunks of boot against stone. Two-Eyes walks as if he has caught his prey already. Maybe he has, but like any cornered animal, I will not let him take me without a fight.

Crouched against the wall, I clench my rod and watch the top of the stairs for the first shadow of Two-Eyes. A knot in the rod's wood digs into my hand. My insides shudder at each step and huddle closer together.

The steps stop. Two-Eyes leans into the hall. He hunches forward, face tense, his eyes darting from side to side seeking prey. In his hand the whip is coiled, ready to strike.

My insides scuttle into my feet, trying to drag me away from him. I clench my teeth. Majesty needs more time.

When Two-Eyes sees me, his shoulders lose some stiffness and his eyes half-close. "Now here's a nice predicament. I've come hunting for a challenge, and I find he has run, leaving behind a lowly beast to fight his battles. It's almost not worth the effort." Stepping into the hall, he opens his fingers and the coils of the whip slap against the floor.

I crouch lower, shifting the stick in my hand. His words dangle bait, but I won't bite. Must not bite. They are there only to lure me into hurt.

His lip curls up, a low chuckle escaping his mouth. "Go on. Growl. I know you're only a beast, even if Elroy is too blind to see it."

Retreating a step before him, I eat my growl. He is making me do what he wants. I know it, but I can't stop.

He edges nearer, backing me up farther. "You don't want to admit it, do you? Even though we both know the truth."

"Truth?" My growl finds voice in words. "Truth is . . . we won."

"Won? Is that what you think?" His chuckle blooms into a full roar of laughter. "If you believe that, you're more stupid than I thought. So your precious Elroy sits on the throne. If I kill him—and I will, slowly, painfully—I have won anyway." He snaps his whip above my head. "Harboring the weak has destroyed him, just as I said."

Coldness starts in my middle and spreads out through my arms and legs. That is why he said he would do this. To him, he would win no matter what we did. He only wanted to hunt. My air hisses out through clenched teeth.

"I guess that just proves what a beast you are." He swings the whip forward.

I spring to the side. The whip cracks against the floor.

Two-Eyes yanks it back for another strike. "Face it. Elroy may dress you in pretty clothes and make people serve you." Crack! The whip hits the floor on my other side. "He may teach you how to act and sit at a table and talk." Crack! "He may even convince others that you are a princess." Crack! "But it won't matter how you look on the outside, will it? On the inside, you will always be a raging, ravenous beast." Crack!

I duck backward at each strike, but the last one bites into my shoulder anyway. With a yelp, I jerk back. My stick jumps from my hand and rolls out onto the balcony over the throne room. No. I need that. It's all I have against Two-Eyes. I lunge for it.

"Not so fast." Two-Eyes grabs my shoulder and flings me across the hall.

I hit the wall and crumple to the floor. Pain spikes through me. I roll facedown with a groan. Why did I stay behind? I knew I was not strong, not like a master predator.

He strides toward me. "Why do you run? Why not let me end all the hiding?"

Shaking my head, I scoot back around him, trying to reach the balcony. Rod. Get to the rod. Fight.

"It will only get worse. The more people who know you, the more you will have to hide. But no one can hide forever, can they?"

I bump against the balcony's edge. Shouting rises from the floor, so far, so very far below me, with nothing but air between. My whole body shudders. There is nowhere else for me to go, and my stick is still out of reach.

"They *will* discover what you are." His words are low, thick, coiling. "And they will loathe you—and Elroy will turn against you."

Immediately I see in my head the Others attacking an animal. Teeth gnashing. Fur flying. The torn, still body afterward. I grab my middle.

"Do you really want that, Beast? To face Elroy as your enemy?"

Enemy. I gasp, Majesty's warning to Tabby loud in my head. *"Never trust the enemy's words—no matter how good or right they sound."* Unlike Majesty. His words have always been true.

Two-Eyes raises his whip. "Trust me, Beast. Elroy will hurt you far more than I ever could."

"No!" I roll over, grab the stick, a hand on each end, and thrust it up. The whip wraps around it, its tip barely missing my face. "Majesty loves me." With a twist of the rod I yank the whip out of his hands and send it flying over the edge of the balcony. Pushing up, I shift my grasp on the rod, ready for the next attack. "He loved me when I was Beast, and he will love me if I stay Beast." Somehow the words rush from my mouth, like water leaping over a cliff, as if they have hidden inside me for a long time but cannot stay there any longer.

Below, metal clashes against metal—Majesty is fighting too. Locking swords with a man in red and black, he smiles up at me. He heard my words.

My insides swell. He loves me, whether Beast or Sarah. And because of that, I am no longer Beast but Sarah. Using the rod and the railing, I pull myself to my feet.

"So now princesses walk on all fours, have matted hair, and scarred faces." Hunching like a predator ready to spring, Two-Eyes slides out his hunting knife. "Or do you think you will never act as a beast again?"

"No. I will act like Beast sometimes." I dip my face away from him. A shadow creeps along another balcony. Tracker? What is he doing? "But what I look like is not who I am." I shift where I stand, to keep Two-Eyes from seeing Tracker. "What I do is not who I am." Balancing on one foot, I hop a step toward Two-Eyes. "I am what Majesty says I am. And he says I am Sarah. Princess Sarah." I lift my head higher. "And I will be that until I am no more." I grip my rod with both hands, ready for whatever he does next.

He shrinks back with a snarl. "That can be arranged." And he springs toward me, knife flashing.

A bowstring twangs. I drop to the floor. An arrow whizzes over my head. Two-Eyes chokes and clutches at his throat, his knife clattering to the floor. Between his fingers two arrows stick out, each pointing a different way. I want to look away, cannot look away. His eyes roll back. He stumbles against a wall. Shivering, I clutch one of the short bars holding up the balcony's railing, as if that will protect me.

"Sarah!" Tracker bursts in from the hall behind Two-Eyes. "Watch out—behind you!" He fumbles for his bow.

I twist around.

A bowman aims at me from the balcony across the throne room. I tell my body to move, but it has turned to stone.

An arrow flies from the floor below and buries itself in the bowman's shoulder. Where did that . . . Majesty. He stands below me, another arrow in the bow, ready to fly. The bowman stumbles away.

The two arrows. I look back at the man who has hunted me so long. One arrow from Majesty, one from Tracker. They both were protecting me the whole time. *Me*.

Tracker crouches before me. "Are you well, Princess Sarah? He didn't . . ." He wraps his hands around mine.

I shake my head and let him help me to my feet. Past Tracker's shoulder, Two-Eyes lies on the floor, his two colored eyes glazed over, all fire now gone.

Tracker sees where I look. He pulls a tapestry from a wall and covers him. "Don't worry, Princess. It's done, finished. He will never bother you again."

Done. Finished. I wait to feel something. Anger. Sadness. Joy. Relief. *Something*. But nothing comes. My insides are empty, as if it doesn't matter whether Two-Eyes is dead or alive.

A man pokes his head around the corner from the stairs. He wears plain brown clothes, not red and black—a castle servant. "Do you—would you like some help? His Majesty King Elroy . . ."

Tracker waves him away. "No. I have her. Tell him we will be down as soon as the princess is able."

Something ripples inside me. I am not empty, but full—full with the quietness of water unmoved by wind or animal. I feel like Two-Eyes does not matter, because he does not, never did. I belong to Majesty, and Lord Avery and all his words could never change that.

"Able?" The servant steps toward us, tipping his head. "Is she unwell?"

Unwell? My mouth uncurls a smile. Oh no. I am quite well. Better than well.

Tracker nudges the servant back. "The princess has suffered no major injuries, but is naturally shaken. We should be only a moment longer."

"I understand. I will inform His Majesty." After a quick bow, the man disappears down the stairs.

Tracker turns, and a smile washes away the wrinkles of concern on his face. "You understand at last."

I nod and duck, feeling like an animal caught out in the open. Below us, Majesty fights off the last of Lord Avery's men with some castle servants that came to help him. But neither Tracker nor I hurry down. Majesty is in control, as he always has been from the beginning. How did I not see that sooner?

My eyes lift to Tracker. He watches me, not the fight below, his eyes so dark, so deep, yet so known to me—now. "Why?"

He tips his head, a frown forming on his face. "Why? Because I am the protector of the royal children. I am supposed to—"

"No." I shake my head. "You called me she, her. Even the first time."

The darkness disappears from his eyes, though his mouth stays straight. "What else was I to call you?" He settles on the railing's edge.

"It. Like the others."

A glint lights his eyes, as if he finds something he could laugh at in my words. "Do you think you are the first to find a monster inside—or to have His Majesty see beyond it?"

His words do not sink into me at first. Then I know. "You—that's why you could . . ." I sit on the railing. He knew, understood, even that first day.

"Why do you think I was so determined to take you?"

On the throne room floor, the ring of swords quiets into commands to create order again. Majesty stops near our balcony. "You two are welcome to come down any time now. It's quite safe, I can assure you." His clothing is wet and crumpled, and dirt and fire's blackness streaks both cloth and skin, but he is still Majesty.

Tracker chuckles and rises to his feet. "I think that was a gentle reminder we are to join him."

Nodding, I stand and reach for the nearest wall to lean against. My legs are still tired from my fight with Lord Avery.

Tracker holds out his hands to me. "Would you like me to carry you?"

"Only if no trouble."

"Princess, pardon me for saying so, but you are nothing but trouble." He lifts me up in his arms. "And none of us would want it any other way."

ONE OF THE PACK

Light and laughter have finally returned to Majesty's castle.

Firesticks and lamps brighten every hall. People bustle from room to room. Chattering voices and gladness and songs fill the air inside and out. Gone are the whispers, the cursing, the threats and shadows of Lord Avery's time.

It has not been easy. Days and days have passed since Majesty won the wager. Lord Avery's men didn't want to let go of their territory and fought hard to keep it. But Majesty was stronger and they had lost their leader. Now only a few strays linger, and the castle is fully under Majesty's care again.

"Good evening, Sarah. Ready for tonight?" Tabby invades my room with bouncing steps.

I shrug a shoulder and twist around to greet her. I was ready to be done with this fuss yesterday.

The she-cub—the girl—preparing me for tonight, nudges my head back around. "Just a minute longer, please, milady." Arianna weaves the last flower into my hair and with a pat, steps back. "There. All done."

Finally. I thought maybe she would take half the night. But what could I say? Arianna can twist and tug my hair into forms my hands could never do.

Tabby walks behind me and fingers my hair. "How beautiful, so intricate. You'll have to show Emma how to do those little twists for me."

"If you wish, milady."

"I do, very much so."

I only shake my head and turn around on the stool, tugging on the thick skirts wrapping around my legs. I eye the boy's clothes folded on the end of the bed. But tonight is special, and that means a new dress of gold and white with green stitching made just for me.

Arianna picks up a few things scattered around the room and goes to leave. I should say something too, something nice like Tabby. "Arianna, I . . ."

She stops in the doorway.

My tongue sticks to the top of my mouth and my face burns.

"Did you need something, milady?"

I shake my head. "No, I . . . thank you. For your help." My words trip over each other. Maybe I should have not tried to say anything.

A small smile curves up on Arianna's face. "It was my pleasure, milady." She dips a curtsey to Tabby and me before slipping out.

I sigh. And I am supposed to get through a whole night of this? And with many, many more people too.

Tabby sits on the bed, her green and gold dress rustling around her; Majesty wanted us to match yet be different tonight. "Are you unwell, Sarah?"

I dip my head. "No, but . . ." I pick up the gold rod Majesty had made to help me walk, and my fingers rub across every dip and bump. Tonight Majesty will claim me as his. Tonight the strongest pack I've ever known will take me into its innermost part.

Me. It's enough to make my insides tumble over each other.

"We both want this; we have wanted it for a long time." Tabby offers me a small green pouch. "The question is, can you accept it now?"

I open the pouch, and the gold feather necklace spills out

onto my lap. So much has happened since she first offered me this. Bad things. Because of me.

She scoots off the bed and kneels on the floor beside me. "Yes, there have been some long days. Some hard days. But there have been good days too, full of fun and laughter." She reaches up and rests her hand on my arm. "And I don't want those times to stop, even if we must have some bad ones in between. After all, isn't that what family is about? Sticking together through good and bad?"

I finger the gold feathers. My eyes look down into hers and I know. I close her hand around the necklace.

Her face falls. "Sarah—"

"Would you do it? My hands . . ."

Her head jerks up, she stares at me a moment, and then she is up, arms around my neck. "Oh Sarah." She pulls back, eyes blinking rapidly. "I'd be honored to." Sliding behind me, she puts the necklace on me. Then she leans forward, wrapping her arms around me from the back this time. "Welcome home, Sarah."

The red light from the setting sun reaches in from the window and curls around us, and outside, a dog howls. One, then two howl back. I smile. Even the dogs are not alone tonight.

There's a knock on the door.

"Come in." Tabby and I say the words at the same time. We look at each other and giggle.

Tracker—the name Mason still does not sound right in my ears—steps in and bows. "Princess Tabitha, Princess Sarah, your father the King—may his rule be long and prosperous!—awaits your arrival in the throne room."

"Thank you." Tabby rises and heads out the door.

I am slower, and Tracker steps closer to help if I need it. These days I cannot leave my room without him always a few paces behind. But I don't mind. With him and his mate, Evie, I have found that my pack does not stop at Tabby and Majesty but goes much, much farther.

By the time I arrive at the throne room, the doors are partially open and Tabby is halfway down the aisle. Majesty waits for her at the bottom of the stairs leading to the throne. He now stands strong and tall, his face without lines and his eyes full of sparkle.

Tabby reaches him, and Majesty takes her hand, guiding her up the steps to her seat at his right. Then he stands before the middle chair, leaving the one on his left empty. For me.

"It's time, Princess." Tracker pulls the doors open all the way.

Every eye in the crowded room turns toward me. So many people. My insides stutter, and my feet put down roots into the floor. I can't do this. I don't belong here. My gaze flits around the room, looking for a place to run, a place to hide, but lands on Majesty instead.

He smiles at me, and that smile pulls me forward, up the aisle, up the stairs until I stand before him.

"Please kneel." Majesty's voice booms out, even this large room too small to contain it.

I slide to my knees and dip my head, trembling. Majesty lifts high a circle of gold just like Tabby's and lowers it onto my head. A crown. For me. Clapping thunders behind me.

"You may rise." Majesty holds a hand out to me.

For a moment I can only stare at it. So many days I still feel like Beast, an animal, a monster no one wants. Then I see Majesty's eyes—their fullness, their tenderness, their love. For though I may *feel* like Beast, Majesty sees Sarah and will only see Sarah. My hand slips into his.

He helps me to my feet and gently nudges my face up so I must look him in the eye. And though he does not say the words, I hear them anyway: *I love you, for always and always.* My face lifts as he turns me toward the crowd.

For I am Sarah, daughter to the king.

———✦———

For you did not receive a spirit that makes you a slave again to fear, but you received the Spirit of sonship. And by him we cry, "*Abba*, Father." —Romans 8:15

Long my imprisoned spirit lay fast bound in sin and nature's night;
Thine eye diffused a quickening ray, I woke, the dungeon flamed
*   with light.*
My chains fell off; my heart was free. I rose, went forth, and
*   followed Thee.*
Amazing love! How can it be that Thou, my God, shouldst die for
*   me?*

No condemnation now I dread; Jesus, and all in Him, is mine!
Alive in Him, my living Head, and clothed in righteousness divine;
Bold I approach the eternal throne and claim the crown, thro'
*   Christ, my own.*
Amazing love! How can it be that Thou, my God, shouldst die for
*   me?*

—From "And Can It Be?" by Charles Wesley